OH BABY!

Randi Reisfeld and H.B. Gilmour

SCHOLASTIC INC.

New York   Toronto   London   Auckland   Sydney

Mexico City   New Delhi   Hong Kong   Buenos Aires

Thanks to my peeps on the East Coast—AF, HB,
MR, SR, and SR—for keepin' it real.
Thanks to my peeps on the left coast—MS and RPM—
for schoolin' me in the unreal!
Thanks most of all to Steve Scott, for creating the MOST
AWESOME cover ever in the history of books! You rock!!
—RR

For Isabelle Savage, with love and gratitude.
—HBG

ISBN 0-439-67705-X

Copyright © 2005 by Randi Reisfeld and H.B. Gilmour
All rights reserved. Published by Scholastic Inc.

SCHOLASTIC and associated logos are trademarks and/or registered
trademarks of Scholastic Inc.

12 11 10 9 8 7 6 5 4 3 2 1   5 6 7 8 9 10/0

Printed in the U.S.A.

First printing, November 2005

Prologue

The Summer of Our Discontent

Jamie

"I'm cooked, I'm done, I've had it!" I raged at my best friend, Abigail Burrows.

After the grope session that passed for "a date" in our janky hometown of Shafton, Ohio, I'd gone straight to the house where Abby was babysitting.

It was the summer after our high-school graduation. "We've got to get out of here!" I insisted, falling back into the scruffy recliner opposite the tweed sofa where Abs was sitting. My father had a recliner, Abby's father had one, practically everyone's father in Shafton had one—a watch-the-game, zone-out-in-style, king-of-the-remote recliner. In that moment, it seemed to represent to me everything that was *wrong* with Shafton.

Legs tucked under her, Abby rolled her hazel-colored cat's eyes. "You're always saying that, Jamie."

"I mean it this time," I persisted.

She shifted her bod and said exactly the wrong thing. "I know, Jamie. And we will...someday."

Someday? That was the issue, the problem, the fantasy!

Shafton—as in, you live here, you get shafted—is a small

town. The sidewalks roll up at nine PM, the kids roll joints and, after graduation, roll straight into mind-deadening lives where the biggest decisions they ever have to make are: extra-large or supersize? Kmart or Wal-Mart? Target or T.J. Maxx?

The other option, of course, is college. But our choices are limited. The only place within financial reach for most of us is the local community college, Shafton-Oaks, which is a two-year trip, and not quite right for anyone who wants to possibly be a doctor (me, potentially) or a published book author (Abby).

Abs caught the look on my face and my disillusioned sigh.

"Okay, James," she said sympathetically. "What happened?"

What happened was my last date in Ohio — hopefully!

It was with Sean Axton, but feel free to substitute the name of any straight guy from Shafton High. Cookie-cutter, hormonal morons, all.

It went like this:

"Come on, Jamie, don't be such a prude." Sean always thought whining would get him to second base.

We were in his pride ride, a beat-up Ford Explorer he'd inherited from his brother. The only thing that kept Sean's heavy breathing from fogging up the windows was that it was mid-August and they were open.

"I'm not a prude, Sean. I'm just not that into you," I tried to explain. It was a moonless night and we were miles from my house, which was why I was still sitting in the front seat with him.

"What's that supposed to mean?" he challenged.

I sighed. If he'd had something on his mind besides scoring that night — anything! — I *might* have been into him. Sean was your basic Shafton stud. Tall, blond, and buff in Levi's, a T-shirt, and date-clean Nike Just-do-its. He was a C-average good guy, except when his testosterone kicked in. Which it clearly had. He moved in closer and clumsily tried to lift my T-shirt.

I moved his hand away. Which did little to discourage him.

"It's Saturday night, Jamie. And in case you didn't realize"— he lowered his voice —"we're alone."

Not so much.

We were in a lineup of cars banked along the river, where the passionate giggles and moans of, like, a hundred other couples could be heard above the rushing water.

So romantic.

I reminded him. "You said we were going to the movies. Instead, you stopped here. I never agreed to this."

Sean shot me the helpless orphan look. "Come on, Jamie. You're killin' me here. We should be celebrating. I got a raise today."

I wasn't sure how Sean's raise at the Stop-n-Shop translated to me giving him sex. I gave him a look that said as much.

"We've been together for three months, Jamie." Sean switched strategies. "It's time to, you know, move on. Take it to the next level."

"I didn't know there was a deadline," I deadpanned.

He moved in to kiss me — I didn't move away fast enough. Our lips met for a nanosecond. One nanosecond too long.

"Sean," I said as gently as possible, "I'm not seeing our relationship the same way you do. I never thought of us as being, uh, together."

This puzzled him. "Of course we're together. We hang out all the time. Stop playin' me, Jamie. Hanging out with someone means something. Like sooner or later, you're going to go all the way. That's how it is."

Sean had a point. In Shafton, that *was* how it worked. There was not a lot of wiggle room in relationships. You were seen talking or laughing with someone more than three times in a week, and everyone assumed you'd found your life partner.

Sean's desperate "Come on, Jamie" brought me back to the present. "Sean," I said, "I know what you want, but try and get this through the part of your brain that resides north of your belt. I don't want to do this."

Not with you was the part I didn't say out loud.

Borderline annoyed, though not willing to accept defeat, Sean tried reason. "What are you waiting for, Jamie?"

Good question.

I was waiting for someone I was at least attracted to, if not actually in love with.

I was waiting to feel tempted by someone who cared about something beyond where the next six-pack was coming from.

I wasn't holding out for a hero, as that old song goes. I was holding out to *be* the hero.

I was waiting for my life to begin.

And the wait could be over, I suddenly thought, as an idea dawned. A brand-new idea that I had to share with Abby as soon as possible.

"And your idea is what?" my best friend asked.

"We don't go straight to Shafton-Oaks in September," I told her, crossing the room to plop down beside her on the sofa. "We take time off, as much as it takes — a semester, a year, whatever — to make enough money to go somewhere better — like Ohio State. We go away. *Away*: as in, bright lights, big city. Where, if you do hook up, it really is hooking *up* — as opposed to hooking down, which is what happens in Shafton.

"*Away* as in New York City, babe," I concluded.

"But what would we do there?" Practical-Ab asked.

"What are we doing *here*?" Rhetorical-me answered. "We're babysitters. That's what it's called in Shafton when you get paid to watch someone's kids. But in New York we could be nannies! Plus, the pay is so much more."

"Nannies." Abby taste-tested the word, then smiled large as if she'd just discovered a fabulous new flavor of ice cream. "I like," she confessed. "Anyway," she added, "Ethan's gone till January."

Ethan. That would be Abby's boyfriend. I was the one who noticed him first. Noticed him noticing Abby, that is. "You're crazy," she'd insisted. "I helped him with his English paper. He's just being nice to me."

It took them till senior year to go out together. He finally got the nerve to ask her to a basketball game. After that, they were a solid item. Holding hands, doing goofy smile stuff, passing notes in class, for God's sake.

A week before graduation, Abby told me she was thinking about "doing it." She was going to have sex with Ethan at some point. In typical Abby style, she said she wanted him to be her first — and only.

Then Ethan broke the news that he was going to California for six months with Justice for All, this totally PC program to help migrant workers. And Abby decided to hold out till they could be "together again for good."

With Ethan away — or out of the way — the coast was clear to start our campaign to be New York nannies. So here's what we did:

We nagged, reasoned, and begged our parents into giving us the go-ahead — which they did, reluctantly at first, expecting nothing to come of our "wild scheme." They thought we were too young to pull this off.

But we were growing up, and fast. I was five-three, freckle-prone, with brown eyes, wavy light brown hair, and boobs that were underwire-worthy — but I'd always been more interested in science and the environment than in looks or fashion. At five-eight, Abby was tall and slim with gray-green eyes and silky straight dark hair, but her self-image was stuck somewhere back in seventh grade when a sudden growth spurt put her head and shoulders above the shrimpy thirteen-year-old boys in our class.

Anyway, after wearing down our parents, we registered with a Google-approved nanny agency. And things fell into place, with amazing grace and speed. By the middle of August, we'd both found our dream jobs.

I got hired by a husband-and-wife team of doctors, extremely cool.

And Abby got a gig working for Lila Matheson, a hotshot New York book publisher. Our new lives were scheduled to begin on September 1.

How perfect was that?

Chapter One

Shock and Awe

Abby

He was disgusting! A drunk perv pressed up against me, breathing vodka fumes into my face.

I couldn't move. There was no room to back up or wriggle sideways. The incredibly jammed subway train that the human Breathalyzer and I were riding was stalled between two stations, and miles from my destination!

I was supposed to be at Lila Matheson's penthouse by nine A.M. It was already nine-thirty, and I was trapped — getting what felt like an alcohol face peel, in a rancid tunnel under Manhattan.

This was so not the way I imagined my first day on the job!

I'd always wanted to go to New York. And I was totally blown away when the nanny agency found positions there for me and my best friend, Jamie.

For starters, I'd be able to leave what was once my home but had recently turned into Menopause Central, a house haunted by my mother's sudden and unpredictable weirdness — which my father handled with anger, confusion, and slammed doors. Day after day, they each downloaded their woes on me — and my hard drive was full. I'd become, as Jamie put it, my parents' live-in "Dear Abby." But no matter how off-the-wall their rants got, I zipped my lip, tried to look sympathetic, and just bobbed my head.

Splitting Ohio was all that stood between me and a meltdown.

Plus, I love books. I've written stories, poems, and articles for our school paper practically since I could clutch a crayon. I had even started a novel. It was about my great-grandmother coming to America when she was sixteen, and I was going to try to work on it this fall. So, being hired as a nanny by Lila Matheson, of Matheson Press, a small but major New York book publishing company, was the best possible setup.

Until reality bit. I flew east — first class, compliments of Lila — for what was supposed to be my dream job, only to get caught up, my first day out of the box, in a New York nightmare.

Which was getting worse.

Trying to twist my head out of the drunkard's way, I felt a tug on my backpack. If the train hadn't been at a dead stop, I might have chalked it up to someone accidentally bumping against me and grabbing my backpack to steady him- or herself.

But we were standing still.

So, I said, "Hey!" And then a woman in back of me also said, "Hey!" And then I managed to turn around.

There was a sudden rustling through the crowd, as if a giant snake were racing through tall grass. People fell back, cursing and muttering. And, as I strained to see what was going on, the reeking guy who'd been in my face a minute before took off in the opposite direction. With my backpack!

I barely had time to freak. A second later, a tall, hot guy at the far end of the car was waving my backpack in the air. "He got it!" people were assuring me. "The creep got away, but that guy got your bag."

That guy was amazing. A tall, dark, and handsome hunk with biceps bursting from the rolled-up sleeves of his faded denim workshirt. Orange hard hat in one hand and my backpack held high in the other, he plodded toward me in sexy blond work boots. Practically everyone he squeezed past patted him on the shoulders and congratulated him. And he got redder and redder with each compliment.

If Ethan and I hadn't promised not to date other people while he was away, I'd have seriously considered flirting with the guy.

Not that it would have done me any good.

I am *horrible* at flirting. If I like someone, I become an instant idiot. I get totally self-conscious and forget how to talk. Thank God Ethan had made the first move.

Hard-hat Boy looked as flustered as I felt. "That's how they work it," he explained to me. "One guy'll distract you while the other one rips you off. You gotta be careful."

I nodded, blushing.

He paused and checked me out. "You're not from around here, are you?"

"Shafton," I said. "It's in Ohio."

"There you go," he replied, as if the word Ohio explained

it all. A couple of people near us grunted their agreement. "Ohio," they told one another, nodding knowingly.

With a squeal of angry iron, the train finally lurched forward. And I lurched into my hero's arms.

I could feel his toned abs as he held me, the strength of his arms, the heat of his body radiating right through his fresh denim shirt. My face was squished into his neck. I caught a whiff of aftershave and the sweet soapy remains of his morning shower.

Just as I was getting comfortable, he released me. He stepped back, his face flushed and grinning. "Welcome to New York," he said.

I lost him in the crowd that pushed through the subway doors at the next stop. Not wanting to take another chance on the train, I got out at Forty-second Street, too.

Where I discovered that I'd forgotten my cell phone.

I knew right where it was — sitting on the dresser in the guest room at Aunt Molly's house, where I was staying for the summer.

Of the first three street phones I tried, two ate my quarters and one, decorated with graffiti and smelly beyond belief, kept spitting them back. None worked. There was nothing to do about it except walk uptown as fast as possible.

Fat chance.

The streets were almost as jammed as the train. And, of course, I was gawking at everything and everyone. Black was the uniform of the day. Skinny was the body type. The sidewalks rang with the quick clacking of high-heeled shoes and pointy-toed mid-calf boots, to say nothing of the chirping of multiple mobile phones.

Elbowed and buffeted, because I was apparently walking too slow, I made it to West Seventy-second Street at a quarter after ten. More than an hour late.

Edith, the Mathesons' housekeeper, seemed incredibly happy to see me. She waved away my apologies. "I thought you'd set a record and quit," she said, ushering me through a marble-tiled entrance hall that was twice the size of my bedroom.

"Dylan was supposed to be at day care at nine-thirty. They don't like it when he comes in late. So I'll call them and make an excuse and you can take him to the park."

"Hi, Dylan." I waved at the chubby five-year-old who was waiting on the wraparound gold silk sofa in the living room. "Hey, you're not dressed yet. Come on. Let's get you ready and then we can go to the park!"

He glared at me, a dwarf Jack Black in cowboy-print pajamas. Little dark eyes scrunched in judgment. Juicy lips curled in a superior snicker. "Go 'way," he said in a nasal whine.

He turned his back on me and stared out the huge picture window. And what a picture it was.

From the penthouse, the lush lawns and playgrounds of Central Park were visible. It was September and the trees had just started to turn. The lake in the middle of the park sparkled in the crisp sunshine, reflecting the early autumn colors and, from the other side of the park, the tall, gleaming buildings of the Upper East Side.

Softly, I knelt beside the sofa. "Dylan, don't you remember me? I'm Abby. I'm your new nanny."

He flounced around to face me. If eyes could smirk, his did. "You're not my nanny. You're a doody head and I hate you," he announced.

I was somewhat freaked. This was not the same shy little guy who, a mere three days ago, had peered at me angelically from behind his mother's black cashmere DKNY skirt.

"Don't start, Dylan," Edith ordered with an experienced sigh. "You be nice to Miss Burrows. She's going to take you to the park."

"I won't go. I hate her," Dylan declared, louder and with more conviction.

"It'll be fun," I promised.

This time he shot me the bird. A five-year-old saluting me with his stubby middle finger!

"I'll get him dressed," Edith said, grabbing his wrist and dragging him into his room.

Dylan glowered at me over his chunky shoulder. "You thuck!" he said. "Peenith faith."

When Dylan returned in Tommy cargo pants, an Eddie Bauer Kids hooded fleece, and adorable little work boots that looked like — but probably cost ten times as much as — my subway hero's, Edith pointed out the playground to me.

"Oh, it's practically across the street from the apartment," I noted.

"This is not an apartment, it's a *co-op*," Edith corrected me.

The Mathesons didn't rent; they owned the place. "Wow," I said. "It must be worth a million dollars."

Edith raised her dark eyebrows. "Times six."

Like everything else in the city, the playground was crowded. Kids of every size and shape were charging around, racing up the steps of the slide, crawling through jungle gym cutouts, and messing around in a mammoth sandbox.

The benches were filled with nannies. Some in uniforms, most not. They called out in a variety of accents and spoke to each other in different languages. The playground was like a mini United Nations with representatives from various countries — Mexico, Guatemala, Haiti, Trinidad, Ireland, and Russia — grouped together.

I asked Dylan what he'd like to do. Bad move. "Go home," he groused. "I hate it here. It thuckths."

"Well, I don't know why," I said. "It looks like fun to me. Let's just stay for a little while and see how things work out."

He plopped himself down on the concrete lip of the sandbox and stared angrily at the kids playing with plastic dump trucks, sand strainers, pails, and shovels.

"Why don't you ask someone to play with you?" I encouraged.

"Dylan, don't do it!" a deep, male voice hollered. I looked

around. If that baritone cry had come from a preschooler, the kid was probably already shaving.

But no. The voice belonged to a guy who was easily twenty. A green-eyed redhead in worn jeans and a Yankees jacket. Cute in a G-rated sitcom way, he was standing a foot away from me at the edge of the sandbox.

Several little heads perked up at his call. "This place is so sick," the redhead confided to me. "There are half a dozen Dylans playing here on any given day — about half of them are girls."

Redhead was the only male over ten in the playground. "Oh, which one is yours?" I asked.

He pointed to the tallest boy in the box, who was pouring a bucket of sand over a cringing, crying little girl. "Dylan Conyers. I usually call him DC to avoid confusion."

"How old is he?" I asked. "Ten, eleven?"

"Six. He's big for his age." He smiled at me. "I'm Garrick. I'm his manny."

"His nanny?"

He shook his head. "*Manny,*" he emphasized. "You know, there are lots of guys in the profession now."

One of the benched nannies had waded into the sandbox and was trying to comfort the unhappy receiver of DC's sand shower. "Gaah-rick!" the nanny called in a lilting Caribbean accent. "Ya better keep an eye on DC. Ee's being nasty again."

"Get over here," Garrick called to the first-grade giant.

The other nanny, young and pretty with peroxide-lightened

dreads, swung her charge up into her arms. "Dis is Daisy," she said as she marched past with the wailing child. "And I'm Margaritte." She indicated *my* Dylan with her chin. "Good luck with that one, girl."

Swinging his now empty pail, DC skulked toward us. As he passed my Dylan, without warning, he whacked him in the head with the pail.

Instant pandemonium.

Dylan wailed and clutched his forehead, which was suddenly bleeding profusely. Garrick snatched DC and yanked him away. The Carribean nanny, Margaritte, still hugging her hysterical little girl, hollered to Garrick, "Ya a damn fool, boy, to think ya can tame that mad little beast."

Clutching the hand of a frightened-looking little girl with jet-black ringlets, another nanny, in a starched gray uniform and sensible shoes, was suddenly at my side. "Dot child needs to be punished. If he ver mine, he vould not act like dot." She aimed her sour face at me. "No. By Ms. Farber, der boy vould learn discipline!"

Talk about no nonsense. *By Ms. Farber,* I thought, *DC would do hard time.*

"Hit him!" Dylan ordered me between snot-soaked sobs. "He hit me. You have to hit him back!"

"Let's see that cut," I said, my fingers trembling.

"I'm gonna tell my mommy that you didn't hit him back," Dylan threatened.

I moved his hands so that I could see the damage DC's pail had caused. Mopping his forehead with the hem of my brand-new blazer, I was relieved to see that the blood was flowing from a pretty small cut.

"I guess we'd better go home," I announced to no one in particular.

"Hey, what's your name?" Garrick the manny called to me.

"Abigail," I answered, blushing ferociously at my own incompetence. Here it was, my first day as a nanny, and I was going to be returning to Lila Matheson's spotless penthouse with her bleeding child.

That was, if I could get him to leave the crime scene. Dylan clamped his forehead again. Blood trickled through his pudgy fingers, as he wailed his mantra: "I'm gonna tell my mommy. I hate you. I'm gonna tell my mommy. . . ."

Ms. Farber shook her head in disgust and marched her charge back to the folding chair she had brought to the playground.

"Get up, child! And go on with Miss Abigail. Go on now," Margaritte commanded, hands on her hips. Leaving Daisy on the Caribbean nannies' bench, Margaritte had rushed to my aid. "Don't sass that girl. Get your little bum up and go with her. Now!"

Dylan got his bum up. Grumbling all the way and refusing to hold my hand, he trudged alongside me. At the gate to the playground, I turned to wave good-bye to Garrick and Margaritte, but they were already busy with their own kids.

I was terrified. Groaning and whimpering, Dylan did everything possible to call attention to his tragic, injured self.

He shrieked up a storm when I took his hand so that we could cross Central Park West. People on the street stared at him with shocked sympathy, then glared at me as if I were doing the perp walk at my child abuse arrest.

But the uniformed doorman at the Mathesons' building barely blinked when I dragged Dylan past him. The smartly dressed, elderly elevator operator just shook his head and rolled his eyes. I asked nervously if Mrs. Matheson had come back yet. "No," he answered. "This must be your lucky day."

"I see you've met DC," Edith said, welcoming us back.

It turned out that this wasn't Dylan's first face-off at the playground. Edith had heard from Miss Skearitt, Dylan's British former "au pair," all about DC's bullying. And he wasn't the only child in the park who treated Dylan as though he had a bull's-eye painted on his back. She also knew that Dylan had commanded his former nanny to fight his battles for him. Somehow, Miss Skearitt had managed to frighten Dylan's tormentors enough to keep them in line.

Clearly, the fearsome Miss Skearitt's absence — and my wimpy presence — had changed things.

I cleaned Dylan up and put a neon orange dinosaur Band-Aid over the minor cut. The bright Band-Aid might as well have been an arrow pointing to damaged goods just in case anyone — like Dylan's mom — happened to miss it. Not to worry, Edith assured me. No big deal. Lila would probably not even notice it.

My so-called "lucky day" continued with me running into Lila as I left the building.

The doorman was helping her out of a cab. She was wearing strappy stiletto heels, with a short tweed skirt, and a plum turtleneck under a cashmere poncho. Her blonde hair was stylishly messy, casually swept up and anchored with a big tortoiseshell barrette. If diamonds weren't her best friend, they were at least close acquaintances. Lila Matheson had more rocks than Stonehenge.

Someone inside the cab handed her a package, which was bound in bubble wrap like a mummy. She gave it to the doorman and bent to say good-bye to the guy in the cab. He put his head out to receive her chirpy little cheek kisses.

I gasped. Lila's friend was Curt Gordevan, a famous writer whose Pulitzer Prize-winning novel we'd had to read in English class!

If I'd had my cell phone on me, I'd have called Jamie right then and there. Instead, as the taxi carrying the legendary author pulled into traffic, I waggled my fingers at Lila and tried to prepare her for what to expect when she got upstairs.

Edith was right. It was no big deal.

"I'm sure you did whatever you needed to do." Lila cut me off in the middle of my confession. She had a smoky hard-edged voice — deep, clipped, and all business. "You've got to see this." She signaled to the doorman and he held out the mummy-wrapped package, which Lila began to tear open. "Curt and I were at the auction this afternoon. And when this fabulous little horse came up, I had to have it."

"I bet Dylan will love it," I said, imagining a miniature antique rocking horse or another kind of toy.

Lila gave me a look that said, "You have two heads *and* you speak?"

"Darling," she said, "this little filly set me back a small fortune. And it's not kid stuff."

She'd pulled off enough bubble wrap for me to get a peek at the horse. "It's porcelain. Fifth-century. Fabulous!" She pointed a French-manicured fingertip at me. "Darling, do you think you can stay late next Friday? I know it's the weekend and I'm sure a pretty girl like you has probably got other plans. But we're having a dinner party. And it would be so fabulous if you could be with us till, oh, about ten-ish."

My mind raced. Dylan would probably behave better at a party with his mom around. And it would be good for him to see me with her. Might give my credibility a boost. What would I wear? (So shallow!) How many famous authors would show up? And, face it, did I really have the nerve to mix and mingle with Lila's A-list?

"It should be an easy evening," Lila said, uncannily reading my mind. Her fingers tapped the bubble wrap impatiently.

"Sure," I said. "Sounds like fun."

TO: Jamie_the_lionhearted@OH.com
FROM: ABS@OH.com

Hey, best. Just checking in. God, I hope your gig starts smoother than mine. My first day? Brutal does not begin to describe it. I'm home now, at Aunt Molly's in New Jersey, getting ready for a healing bubble bath before I totally crash. But I've gotta give you one hot tid-bit: Lila Matheson knows Curt Gordevan! She shared a taxi with him this afternoon and gave him the Euro trash, two-cheek buzz good-bye. She's throwing a party on Friday and who knows who could be there? I will. Lila invited me!

Oh, James, I miss you already. And speaking of missing — I'm about to put Ethan's face on a milk carton. It's day four since my last contact with him. No e-mails, no phone calls, no answers to the gazillion messages I left. Last I heard, he and Sam, this other Justice for All guy he bonded with, were on the road recording migrant worker grievances in the San Joaquin Valley. I looked up Bakersfield in the atlas. It's Justice for All's West Coast home base. As far as I can tell, it's about three hundred miles north of LA. Oh God. The bathtub! I forgot to shut off the water. Help! XXX Abby

Chapter Two

Blinded by the Light

Jamie

"If Los Angeles, California, is not in your travel plans today," chirped the robo-flight attendant, "kindly deplane at this time."

If I freakin' could, I would.

I wasn't supposed to be *on* de-plane in de-*first* place. And Los Angeles, California, was not in *my* travel plans, today or any other day.

Yes, I wanted *out* of mind-numbing Shafton.

Yes, I wanted a gig that paid big, where I could make enough money in one semester to fund two at Ohio State.

Yes, I wanted to meet hot guys with brains and sensitivity.

But the whole idea was to go to open-all-night New York City. Where two ready-for-anything, smart, sexy best friends would explore, discover, meet, greet, and tear up the town.

What part of that did fate not understand?

So, this is me, Jamie Devine: day one, seat 20A, USAir Cleveland to LAX. I snapped on the seat belt and spent the next five hours going west instead of east, completely contra to the plan.

"Want to know how to make God laugh?" My dad answers his own riddles. "Make a plan."

She must be havin' a cow right about now.

Two days before Abs and I were to leave for New York, I get a news flash from our highly rated nanny agency. The doctor couple I was going to work for had a "change in plans."

Translation: My job fell through.

But, hey, Nannies Without Borders had already scored me another position, a "to-die-for" gig. I should feel *honored* they accepted me, they told me. Because, like, omigod!, the mom, Nicole Hastings-Taylor, is a huge TV star! The dad, Christopher Taylor, Esq., is a way famous attorney! How "serendipitous" (their word, not mine) that their regular nanny had to go back to England for a family emergency, and wouldn't return until January. How very lucky for me that I could fill in for her.

And the hits just kept on comin'. Their one little girl, Olivia, is an angel! And because the Hastings-Taylors are loaded, the money I'd earn was nearly double what the New York doctors had agreed to pay. Translation: This September-to-December job would net me enough to pay for two years at Ohio State.

Okay, so that last bit was very cool.

Only, very me without my best friend. Very me alone.

Not that I'm codependent or anything. I'm totally independent, and beyond ready for new vistas. I just hadn't planned on vista-ing without Abby.

The time I could have taken on the plane adjusting to the change in plans was instead spent with headphones in my ears and the volume cranked up so Courtney Love and Ani DiFranco could scream angry songs to me. Enough fuel to power my bad mood for the whole trip.

Robo-flight attendant made me turn off the music just before landing, so I got to hear the prepackaged warning for passengers to "exercise caution when opening the overhead bins, as things may have shifted during our flight."

Here's what they should have said: "Your brain may have scrambled during the flight. We suggest you check it at the California state line. You won't be needing it."

Jet-lagged and pissed off, I forced myself onto the moving walkway. By the time I was actually paying attention to the here and now, the usual low airport din had morphed into something else — mass hysteria, accompanied by a chaotic rush of stomping feet.

I blinked. And everything went . . . *white*.

I'd gone either dead, or blind.

I was now too panicked to be pissed, as my infantile screams of "Help me! I can't see!" would attest. Either the moving walkway had walked me straight into the sun, or terrorists with chemical weapons had struck, or . . . this was a whiteout courtesy of the California energy crisis.

The riotous stampede was practically on top of me now. Close enough so I could decipher the actual shouts: "Oh my God, it's her! Hurry! Get the camera!"

It's *me*? They're coming for me? They've blinded me and now they want . . . a picture?

Hyperventilating, I forced myself to get a grip. I kept blinking. Until, thank you, God, I saw something. Dots.

Lots of dots. Dots that grew into halos. And then sunbursts, like when you look straight into a camera flash. Imagine, then, staring into a hundred of them.

A camera-toting flash mob had materialized. I was swallowed in a frenzy of clicking shutters, waving arms, and shouts of, "It's her!" "Jewl-ya!" "Get a picture!"

Jewl-ya. Not *Jay*-me.

Just like that, everything came into focus. I'd landed in a place where the welcoming committee was a herd of paparazzi and gaping fans, all in a single-minded quest to snag a picture of some random movie star.

"Julia! Julia! Look this way! Ms. Roberts! Over here!"

Julia Roberts? World-famous movie star? Not so random. And about twenty feet behind me? On *my* moving walkway? Cool.

That is, not cool for me personally. I couldn't care less about movie stars. But to my little sister, this would've been *big*. And bagging an autograph for her? Sweet.

Julia Roberts, like me, was just off the plane. Unlike me, she was radiant. Being mobbed by photographers and autograph hounds was just another day in the trenches for her. She gave them exactly what they wanted, a toss of her luxe curly locks and that megawatt smile. I started to walk toward her, forgetting that the moving walkway was still moving — the other way. And that it would come to a stop. When it did, it was too late. The humiliatingly stupid backward tumble I took was a total non-event in light of the Julia sighting.

By the time I dusted myself off and retrieved my wheelie-suitcase and backpack, the commotion had subsided. The movie star had been whisked away, along with her million-dollar smile — and my big chance to make *my* kid sister smile.

"Miss Devine? Jamie Devine?"

I turned in the direction of the name-check. And blinked again. First, Julia. Now . . . Brad Pitt? And he knows my name? The guy approaching was probably thirty-five at least, but he wore it well. Rock-solid bod, chiseled cheeks, twinkling eyes bracketed by tanned eye-wrinkles. He offered a friendly smile and a handshake. "Hi, I'm Kip, your chauffeur."

"My chauffeur?" I repeated stupidly.

"You *are* Jamie Devine? The nanny for the Hastings-Taylors?"

I nodded, slo-o-o-w on the uptake. They'd sent a chauffeur for the substitute nanny.

"You okay? You look like you just got a scare."

"I . . . I saw . . . Julia Roberts," I stammered, pointing in the direction of her leave-taking. "I got caught in the stampede."

He smiled and took my suitcase. "Welcome to LA, Jamie."

Enviro-nightmare number one: We walked outside, and I breathed. The air was choked with humidity so heavy, just inhaling made you feel full. Maybe that's why everyone here was so thin. It's not anorexia. It's smogorexia.

Limousines lined up at curbside. A red stretch Hummer was in the lead, then came a snazzy silver one, a pearlized white, and finally, your basic black. Kip strode up to the nearest, a relatively simple white stretch, with contrasting darkened windows.

"The family ride," he explained genially. "Please, get in."

I flashed on the Academy Awards. How do the stars do it? Back in, butt first, or the dainty head-duck? I didn't have a chance to choose. A big-haired woman — wearing a "Cleveland Rocks!" sweatshirt — came crashing into my personal space and shoved a disposable camera in my face, demanding excitedly, "Are you anyone?"

My jaw dropped. I was horrified. It really didn't matter who I was — or wasn't. This random tourist was in Hollywood, and indiscriminate. "Anyone" getting into a limo must be *someone.*

A dozen sarcastic responses came to mind — and stayed there. The hope in her eyes, the excitement of taking a picture of . . . somebody . . . was just too bizarre and sad. I couldn't bring myself to insult her. So I put on my sunglasses, tossed my wavy hair, and shot her the biggest smile I could manage, as she joyfully snapped away.

I'd channeled my inner Julia.

Now I was really horrified.

Kip was amused. "Look at that, a pro already."

"No," I protested, climbing into the backseat. "That was a goof. I'm not like that."

"Well, better get used to it," he said, starting the car and easing us out of the airport. "Nicole Hastings-Taylor is a big star in this town. Where she goes — the stalkerazzi follow." He stopped at a light and glanced back at me. "But I'm sure you know that."

Here is what I know.

While Abby's in New York, living her dream, I'm playing nanny for some pampered, plastic TV star and her spoiled spawn, three thousand miles from everything and everyone.

To: ABS@OH.com
From: Jamie_the_lionhearted@OH.com

I'm reading your e-mail — from the back of a limousine. A smog-spewing monstrosity on wheels equipped with a wireless Internet computer. We're deep in the heart of the material world, my friend.

I'm in pity city. Okay — wait, hit pause for the proper response. I should feel lucky!!! Paste picture of me, phony smile here. A semester in Hollywood. Living with the stars! Glamour, glitz, 'Benzes, beaches, and bling!

About Olivia, the kid I haven't met yet. Bet she'll be a total entitle-tot, a Paris Hilton waiting to happen. Her middle name is Cristal, same as the champagne. I can hear the kid now: [To be read in whiny voice] "I can have everything I want because my mommy's a star, and my daddy's a lawyer. They'll sue you if you don't do everything I say."

Can't wait to meet her.

About Ethan. Possible he's suffering from left-coast amnesia? Here's my bff promise: If he doesn't connect soon, I'll personally hunt him down and kill him. Joke! Joke! But seriously, if it's Cali-recon you want on your beloved, color me: Spy-girl.

Hey, I just discovered the minibar in this cabinet. It's stocked with wraps and chips and bottled water. It seems wasteful not to partake.

"Here we are," Kip announced, "Casa Verde. Our little corner of paradise."

I looked out the window. *Verde* is the Spanish word for green. The color of money. Suitably, a towering wall of sculptured shrubs was protecting the Hastings-Taylor hacienda from inquiring eyes.

Kip steered the smog-mobile up to a set of imposing wrought iron gates.

"Look up," he instructed, pointing at a video monitor. "The security camera has face recognition. It'll scan you in and approve you now."

Will they also run my fingerprints, like a CSI background check?

The gates to the kingdom opened, and we rolled into an enormous tile-paved circular driveway, where I got my first look at the place I'd call home from September to December.

The main house was colossal, all creamy white, sporting marble columns, high arched windows, and a tamale-red Spanish-tiled roof. And then there were the grounds, which Kip proudly drove around, so I could see what I was really in for!

Flower-lined stone paths wound around acres of lush landscaping, leading to pools (yes, plural!): one with cabanas and an outdoor Jacuzzi, another a lap pool with cordoned-off lanes, and yet another a kiddie pool with its own playground. And we were only partway around!

We'd yet to reach the tennis court, golf course, the koi pond (koi being goldfish on steroids), and an entire motor court. Which in normal language is a "garage." Except this one had so many parking spaces, it resembled a Motel 6.

There was a guest bungalow — the size of my entire house — to accommodate such recent guests as "former President Clinton, future President Hillary, and Bono of U2," Kip explained.

Of course, there was a "staff wing," the housing area for the twenty or so live-in butlers, maids, chefs, and the "personals" — assistants, trainer, stylist, et cetera.

This is me, rewording that poem "The Rime of the Ancient Mariner": *Servants, servants everywhere, yet not one's a nanny, ya' think?*

Where did I fit in?

We circled back to the main house, and Kip walked me up to the mahogany double doors. It was now or never. I could click my heels three times and —

"Hello! You must be Jamie!"

And you must be . . . *Hugh Grant?* The tanned guy who opened the door surely resembled the rumpled, yet gorgeous star, complete with the bed-head chestnut hair, sparkling blue eyes, and sheepish, self-effacing grin. "Welcome! I'm Topher, Olivia's dad." In the crook of his elbow a small child nestled. Her back was to me so all I saw was a cascade of ginger curls and a frilly dress.

This is Christopher Taylor, barracuda attorney, rich, powerful, connected? Christopher Taylor, Esq., lord of the manor, second-or-is-it-third? husband of Ms. Nicole Hastings, star of the TV sitcom, *Nikki's Way?*

He was shorter than I'd expected. And messier. A wrinkled shirt hung loosely from his wiry bod, and striped shorts stopped at his knobby knees. But some gator minding its own business had clearly died to provide those loafers and the casing for his cell phone.

I was all ready to hate Christopher Taylor, the embodiment of phony. But I didn't. He seemed *sincere.* And — incoming Hollywood cliché — he had me at hello, when he tenderly tucked the child's curls behind her ear, and whispered, "We're so glad Jamie is here — aren't we, Olivia?"

I was moved; the child remained still. Had she even heard him? A wild thought came to me: *Maybe she's mute.*

Topher Taylor gently said, "Our Livvy can be a little shy at first. Don't take it personally, Jamie. She really has been looking forward to meeting you."

"Me too," I lied clumsily to the child's back.

Waving Kip off, Topher took my suitcase with his free

31

hand, and ushered me into what appeared to be a living room. How naïve. This, I was about to learn, was the Guest Reception Area. It was like a doctor's waiting room, down to the sleek couches and artfully arranged magazines on the coffee table.

"Follow us," Topher instructed.

In doing so, I got my first good look at my summer charge. I melted. She looked like an *angel,* all strawberry blonde curls and ringlets around a valentine-shaped face, apple cheeks, button nose, and rosy lips. Her manga-sized blue eyes locked on her dad's shoulder the minute she caught me trying for a direct-connect, and her dimpled chin tucked quickly beneath his shoulder blade.

Memo to self: This whole bashful baby thing is probably an act, put on for her father's sake. When we are alone, her true colors will come out.

"This way to the Great Room," Topher was saying.

Pretty great, truly. It was two-story, with cathedral ceilings and floor-to-ceiling windows. The "conversation pit" (dumb term alert) included a cushy sofa, wing chair, and bronze and leather chairs arranged around a glass coffee table bearing a glass vase with an autumnal bouquet.

"Sit down, Jamie, make yourself comfortable," Topher invited me.

"Um, sure," I started to say, but he interrupted again.

"Unless you're hungry? We should probably get you something to eat first."

I shook my head. "Not really."

"Thirsty, then?"

Without waiting for an answer, he hit an intercom that was set into the brick wall of the fireplace and requested a bottle of Perrier.

Topher planted himself on the wing chair, forcing Olivia to adjust her position. "Come on, sweetie pie," he cajoled, twisting her around and planting her feet on the uber-polished bamboo floor. She resolutely buried her head in his chest.

I shrugged, indicating that I was used to shy kids. But I was thinking, *She hates me. I can leave!*

Topher seemed flustered. This was obviously not starting out the way he'd hoped. I must've looked royally uncomfortable and out of place, and Olivia was definitely not helping. Yet, he wasn't out of ideas.

"I'm going to call Tara. Livvy'll brighten once she sees her big sister. She worships Tara."

There's a sister? Why hadn't anyone mentioned that? Was I expected to deal with two of them? Unless Tara had her own personal nanny.

He plucked the cell phone from his belt loop and hit speed dial. "Tara's my stepdaughter," Topher informed me. "She's 18, same age as you are."

"And she lives here?" *Maybe she could've filled in for the nanny,* I thought.

He laughed. "Tara graces us with her presence when the mood strikes. Same with my son, Tripp. He's 18, too. Actually" — he lowered his voice, as if the info was strictly need-to-know. "They're supposed to split their time, respectively, between my ex and Nic's ex, but they seem to prefer being here."

"Tara," he said into the phone, after what had to be several rings. "Come down and meet Jamie." Awkward pause, as Topher tried to turn his head. "Olivia's nanny, that's who."

Chapter Three

Reckless Infatuation

Abby

Lila's party? Amazing!

Why?

One word. Simon.

Six-foot-two, eyes of blue, the boy was museum-worthy gorgeous.

And he acted like he thought *I* was hot stuff. Oh God.

Friday was a Dylan Lite day. The demanding little dude spent the morning at Elysée Félice, this posh preschool near Lincoln Center.

I killed time scoping the center. Then I crossed a wide, dangerous avenue with confusing traffic signals — and was assaulted by swerving cars, rude shouts, bleating horns, and clouds of grime spewing from the tailpipes of buses. I wound up in a huge Barnes & Noble; checked out the New Fiction section; took an escalator to the second floor and had a "latte" — which is basically espresso coffee, steamed milk and, judging by the price, a heavy infusion of liquid gold. Hello. Three dollars for a caffeine hit? Never in Ohio.

When I arrived back at Dylan's preschool, hyped on pricey espresso and sightseer shock, Mademoiselle

Félice — the overly mascaraed, clownishly blushed, seventy-something woman who ran the place — latched onto me.

"Deelyn," she said, "'as been naughty." Apparently, he'd refused to lie still on his cot during rest period. Rest period? The kid had just gotten up from a solid eight hours of sleep. Who wouldn't have a hard time taking a nap in the middle of the morning?

His penalty for wriggling, Mademoiselle informed me, was to sit on the sidelines during his favorite activity, art. He'd become furious, of course. He'd told her that when I came to get him I'd punch her in the *boobies*. He'd also called her a doody head.

I went to the school's office and sprang Dylan. He'd been crying. His throat was clogged and he was wiping his runny nose on the sleeve of his Polo Ralph Lauren Childrenswear sweatshirt.

Mademoiselle wagged a finger under my nose and announced that "Ee 'as just one more shance." Did I understand her? she demanded.

"If when you say shance, you mean *chance*," I said in my snottiest tone, "I do."

After lunch at home, we headed crosstown for Dylan's swimming lesson. It ended half an hour early when he panicked in the pool and snarked up a mouthful of chlorinated water.

Then on to Eighty-sixth Street for Martial Arts.

Dylan looked adorable in the little white karate jacket and pajama pants they call a "Gi." He was so-so at the kicking and hand-slashing stuff, but had the shouts and grunts down pat. In spite of his trademark scowl, he seemed to be enjoying himself — until another five-year-old, a girl who was slightly taller than Dyl, kicked him by mistake.

It was a total love tap. Her big toe kind of brushed his arm. But it was enough to throw him off balance. He hit the mat like a hunk of raw beef hitting a cutting board.

Dylan lost it.

First he yowled as if she'd drawn blood. Then, fighting back tears, he stomped off the mat, plopped down in a corner of the room, and refused to even look at me when I tried to encourage him to get back into the game. Only when the instructor came over at the end of class and told him he was really improving did he heave his little booty off the floor and get ready to leave.

The penthouse was like a beehive when we got back. Caterers and florists were buzzing around the place, setting up extra tables and chairs in the dining room and positioning scrumptious arrangements of pink and white roses, lilies, and white orchids everywhere. A manic battalion of worker bees scurried to prepare the Mathesons' home for Lila's "very easy" dinner party.

"Dylan's clothes are laid out on his bed," Edith told me in passing, "and so are yours — in the nanny's suite."

I was thinking how thoughtful it was of Edith to find the clothes I'd brought to change into for the party and set them out for me. "Thanks," I called, ducking out of the way of an immense basket of lilies.

I wrestled, pleaded, and promised Dylan into the bath-tub. I agreed that he could keep his underpants on while I bathed him. And that I'd sneak into the pantry and score him a couple of Godiva truffles if he dried himself and changed his underwear while I was gone.

Before I hit the chocolate stash, I ducked into the nanny's suite to check on the outfit I'd brought for the party. The missing Miss Skearitt's quarters were small, but only by comparison with the other cavernous rooms in the apartment. And it was beautifully decorated. A blue-and-white ruffled quilt with matching shams and a gazillion throw pillows of every size and shape rested on the polished mahogany sleigh bed.

And there, laid out on the Laura Ashley gingham, was an outfit — but not *my* outfit!

There had to be a mistake. It wasn't my slinky red strapless lying there in its plastic dry-cleaning bag. It was a *uniform*! A black-and-white servant girl costume. Someone had even thrown in a still-in-their-Dior-wrapper pair of stock-ings and a brand-new pair of Nine West black loafers, just my size.

I hadn't been invited *to* the blowout. I'd been invited to take care of Dylan during the festivities. I swallowed back the lump in my throat and zigzagged through the pre-party pande-monium to find Edith.

"I know, I know," she said, holding up her hand. "Miss Skearitt liked dressing up. I guess Mrs. Matheson figured every nanny was a uniform nut like her — although, God knows, we've had enough nannies marching through this place for her to know better."

"Do I have to wear it?" I asked, hoping I didn't sound as pathetic as I felt.

Edith shrugged. "I wouldn't," she said. Then, realizing that she actually was wearing a uniform, she added, "Not if I were seventeen."

If Edith hadn't given me permission, I probably would have crawled into the humiliating costume. But because of her, I decided on an uneasy compromise. I wouldn't wear the black-and-white outfit. And, since I was not a guest, I wouldn't wear my favorite slinky dress either.

Which left me with hip-hugger, boot-cut jeans and the black V-neck I'd worn to work. Just to ramp it up a little, I thought I'd wear my dangly faux ruby earrings and the silk red jacket that Aunt Molly had picked up for me in Chinatown. It had a Mandarin collar and was embroidered with gold-and-pink dragons.

That's how I was dressed when I finally met Dylan's dad, and Lila's ex, Spence "Call-Me-Speed" Matheson.

I was reading to Dylan, who was popping truffles and wiping his chocolate-smeared fingers on the arm of his kid-sized sofa. We were in his playroom, the one with the trampoline, plasma TV, video games, battery-operated ride-in Hummer, and life-sized plush tiger — not to be confused with his toy-filled bedroom, or the duck-wallpapered bathroom with its plastic barrel full of bath toys — when Lila dragged Speed Matheson in. He was very tan and tall and handsome. And his teeth were unnaturally white. I'd heard from Edith that he lived in LA.

"She's a big improvement over Skearitt," he told his ex-wife, giving me a blinding grin. "Great jacket. Whose is it?"

"Mine," I said, a little defensively.

"No, whose label?" Speed clarified.

"He always asks that," Lila announced as if her ex wasn't there. "It's a family thing. Speed comes from a long line of filthy rich garmentos. Like his father before him, he designs and manufactures high-end knitwear." She elbowed her beaming ex-husband playfully. "Did I tell you? Isn't she fabulous?" she said, elegant arms outstretched, displaying me as if I were a pricey antique she'd bid on and won. If she noticed that I wasn't wearing the uniform she'd put together for me, she never mentioned it.

"Welcome aboard, Abby," Speed said, sounding as jaunty and nautical as the yacht-racing emblem on his charcoal blue blazer and the yellow silk ascot at his throat. "Hey, big guy." He bent to give Dylan a hug.

Lila shrieked, "Speed, watch out! His fingers! Darling," she said to me, as Speed fell backward. "In about twenty minutes, bring Dyl into the living room. And get him into a clean shirt before you do."

She was wearing this spotless white, bare-backed, Michael Kors dress, so I was impressed when she bent to kiss Dylan. If he'd laid a paw on her, the costly garb would have been history. But Lila had the touchless embrace down. She managed to air-kiss Dylan's freshly washed, shiny dark hair without actually touching him.

As requested, Dylan and I hit the party twenty minutes later.

The cocktail hour was in full swing. Guys in crisp white shirts with black vests and slacks were passing out hors d'oeuvres. Glasses and ice cubes clinked, and a tinkling piano tried to ride above the mounting noise of small talk. Lila saw us and glided over on her mile-high Jimmy Choo's.

She checked Dylan out before taking his just-washed hand. "Dyl," she whispered, "these are Mommy and Daddy's friends and I want you to be polite to them."

To my surprise, Dylan just nodded. No convulsion, no screaming fit, no going suddenly slack and having to be dragged around the room.

Lila walked him through the crowd while I stood awkwardly among strangers whose coifs, cosmetics, and clothing probably cost more than the national budget of a small country.

I spotted Curt Gordevan with a drink in his hand. He was splayed out on the gold sofa lecturing to a bevy of worshipful women and wistful men. A few other people looked familiar — not because I'd met them before, but because I'd seen them on magazine covers, TV talk shows, or on the back jackets of books they'd written.

I felt incredibly excited at first, and then awestruck — which led to a familiar panicky dip in self-esteem because I knew I didn't have the guts to talk to any of them.

I figured I'd duck back into the playroom when suddenly this outstanding guy, easily over six feet, in a white shirt, dark slacks, and a pair of ratty Adidas was in front of me. Before he said a word, my heart went flamenco — castanets included. He asked if I'd like a drink or an hors d'oeuvre.

I croaked, "Diet Coke."

He laughed. "Ah, the designated driver." Then he got serious. "Don't go away. I'll be right back."

In the minute it took him to get me a Coke, Ethan crashed the party in my head. *Don't even go there, Abby,* my mind said. *What?* I countered. *I don't even know this guy.* But what I did know, which totally freaked me, was that my pulse was banging away, my face had gotten ridiculously hot, and I was shaking. Three symptoms, it occurred to me, I'd never experienced around Ethan.

"So, who are you?" the cause of my elevated heart rate asked, handing me a Coke with a cherry and a Mai Tai paper umbrella stuck in it.

I laughed at the Shirley Temple he'd delivered. "Abigail Burrows. How about you?"

If he wasn't one of the catering crew, I thought, *I'd never have the nerve to talk to him.* But despite my physical meltdown, I wasn't as tongue-tied as usual.

"Simon," he said, offering his hand. I took it, expecting to shake. Instead, he covered my hand with his, and held onto it. "Cool jacket."

"Chinatown's best," I said. "Do you do this often?" I meant working at parties, fetching drinks for people.

"What? Become recklessly infatuated? No, not too often," he said, his blue-blue eyes sparkling. "Where did you come from? I don't think I've seen you at any of these blowouts before —"

"Probably not," I said. My mouth had gone dry, as my captive palm grew clammy. I took a sip of the Coke and slipped my hand out of his, reluctantly. "I'm from Ohio," I confessed, my freed hand tingling with warmth. "I work for Lila — Mrs. Matheson," I corrected myself.

"Speaking of," Simon said, as Lila came toward us, a frowning Dylan at her heels.

"I see you've met Simon," Lila beamed. "He's one of my absolute favorites. Darling, can you tuck Dylan in? He's getting a little —" She spelled it out: "C-R-A-N-K-Y."

"Of course," I said, reaching for his chubby paw.

He jerked his hand away. "Doody head," he growled at me.

"Dylan!" Lila was shocked.

"Whoa there, little guy. That's not very cool," Simon observed.

"Come on, Dyl," I said, shooting Simon a smile. "I'll read to you. Better yet, I'll tell you a story. I'm really good at making up stories. And guess who's going to be the star of this one? You."

His guard was down. I took his hand. He squeezed my fingers with surprising strength — definitely more than he'd shown at karate — and glared up at me. I knew what was coming next, and there was nothing I could do to stop it. He dropped to the floor, or rather to the Oriental carpet beneath our feet. And there he hung, dangling from my hand.

"Dylan!" Lila hissed. "You get up this instant. What's wrong with you?"

"Abby's a poo-poo turd. I hate her."

Before he could offer a second opinion, Dylan was swept up into Simon's arms.

He kicked his feet in protest, but Simon swung him up onto his shoulders and jogged behind me into the playroom. Simon ducked and let Dyl tumble over his head onto the trampoline; then he plopped himself down on Dylan's little couch.

He looked adorably zany sitting on the peewee-size sofa, his thick dark hair spiked and messy, his legs so long his kneecaps practically brushed his chin. "Whew, the kid's got issues. You okay?" he asked.

"Thanks to you," I said, casting a responsible eye on Dylan, who was taking his misery out on the trampoline, jumping, kicking, and flopping with grumpy gusto.

Simon laughed. "Yeah, it was getting pretty ugly out there. Guess you owe me."

I was smiling. Actually, I realized, I'd been smiling almost from the moment I saw him. "Guess I do —" I took a breath and smelled the clean scent of his cologne. Sniffing, I blurted, "What *is* that?"

"My cologne?" He rubbed his neck. "Too much?" he wanted to know.

"No . . ." I burned with embarrassment but couldn't stop myself. "Just right," I said.

Simon's satisfied grin raised the heat. *"L'homme."* He pronounced it *Lum*. My third year French kicked in: *L'homme*. As in "The man." Oh yeah.

Someone in the doorway cleared her throat. We both looked up. A beautiful blonde, in her mid-thirties, I guessed, was tapping her hot red fingernails on the doorjamb. "I hate to interrupt your fun, baby, but we've got work to do."

Simon made a face and groaned. "Yes, Boss." He hoisted himself up out of the little couch. "I'm all yours," he told her, glancing at his watch. "For the next fifteen minutes anyway. But remember, I'm not doing dinner. Agreed?"

She gave Simon a curt nod, then turned her green eyes on me. "I'm Jacqueline," she said, looking me up and down. "And you are?"

"Abigail Burrows," I responded. "Nice to meet you."

Liar, liar, pants on fire, an insane little voice in my head chanted. Meeting a blonde who could snap her fingers and make Simon jump was not on the agenda I didn't know I had until she showed up. *Excuse me. You have a boyfriend,* I reminded myself as Simon strolled over to Jacqueline.

She took his hand and started to leave, with him in tow. *I'll be back,* he mouthed over his shoulder.

To my surprise, I was still smiling . . . until the rhythmic thumping of trampoline action suddenly stopped, and a tug at the hem of my jacket signaled that Dylan had returned. "You have to tell me a story," he whined.

"Right." I headed for the stack of books that shared shelf space with his impressive video game collection.

"No, you can't read to me!" he grumbled. "You have to make one up — about me! You said so."

"Silly me." I sat down on the little sofa Simon had abandoned and patted the cushion next to me. "Once upon a time, there was a boy . . . named Dylan."

He scrambled onto the couch. "And he was —?" His forehead, with its bright new Band-Aid, wrinkled in thought.

"Help me out here," I said. "And he was?"

"Big fat!" Dylan hollered.

His answer caught me totally off guard. I kind of gasped and felt my heart fall. "No, I don't think so," I told him. "Not the Dylan I'm thinking about. The one in my story is not too big and not too little. He's just right and very nice."

"Okay," he said, settling back.

"But he was lonely," I continued. "He was lonely because —?" I waited again for him to finish the sentence.

"'Cause he could beat up everybody and they was a-scared of him," he suggested.

"Do you think it was because he was good at karate? And his teacher said he was getting better every day?"

"Yeah!" Dylan agreed. "And he could beat up DC —"

"Definitely. Because he practiced and practiced and didn't cry when someone made a mistake and accidentally hit him. He just said to himself, 'Oh, well, everyone makes mistakes. Even my mommy and daddy and Edith and — who else?'"

It took him a minute, then he got it. "And you!"

"Yes, even Abby can be wrong sometimes. Not a lot, but sometimes," I allowed.

46

"Yeah. And you know who else does big stupid mistakes?"

"DC?" I guessed.

Dylan practically jumped for joy. "DC is a big, fat, peenith faith!"

"A total poo-poo head," I agreed. "So Dylan decided to practice karate with his friend who sometimes but not often made mistakes. His friend was a brown-haired, hazel-eyed girl, who made up fabulous stories —"

"You!" Dylan yelled.

I leaped up and struck what I hoped looked like a threatening karate pose. I put my hands flat in front of me and held one leg off the floor.

Dylan jumped up, spun in front of me, and kicked me in the shin. I yowled exaggeratedly and fell to the floor, hollering, "No. Stop Dylan. I'm DC. I give up. I'm 'a-scared' of you! Don't hurt me!"

He tried to harden his round little face but couldn't hold the ferocious scowl. A giggle escaped his clenched lips. I grabbed his ankles and pretended to try and fail to pull him off his feet.

"Ha!" he exulted. He threw himself on top of me, landing on my exposed stomach like a fifty-pound mackerel, and knocking the air out of me.

I was on my back, trying to catch my breath. Dylan was draped across my middle, kicking his feet triumphantly. All of a sudden, someone was kneeling next to us, pounding the floor like a wrestling referee.

"And the winner and still champion is —" The cheerful voice belonged to Simon.

It hit me then that my cropped sweater had ridden up and was practically wrapped around my neck. And my hip-huggers were riding low. The only thing covering my bare belly was Dylan.

"— Dylan Matheson!" Simon announced.

Dylan jumped up and began a victory lap around the play-room. I rolled over quickly.

"Gotta split," Simon said, "but I need your number."

"I can't," I told Simon, feeling like an idiot. "I mean, I've got a —"

"Can't?" he cut me off. "What do you mean 'can't'? I leave you with Jackie Chan here for ten minutes and you forget?"

"Forget what?"

"That you owe me," he said, his grin sweet and sexy.

TO: Jamie_the_lionhearted@OH.com
FROM: ABS@OH.com

Hey, limo girl. Gotta sec? I know you call me "Dear Abby," but right now, James, I need *your* advice. Urgently. I met this guy at Lila's little blowout. (Please note: an "easy" party is New York-ese for a bash of about a hundred, mostly skinny, designer-outfitted beau-tiful people. Lila's mammoth co-op was wall-to-wall celebs tonight, with one cater-waiter for every three guests and enough finger food to stamp out famine in Africa.) Speaking of cater-waiters, one asked for my number. His name is Simon, and he's a twenty-some-thing, dark-haired, and blue-eyed. And, shame on me, I gave it to him. Before you judge me — which I know you won't — here are the facts: No contact from Ethan at all. I was starting to get worried so I called his parents a little while ago and they said, yes, they'd heard from him and he's fine. What to make of this info? Are Ethan and I still an item? And if so, why won't he return my messages and e-mails? Can I go out with Simon — just as a friend — if, *big if,* he actually does call and ask me out? Whaddya think? XOXO. Ab

Chapter Four

She's So Vain, She Probably Thinks This Chapter Is About Her

Jamie

I watched Tara Hastings drift down the stairs, her finger lightly brushing the banister. You know that lame expression, "You never get a second chance to make a first impression"? So unfortunate. Here's my impression: contempt at first sight. And, from her expression, it was mutual.

A tall, swizzle-stick thin cliché, Tara was so . . . LA! I bet her idea of heavy reading was the fall issue of *Vogue*. She was all shiny and metallic. Bronze skin, platinum hair, topaz eyes, slinky silver minidress, diamond bracelet, and gold-star attitude. As she got closer, I nearly had to shut my eyes.

Over Topher's fumbling introductions, Tara actually *sniffed* me! Like a rude Afghan hound making sure I knew who was alpha bitch in this house. She oughtn't have fretted. Her points — all of them, from her sky-high slides to her little boob-ettes — were well taken. I'd call her an ice princess, except ice eventually melts. I was pretty sure Tara would not.

She didn't even pretend to be nice. Or even courteous. Her opening salvo: "So your luggage is coming later?"

I gestured to my carry-on–size suitcase and backpack. "This is it."

She cocked an eyebrow. "*This* is all you brought? Are you already planning to quit?"

"I have what I need."

Gingerly, Topher tried to engage Olivia in our meeting, but Tara stayed on topic. "So, it's like what you're wearing . . . and whatever's in there?" She wrinkled her nose at my suitcase, as if a pile of Dumpster-rags might be inside.

For the record, I was wearing Levi's recycled jeans, Birkenstocks, my "Cure It Fast" T-shirt, and the peace-symbol necklace my mom had given me years ago. So why did I suddenly feel like some lower being? Why even care what this vacuous viper thought of me?

Alert to potential hostility, Topher played peacemaker. He urged us to relax and get to know each other.

To which I could totally hear Tara thinking, *Why? She's the nanny.*

To which I was totally thinking, *Why? I'm only here for a few months.*

For Topher and Olivia, I smiled and took a step toward the couch. Tara intercepted, circling me like a predator.

Topher kissed the top of Olivia's head and offered, "Jamie came a long way to take care of you, Livvy, isn't that nice?"

Tara snickered, "Yes, our very own Midwest milkmaid. From Ohio."

"Never heard of it?" I guessed.

"Oh, please, it's like all the other flyover states," she responded with a dismissive wave of her hand. "Why anyone would live there is beyond me."

I imagined a lot was beyond her.

Olivia suddenly giggled. Topher, clearly searching for a way to lighten the moment, was tickling her. Olivia's giggles got louder, and more insistent, as if she was forcing them. Topher stopped immediately, and stroked her hair, but that only made her giggles turn into hiccupy laughs, which she didn't seem to have control over.

"Uh-oh," Topher said soothingly, "I think we might be having a giggle-fit."

Tara's eyes flashed dangerously at Topher. "Why'd you start that? You know how she gets! She's practically four years old. She should be over this infantile behavior by now. Even the shrink says so!"

Tara's outburst had the desired effect. Olivia had stopped giggling, all right. And started to pee. A wobbly stream leaked down the child's chubby legs, puddling onto the shiny bamboo floor. Horrified, Livvy turned red and started to sob.

This was not an act. This child was deeply ashamed.

Topher leaped up. "Come on, sweetie," he said. "It's okay. We'll get you all cleaned up." He seemed all too accustomed to this incident. He shot us a chagrined look, swept the baby up in his arms, and rushed off with her.

The ice princess folded her spindly arms and rolled her eyes.

Over his shoulder, Topher called out, "Tara, show Jamie to her room."

Tara looked startled, as if he'd ordered her to lug me on

her back. "Now," he added, through clenched teeth. "It's the one next to Olivia's."

I was stunned. I hadn't expected Tara to lower herself and clean up the mess, but I thought she might at least show an ounce of empathy for her little sister who, at age three, already knew how it felt to be humiliated.

But Tara just tossed her long silky locks regally, and made a show of applying lip gloss.

I hitched up my backpack, grabbed my suitcase, and started toward the stairs. Actually, it was one of those twin butterfly staircases. I chose one, Tara deliberately went up the other, then brushed me aside rudely at the top and headed down the corridor.

Out of the corner of my eye — just for an instant — I saw a tall, thin guy in a hooded sweatshirt slink down another hallway.

"Tripp." Tara, her back still to me, answered my unasked question. "My brother from another litigation. Or as we call him, The Shadow."

A door closed. And latched.

Tara marched into the room assigned to me. One step in, her towering heels sank into the plush creamy carpet.

As Abby would put it: Oh. My. Gawd.

It was an entire suite, done in white and aqua, breezy, open, and airy. Snow-white lace curtains billowed over floor-to-ceiling arched windows, one of which led to my own private balcony.

Tara played snarky tour guide, pointing out everything she was sure I would not appreciate, from the Klaus armchairs, to the four-poster king-sized bed, to the "Frette linens."

By her tone, clearly they weren't made of hemp, like mine at home.

"They get changed daily. By housekeeping." Her tone was deliberate.

Color me warned: Do not attempt to make bed by myself! Was I good enough to even rest my head on one of the dozen or so poufy pillows?

Tara continued to rattle off designer names, indicating the enormous flat-screen plasma TV and entertainment system with DVD and Bose speakers.

I so did not belong here. No human did. This was a magazine layout, not a room you actually slept in.

Then I noticed the cushioned window seat set inside an arched window, looking out over the backyard. Confession: Always wished I'd had one like that.

"Full bar . . ." Tara was now saying.

I twirled. Wow! Polished wood, glass, a nozzle for beer, and a pantheon of pricey wines and hard liquor rounded out a corner of the suite.

"Are you sure?" I stammered.

Tara yawned so big I saw her tonsils. "About what?"

"This suite. I guess it's for Olivia's regular nanny?"

"Olivia doesn't have a regular nanny," Tara informed me. "They come, they go. Like yesterday's Manolos."

"Why?"

"It's obvious, isn't it?" Tara snorted. "Once the bridge-and-tunnel crowd discovers them, it's time to move on to Jimmy Choo's."

She. Is. A. Moron. Slowly, I said, "I meant, why the revolving door nannies?"

"Oh, that. Olivia has issues."

Aside from you? The sister she worships, who berates her in front of a stranger? (Don't worry, I didn't *say* that.)

Tara settled into a chair and crossed her legs so her flimsy skirt edged up to the northern limits of thigh-land. "I suppose you've met Kip," Tara mused, as she fiddled with her diamond bracelet.

Who? Oh, right, the chauffeur-slash-tour-guide.

"You like?" Tara asked, smarm coating her voice.

"He seems OK," I said noncommittally.

"Friendly warning. Don't waste your time. He may be on your . . . level — one of the *help* — but he bats for the other team."

And the English translation of that might be? Whatever. Really, there were only two words I wanted to hear from her: "good" and "bye."

Tara reverse-crossed her legs and fixed a superior gaze on me while I tried not to squirm. Topher had mentioned Tara being my age. *High school or college?* I wondered.

"I take classes," Tara informed me, as if she'd read my mind.

"Where?" Was it too much to hope that she'd be going away to school — far away? Soon?

"At USC," she responded, in an extremely bored tone.

Despite myself, I was impressed. The University of Southern California was a prestige school. To get in, you needed smarts, not just big bucks. "What's your major?"

"Undecided. I'm dabbling."

Rrrrp! That was the sound of "impressed" being rewound. What had I expected? Bio-chemical engineering? Asian econ? Organic chemistry?

Tara's cell phone rang. She checked the caller ID, rose languidly, said something about "nanny-girl," and slowly headed out the door.

I couldn't close it fast enough.

Alone at last, I drifted aimlessly around the suite, admiring a vase of fresh flowers and flipping through the issue of *Los Angeles* magazine on the nightstand. Everything was so opulent, so big. Except me. I felt small and untethered, like a balloon some careless kid had let go.

I floated over to the bar, stocked with brand-named vodka, rum, gin, tequila, and wines with colorful labels. I kept floating. I finally stopped, when my fingers touched the bedside phone.

"Abby?" I said tentatively, incredibly relieved that she'd picked up.

We caught up quickly, filling each other in on our respective stresses.

"Terror?" Abby asked when I'd finished. "The sister's name is *Terror?*"

"Might as well be."

"Let it go," Abby advised. "She's probably dealing with her own stuff. You're the intruder in her tiny little fiefdom, so she comes on strong, messing with you. My guess? You won't see much of her."

As they say in sarcasm-land, "Yeah, right."

Chapter Five

Call Waiting

Abby

I'd done it. I'd given Simon my cell digits. It was okay, I told myself. He'd never call me anyway.

The next day, I checked my cell phone hourly to make sure it was working.

It was Saturday. Dylan's ten A.M. Art Appreciation class had been canceled, Edith told me on her way to the kitchen. I followed her into the bright loftlike space, and was surprised by a weird feeling of disappointment. The spacious room was back to its tidy self, brushed aluminum appliances gleaming, country wood floor waxed to a dangerous sheen. There was not a trace left of last night's frantic doings. Not a trace of the catering staff in their starched black-and-white uniforms. Unconsciously, I sniffed the air, seeking the sexy scent of *L'homme*. Not a trace of Simon anywhere but on my mind.

Dylan was in the breakfast nook, dragging a spoon through a bowl of sticky cereal. "Good morning," I called to him.

"I hate oatmeal," he answered.

"Mrs. M. wants to know, can you stay until nine tonight," Edith said. "She's got a cocktail party she forgot, and I can't do it. She says she'll make it up to you. In cash and prizes," Edith deadpanned.

I was supposed to leave at seven. *Oh, well, two more hours wouldn't really be a problem,* I thought, feeling very Cinderella. Especially since I had absolutely nothing else to do.

"He's all dressed and ready to go," Edith said eagerly. "Mrs. M. left half an hour ago. It's a beautiful day. Nobody should be inside on a day like this."

"You want him out of here," I guessed.

"On the count of three," Edith confirmed.

"Let's go, Dyl," I said.

It was too easy. He scrambled off the breakfast banquette without protest.

"How'd you like to go to the Alice in Wonderland statue?" I'd read about it in a New York guidebook; there were supposed to be storytelling sessions there on Saturdays.

"Is DC gonna be there?"

"Oh, I don't think so," I said, hoping I was right. "He's probably at the playground."

"Torturing someone," Edith grumbled.

"I wanna go to the playground," Dylan decided.

"You don't want to be where DC is, do you? I thought you didn't like him."

"I'm not a-scared of him," Dylan growled.

"Of course not. I didn't think you were," I lied supportively.

An odd thought hit me. Was it possible that Dylan had

taken last night's karate game seriously? Was he now itching for a face-off with the bad boy? *No way. Not my fault,* my mind declared defensively.

"You know what, Dyl? I've never seen the Alice in Wonderland statue," I wheedled hopefully. "I bet it's lots of fun."

"I wanna go to the playground!" he repeated, narrowing his eyes at me, daring me to defy his command.

I folded.

The usual suspects were perched on the nanny benches. I recognized only one, Garrick, the manny. He was leafing through a newspaper, ignoring the sandbox, where DC was busy stealing a little girl's plastic sand-castle mold.

Garrick glanced up. I waved to him and took Dylan over to the jungle gym. Dyl held onto my hand, but kept glaring over his shoulder at DC — who fortunately didn't notice.

"What's wrong?" I asked, heaving Dylan onto the monkey bars. "Why are you giving DC the evil eye?"

"'Cause he's a meany cockabeany," he answered. He crawled out of my reach, heading with surprising nimbleness to the top of the bars.

Garrick strolled over. "How'd it turn out?" he asked me, nodding toward Dylan. "Did Lila go bats?"

"You mean, because of the cut? No. She hardly noticed. What did DC's parents do when you told them what happened?"

"Parent. Single," Garrick said, running a hand through

his crimson curls. "Tess Conyers. Her ex-husband lives in Chicago. Never sees DC. I didn't tell her. Tess is usually so wiped out when she gets home from work that I don't like to give her grief."

I smiled, thinking that was considerate.

"Anyway, I cut him off from his favorite TV show," Garrick added.

"SpongeBob," I guessed, trying to show that I knew what passed for cool in the kindergarten set.

"Survivor, the Final Challenge," Garrick said. "That really tore him up."

"Are you sure he's six?"

"In dog years," he teased. "So, how do you like working for the hottest publisher in town?"

He surprised me. I wondered how he knew about Lila. Although I figured lots of people who knew about books would recognize her name, I didn't think everybody in New York knew who she was. Then I remembered. "Did Miss Skearitt tell you about her?"

"She didn't have to. Ever read the *New York Post*? Page Six?" He opened the newspaper he'd been reading and showed me the gossip column. "There's dish about her in here every other day. Today's column's all about last night's blowout for her new wonder boy."

There, beneath the banner, PAGE SIX, was a blurry black-and-white photo of Lila with Curt Gordevan on her left and, on her right, a tall guy in a dark jacket who was looking over his shoulder, his head turned away from the camera. The

61

caption under the picture read: *Lila Matheson of Matheson Press and her two best-selling authors, Curt Gordevan and S. G. Wagner.*

"S. G. Wagner!" I said. "Oh wow, I didn't know *he* was at the party. I love him. I read part of his novel in *Rolling Stone.*"

That had been two years ago, when the magazine ran a chapter from *Lost in Brooklyn*, which S. G. Wagner had written when he was just eighteen years old. The book was about sex, drugs, and these hot young guys, tight friends, living in this artsy section of Brooklyn — Williamsburg, an industrial area where painters and poets lived in cheap converted warehouses. It was supposed to be the happening place. The little bit of the novel that I'd read was sizzling. The whole book, I'd heard, was even hotter.

So, of course, Ms. Danbury, our school librarian, refused to order it. And, of course, our local bookstore, which carried every romance novel ever published, didn't have S. G. Wagner's bestseller. So I'd never even seen the book nor looked at the author photo on the jacket flap.

"God, I am so lame," I wailed, thinking probably everybody in the world would have recognized S. G. Wagner at a party. But I wasn't from the world. I was from Shafton. "I don't even know what he looks like."

"Join the club," Garrick said. "He's like this 'very private' guy. Practically paranoid. I mean, did you notice that he wasn't even looking at the camera in that shot? He's supposed to be big-time publicity shy. That's probably the only thing he *is* shy about," he added. "From what I hear, the dude's always at the right party with the right blonde."

I looked up from the fuzzy photo and checked Garrick's expression, half expecting to see a sour, jealous look on his face.

But no, he was smiling at me . . . as if he wanted to make me feel better about not knowing what S. G. Wagner looked like. As if he wanted to tease me out of hating myself.

I took in his curly red hair, his green eyes, and his mischievous smile. And it dawned on me that he was pretty darn cute. And sweet.

"I wish I'd known about Wagner's thing for blondes last night," I teased back. "I could have tracked all the blondes at Lila's bash —"

"You were there?" Garrick asked, impressed.

I nodded, then added truthfully, "I was taking care of Dylan. But I can't believe I was at the same party as S. C. Wagner and never even knew it."

"So you're a big fan of his?"

"I guess." I shrugged. "I mean I didn't get to read a whole lot of the book. Did you read it?"

"Nope," he said. "But if you like him that much, maybe I'll give him a try."

I was surprised. And flattered.

A shrill scream from the sandbox announced that DC had fulfilled his mission. The plastic sand-castle mold sailed toward us, followed by the heart-wrenching cries of his victim. In four impressive strides, Garrick was in the sandbox and all over DC.

My cell phone rang. *Oh, my God. Simon,* I thought. Then, *Yeah, right. No way.*

For a second I mused that my mom might be calling to report a killer hot flash, then I remembered with relief that I hadn't given her my new cell phone number.

Ethan? Of course! His parents must have told him to call me, told him how worried I was about him.

Before I answered my phone, I checked on Dylan, who was at the top of the jungle gym, watching DC catch hell from Garrick.

"Ethan?" I said.

"Try again," the caller challenged. "Category: Guys who think Abigail is cute —"

The heat rising from my neck to my face gave me my answer. "Simon?" I whispered.

"Miss me?" he asked. "And by the way, who's Ethan?"

I was waiting under the awning outside Lila's co-op. The forest green canopy was held up by four thick, brass poles, all of them polished to a blinding gleam. I could see myself in the nearest one. I'd swept my dark hair up in an amateur version of Lila's pricey 'do. And I'd done a decent job on my eye make-up. The black mascara thickened and lengthened my lashes, just like the tube had promised, and highlighted my green cat eyes. I was wearing the jeans and blue sweater I'd worn to work, and my backpack was looped over one shoulder.

But, folded over my arm, radiant in its plastic dry cleaning bag, was the killer red strapless I'd left at the Mathesons' last night, and the Chinese jacket that everyone had thought was so cool. And dangling from my fingertips was the pair of five-inch heels I'd worn only once before, a couple of months ago, when Ethan and I went to dinner at Shafton's only nice restaurant and decided that we wouldn't date anyone else.

This is not a date, I reminded myself. *Not officially.*

Which was what Simon had pointed out on the phone. "I'm not asking you up to my place — even though it's been featured in *Architectural Digest* and *GQ*," he joked. "I'm inviting you to a party for The Killer B's." I hadn't heard of the group, but was too embarrassed to say so. "They're a reggae blues band," Simon explained. "There'll probably be a huge crowd."

"I'm working tonight. Till nine —"

"No problem. I'll pick you up about nine-thirty," he said. "Things don't get going in Brooklyn till after ten anyway."

I had to sit down. I put my phone away and balanced my butt on one of the monkey bars. Dylan scrambled down and sat two bars over, kicking his feet back and forth. "Your face is red," he said.

"Yeah, I'm feeling a little warm. You're good on the bars," I told him. "Did you ever take gymnastics?"

He shook his head no. "I think we should check that out," I said.

Dylan shrugged. I followed his gaze to the entrance of the playground. Garrick had DC firmly in hand and was walking him out the gate. "It's no fun here," Dylan announced. "Let's go to Alice in Wonderland."

A shiny, black Lincoln Town Car with tinted windows pulled up at exactly nine-thirty. The back window went down and Simon looked out.

"What are you doing in that?" I blurted, meaning a luxe car with a driver.

"My bike's in the shop, so Mike here is doing me a favor. But I could ask you the same thing." He laughed, checking out my outfit. "Could you dress down a little? Come on, get in, Ohio." He pushed open the door for me.

He was wearing dark pants and a white shirt again; this time the shirt was under a creamy black leather blazer. I didn't notice his signature scruffy Adidas until later. He looked too good to be true. But this was New York. For all I knew cater-waiters made a fortune — and spent it all on clothes and cars.

"You didn't tell me whether the club was casual or dressy, so I hedged my bet," I told him, putting the red dress between us on the roomy seat. "I didn't know the dress code."

He checked out the strapless. "Code red," he said. "Definitely."

"I can run back up and change," I offered, even as the car pulled away from the curb.

"No, you don't have to. You can change on the way down-town, in the car. What?" he said, at my astonished stare. "Believe me, the lead singer of the KBs will be wearing a lot less than you, even if you stripped clear down to your Victoria's Secret thong."

"Wal-Mart. Fruit of the Loom," I blurted. "And they're bikini cut."

Simon laughed. His teeth were perfect. His blue eyes as dazzling as sunlight on water. He had that cool, well-groomed, unshaven look. Just enough stubble to make you want to stroke his cheek. "Go on. I promise. I won't peek."

I glanced at the back of the driver's ponytailed head. Simon picked up on my new concern. "Mike, you don't care if Abby changes her clothes back here, do you?"

"Not if you come up here with me and keep your eyes facing front," Mike said gallantly, pulling over to the curb.

Simon hopped out and got into the front seat, and Mike maneuvered back into traffic. The tinted windows added just enough privacy for me to feel safe sliding into the dress — which I did before pulling my jeans down or my shirt off.

I was wearing a push-up, skinny-strap bra, which was okay with my T-shirt, but didn't go with the strapless. I had this evil little thought as I unhooked the front. I wanted Simon to steal a glance just then. To see my bare boobs. Which, even I have to admit, are not half bad.

Just the thought of it made me blush. And then smile. Which was a startling change from my usual feelings of guilt and regret.

When I called, "Ready," Simon crawled over the top of the front seat and practically fell into my lap.

"You look great," he decreed, pulling my push-up bra out from underneath him. "You ever think about modeling?"

I laughed uneasily, waiting for the punch line. When it didn't come, I said, "Not really."

"You've got the looks. And the height," he said. He studied me for another beat. Then grinned. "You don't know it, do you?"

But I was back a sentence. *He thinks I've got the looks?*

Oh, grow up. It's just a line. He probably uses it on everyone.

But, hey, you never know, I thought. *Maybe he meant it. Jamie's always reminding me that I'm not the gawky, dorky, tallest kid in the class anymore. She says I've got great eyes and cheekbones and that most of the girls we know would kill for my lanky bod.*

Whatever the truth was seemed to make no difference to my skin. Predictably, my temperature went up. I snatched my Chinese jacket — casually, I hoped — and pulled it over me to hide the redness creeping up my chest.

There was a sudden deafening rumble. I looked out my tinted window and saw that the bright lights of Manhattan were below us. We were driving across a wide steel bridge — and a rushing, screeching, swaying subway train was speeding practically alongside us. "Where are we going?" I asked.

"Brooklyn," Simon said.

Brooklyn! "Williamsburg?" I asked excitedly.

"Williamsburg," Simon confirmed, surprised, I guess, that I knew of the place — which of course I really didn't. I'd only read about it in the chapter from S. G. Wagner's book. "I used to live there," he added.

"No. Get out!" I squealed in a heinous lapse of cool — which made Simon laugh.

Kill me, I silently begged no one in particular. Embarrassed, I rested my forehead on the tinted window and pretended to be enthralled with the view. Which, as we reached Williamsburg, was nothing like the colorful, crowded chaos we'd left behind.

We drove into a forlorn-looking area. The streets were narrow, most of the stores were shuttered, a few dimly lit delis were open. But, for the most part, the buildings were either skinny tenements or wide industrial buildings, many of them fronted by deserted loading platforms. Night had settled darkly into deserted doorways, alleys, and empty lots.

So I shrieked when I felt a warm hand on my bare shoulder.

Simon fell back. "Oh man, I'm sorry," he said. "I didn't mean to scare you. I was just going show you where I used to live."

"No, I'm sorry. It's just that it looks kind of spooky out there." Even though his hand was gone, I could still feel its warmth on my skin. I turned to face him. He grinned sheepishly.

"Right up there," Simon said, brushing my shoulder as he pointed at a rickety tenement building covered in grafitti. "We lived on the top floor."

We? Simon and . . . his girlfriend? His wife? Had he been

married? Was he now? I glanced at his hand. No ring. But so what? Lots of guys didn't wear wedding rings.

"Harry, Reef, and me," he went on — and I practically giggled with relief. "Three of us in a two-room walk-up with a bathroom in the hall. We were going to take New York by storm. Reef is the Killer B's main man. Just signed a record deal. Harry is a painter."

And then there's you, I didn't say. *The cater-waiter.* I was pretty sure it was just a temporary thing for Simon, fetching cocktails for the rich and famous. The kind of job wannabe actors took until they were "discovered." I thought about asking him what it was that he planned to be or do in order to take New York by storm.

My wondering was cut short by an awesome sight. We had turned toward the waterfront. Under the soaring arc of the bridge was a spectacular view of Manhattan. And all around us were brightly lit boutiques and bars, vintage clothing shops, and coffee houses, and a big, blindingly lit-up yacht, which turned out to be a café on the water.

"I waited tables there, a couple of years ago," Simon said. "The price of a dinner was more than my weekly salary. Do you want to stop in for a drink?"

And bankrupt you? I thought. "No, that's okay," I answered. To avoid seeming obvious, I added, "I don't really drink." Which was true.

"Me neither," he said.

"How come?" I blurted. "Are you into drugs?"

I'd have taken it back in a second if I could. It was

supposed to be funny. It was supposed to show how cool I was. But Simon's look told me I'd wandered into dangerous territory.

Was he actually into drugs? Why had my joke made him so angry? Was he . . . a *dealer*? I had heard the expression a million times and associated it only with this skinny guy at school who supposedly sold pot.

I was nervous. Confused. "I'm sorry," I quickly murmured. "I was kidding. It was a joke. Not a very good one," I admitted.

"Yeah, not a very good one," he agreed.

Oh my God, what if he actually *was* a drug dealer? What if that was why he got invited to hot reggae shows, and seemed so into New York nightlife?

We were quiet for a while. The limo had strayed back into an area of dark, narrow streets. The few lampposts that were still working threw weak puddles of light onto potholes, wind-blown newspapers, and dirty gutters.

I was a wreck. I was close to tears. I couldn't believe that I'd said something so stupid.

Simon heard me sigh miserably. He put an arm around me and turned my head from the window to face him. "I'm really sorry," I said again.

"It's okay. Let it go," he urged softly. "You didn't know, did you?"

I tried to swallow my tears. "Didn't know what?" I snuffled.

"It's a long story." Simon got quiet again and searched my

face with his sexy blue eyes. Then he smiled. "I don't know why, but I trust you, Ohio," he decided.

His smile was totally contagious. I wound up smiling, too. "That's 'cause I'm trustworthy," I said. *Ethan, this is not a date,* I added silently. "So what don't I know?"

"We're almost there. I'll tell you about it another time, okay? Only I need you not to tell anyone. Seriously, not anyone, all right?"

"Tell anyone what?" I teased, batting my eyelashes innocently.

"That's my girl," Simon said.

Accompanied by another adrenaline spike, my instant response was: *I'm his girl? Don't I wish.* What was it about the boy that made me want to hang curtains, put on a little apron, and play house?

"Let's do it," he added, startling me. "Destiny's around the corner."

Chapter Six

Toddlers Who Lunch

Jamie

TO: ABS@OH.com
FROM: Jamie_the_lionhearted@OH.com

This is me, jealous. Finally read your e-mail from yesterday. You are so "there" — experiencing New York life in all its . . . is rawness a word? Eating it, breathing it, drinking it up! And the Big Apple is bringing out a whole 'nother Abigail. The funny, flirty, adventurous, good-hearted best friend I know — but few others, including you sometimes — even believe exists.

Me? I can't even peel the skin off the Big Orange.

Although, in the plus column, I did finally meet the Mothership: Nicole Hastings-Taylor. What a trip! She sashays through the mansion in a silk robe, cigarette waving in the air, headphones on, trailed by a posse of personal assistants — the primary one being Leee, ("that's with three e's," he informed me haughtily) — publicists, trainers, assorted hangers-on, etc. Topher introduces me, and suddenly, everything stops. She trains her big baby blues on me — grown-up duplicates of Olivia's — and sweeps me into the Nic-iverse.

"How wonderful to meet you! It's just delicious that you're here with us."

Delicious. It's delicious that I'm here.

"I so want to know everything about you!" she exclaimed. "I'll have Leee set some time up for us. But don't let's forget, okay?" And with that, Her Diva-ness was off!

Not that I have any idea what she just said, but color me a new member of the Nicole fan club. Yeah, I hope I get to spend some time with her. She's kinda cool. Abby, if you tell anyone I just admitted that, I'll have to kill you.

Also. She's smaller than she looks on TV. She's my height maybe, half my weight, definitely. Teensytiny. But toned to the bone. Did I mention there's a fitness center right here in Casa Verde? Maybe I'll check it out, if I'm allowed to.

BTW, do you know what it means to 'bat for the other team'?

The official reason Olivia does not go to some pish-posh private preschool like other privileged Tinsel-tots is because Hathaway's Haven is not "progressive" enough for the forward-thinking Hastings-Taylors. The *real* reason is my posh pipsqueak pees on herself at the least provocation. Olivia is not welcome there. She actually got a rejection letter, which I happened to spy on the kitchen counter: *Until your daughter is able to control her bladder, we regret that we cannot have her at Hathaway's.*

He-*llo*! She's a *toddler*. She piddles when she's panicky, which happens frequently. But unless Hathaway's preschool is populated by adult midgets, she can't be the only one. Isn't that why they invented those diaper-undies hybrids?

The Hastings-Taylors have dealt with Olivia's anxiety issues by enrolling her in bumper-to-bumper activities. Instead of playing with her pals in the sandbox, she spends sunny days strapped into the car seat, toted from activities to lessons to classes to appointments. She even "does" lunch! Why? They say it's so she'll be up to speed when she does enter preschool. I say it's so she'll become a socially acceptable Hollywood robo-tot. Olivia's on a schedule — for life.

This is what it looks like:

9:30: Life Coach
11:00: Kickboxing and/or Krav Maga lesson
12:30: Lunch date with Sienna and Sedona Brill
2:00: Yogalates lesson
3:00: Music Rhapsody and/or Great Impressionists
4:00: Swimming class
5:00: Psychologist

Because there was no mention of "park," or "playground," or "story time," when I first got this, I assumed this was Nicole's schedule. Topher sheepishly set me straight. "It's LA." He didn't need to elaborate.

Right. Who *wouldn't* need a shrink after a day like this? Olivia doesn't need psychoanalysis, she needs a life!

The Sunday before my first official day of work, I decided to try and get to know Olivia. Would she morph into the spoiled brat I'd been steeled for, or was she just a traumatized trophy child?

Turns out, I'd picked a good day. Nicole and Topher were "doing" some tennis/cocktails industry event, and Tara, mercifully, was sleeping off the effects of whatever, or whomever, *she'd* been doing the night before. I gave no thought to Tripp, The Shadow. I'd glimpsed him only one other time, wearing shredded jeans and carrying a guitar up the stairs. He'd shot me an odd look, then disappeared.

Around nine A.M., I knocked on the door that joins Livvy's room to mine. There was no response, so I quietly slipped in — and not-so-quietly slapped my hand to my chest.

This was Disney out-Land-ish. Everything twinkled, including the wraparound mural of the unicorn carousel. The name OLIVIA CRISTAL was calligraphied above it. My tousle-haired charge was sleeping peacefully — she really did look like a living doll in her Princess bed, a mini replica of Cinderella's castle. And I wondered: If my sister, Juliana, who has a life-threatening illness called cystic fibrosis, could trade spaces with Olivia, would she feel transported to paradise? Would it make her feel special, improve the quality of her life?

I was inspecting the kiddie computer and video-game library when I heard a barely-there whisper. "Hi, Jamie."

Startled, I whirled around. Olivia was sitting up in bed, staring at me expectantly. She knows my name! And, score — she's not mute.

"Hi yourself, cutie-pie. Wanna hang out today?"

Olivia looked beyond me to the door, as if expecting someone else to come in and tell her what to say.

"Just you and me," I prompted. "You can show me what games you like to play."

I shouldn't have been surprised when it turned out her favorite game was "dress up." All it took was another prod: "What would you like to wear?"

She shot out of bed as if she'd been launched.

"I could choose?" She was on tiptoes, her tiny hand cupping the bureau drawer knob.

"Anything you want. Even . . . two pairs of pants! Or a backward shirt!" I thought I was being such the renegade nanny.

"Noooo!" Olivia's giggle was musical. "No *girl* wears a backward top."

She chose a tube top. Not like a kiddie bathing suit top. This was sequined and elastic. Paired with — I know this is hard to believe, but work with me — low-rider jeans and magenta flip-flops. If it's possible, she looked like a three-year-old version of Tara.

"That's really pretty," I lied.

"It's Versa-*cheese*," she announced, pointing to the top, and did a little spin around the room. "And wanna know what else?"

Not really, I thought, while nodding yes.

"Come." She led me to her closet. A closet the size of Juliana's bedroom.

"I got blotchy and banana jeans, too."

I guess I expected stonewashed yellow jeans. Olivia peeled back the waistband to display the label. Dolce & Gabbana. Blotchy and banana. Versa-cheese. Versace.

Olivia, bless her baby bling-bling heart, thought I was impressed, and really got into it, pulling her clothes off the hangers, tossing them around, all the while doing a squeaky soliloquy on kiddie couture, pronouncing all her clothes, "scrumpdeli-ish-us!"

Oh, God, I thought. *She's gone from mute to motormouth in twenty-four hours.*

I wasn't sure which I preferred.

After an hour of dress up (her) and clean up (me), I proposed breakfast, picturing us in the kitchen, spooning Cheerios and milk. Maybe I'd teach her to bake my favorite organic oatmeal cookies.

Olivia pictured something else: A catered breakfast in her playroom, prepared by a four-star chef, hand-delivered by the staff.

We had it her way.

It wasn't even a bratty thing. Olivia had no concept that there was another way to do things. I'd have to introduce her to the real world. We took our first step a few hours later.

Her computer was state-of-the-art: a chunky keyboard for toddler-sized fingers, *SpongeBob* screensaver, and games galore, from *Clifford the Big Red Dog* to *Dora the Explorer*. Olivia had never used it, since no one had shown her how. We had our first lesson in e-mail and IM. In the bargain, Olivia made a new long-distance friend. I called my sister and told her to log on.

Hey, Juliana! I have someone here who wants to meet you. Write back. Use small words.

OK, came the response. I will. Put her on!

Olivia hadn't aced the alphabet yet, so we worked together, composing the message.

My name is Olivia. What is yours?

They were off and running, and got along famously. Juliana, who was having a good day, even drew a picture of herself for Olivia and scanned it in.

Olivia was really excited, and wanted to draw one back. The new friends traded drawings of themselves, their rooms, and make-believe pets. Juliana drew a cat, and Olivia, a pony. I was starting to feel proud of myself. I calculated: Computer? $2,000. Scanner? $150. The look on Olivia's face as she accomplished something on her own? Priceless.

I took her hand and led her to the bathroom. This accident-proneness was something we could surely conquer.

*   *   *

In the real world, kids eat lunch.

In this alt-verse, they *do* lunch.

The preprogrammed social hour is usually held at some swanky estate of another swanky three-year-old. Edibles are catered by Emeril or Wolfie — Wolfgang Puck, that is. Lately, Whole Foods, with its overpriced all-organic vibe, is very "in."

One of our first lunch dates was on the Great Lawn (seriously, that's what it's called) of the Bel Air manor of Sedona and Sienna Brill, twin daughters of the "hottest" super-producer working in TV. Or, as it was haughtily explained to me by Nanny Leticia, "Lonnie Brill has so much more cachet in this town than Nicole . . . *sniff sniff* . . . Hastings-Taylor."

Which made *me* less "important" than she.

"Really?" I challenged. "Then how come I don't see one paparazzi hovering around? He can't be that important if no one cares about getting his picture in the papers."

So there. I'd used *real* Hollywood currency. And Leticia, not the brightest bulb, had no comeback. She turned and walked away. Me, I did not let the kids out of my sight. I may be less important, but I'm a helluva lot more vigilant.

I almost wished I hadn't been. The trio of tots compared their outfits, already practicing the fine art of one-upping. When they'd exhausted finery, they went to food.

"That," said Sedona, pointing a stubby finger at a veggie wrap, "has too many cawbs."

"Whatsa cawb?" Olivia asked, stuffing a handful of greasy chips into her mouth.

Oh, baby, bad move. Even I knew that "cawb" — from the mouths of these babes — meant carb.

"You do-o-o-n know! Olivia's a dumbie," chortled Sienna.

Sedona had a better one. "No wonda you're a fattie."

Olivia, her cheeks squirrel-stuffed with potato chips, went red. Before she could expose herself as an accident-prone fattie, I scooped her up and called Leticia to come for her mini-vipers.

Was there such a thing as friendship in Livvy's world? I wondered, as I snapped her into her car seat. Or was that little scene just a snapshot of her future? Would she grow up thinking that relationships are only about who's got more or better stuff? Would she ever have a real friend?

In the car ride home, I went nostalgic, remembering how Abs and I first met. She was the new kid, scared and friendless, and had just transferred into our kindergarten, where I was the total leader of the preschool pack. Abby had been watching me and a bunch of girls playing dolls in the playhouse. She'd wanted to join in, but was too shy.

I never thought twice. I marched right up to her and said, "There's a Barbie that doesn't have a mommy. Wanna help us out?"

(Yes, we bonded over Barbies — before, as Abby always points out, I decided they were the anti-Christ and gave little girls a sick impression of what they were supposed to look like when they grew up.)

That day cemented a friendship, a journey taken over bike rides and scraped knees, pop and hip-hop CDs, pizza, braces, glasses, first bras, makeup sessions, perms, and crushes. We had our differences, we had our days of swearing never to talk to each other again. But mostly, we had our secrets, our confidences. When Juliana was first diagnosed with cystic fibrosis, the disease in which your lungs fill with water, the neighborhood kids were afraid to come over. As if CF is contagious. My status as fun-loving leader spiraled to "sister of the sick kid."

Only Abby defied the pack, stayed my true friend. She came over all the time. She played with Juliana, she forged a bond with both of us. She remembered who I was.

We had each other's backs. Who will have Olivia's?

Chapter Seven

Saturday Night Fever

Abby

Destiny turned out to be the name of the club Simon and I were going to — although there wasn't a sign suggesting it anywhere. There was just a fog of cigarette smoke hanging over a loosely lined-up mob of tattooed and pierced club kids.

The entrance to the place was a metal door covered in graffiti. Guarding it, huge arms crossed over his massive chest, stood a steroid-pumped, no-neck giant.

Simon walked up to the bruiser, who greeted him like a long-lost, muscularly challenged brother. "Hey, man, I was at the sound check. The B's are fly. They got a full-blown scene going on in there," the bouncer said, opening the door to allow us to jump the line.

Only a tinge of guilt (brought on by the grumbles of those waiting to get in) marred the nasty thrill of feeling special. Stepping inside the club was like being transported to another country: The Sovereign Nation of Chaos and Noise. The smoke-murky cavern pulsed to a deafening bass beat. Shadowy figures bobbed to the throb. Dim, dark, and beer-dank, the place could have earned a merit badge for conserving electricity. Feeble blue lights highlighted the major sites — the table near the door where a couple of girls were checking names against the comp list, the shelves of gleaming liquor bottles behind the mile-long bar, the glassed-in DJ's booth, the jammed dance area, and the empty stage where the Killer B's electronic equipment and instruments rested.

I could see Simon's mouth moving but couldn't hear what he was saying. Finally, after I'd hollered, "What?" a couple of times, he put his arm around me and pulled me close against him.

"What are you drinking?" he asked, his lips brushing my ear. "I'll get you set up, then I'm gonna go backstage for a minute."

"Diet Coke," I managed to say, my voice hoarse.

With his arm firmly around my shoulder, he steered us expertly through the crowd, toward the bar.

"'Sup, Simon?" the bartender yelled. She was an anemically white-skinned redhead with two-inch black roots, an eyebrow ring, and lipstick the color of blood.

"Hey, Tina," Simon shouted to be heard. "This is Abby." He took my backpack, in which I'd stashed my jeans. "She's comped for everything tonight. Give her whatever she wants, okay?" Slipping the bag over his shoulder, he turned back to me. He caught both my shoulders, and leaned forward, his lips ever so close.

My eyes closed, my mouth opened slightly, my expectations went way out of whack. "I'll stow your stuff in the back, okay? Be right back," he promised, planting a kiss on my forehead.

"He is so cool." Tina the bartender's smudge-rimmed eyes tracked Simon's exit. "So what'll it be, Annie?"

"Diet Coke," I shouted.

"Right, a Coke." She moved away to get the drink.

Two guys pushed up to the bar. "Innkeeper, two Cosmopolitans," the one wearing tinted glasses called to Tina. He turned to me. "Well, hello," he crooned in a British accent. "Fancy a Cosmo?" He was weaving slightly.

"No thanks," I said.

The guy next to him with an Austin Powers shag and teeth to match leaned over the bar to get a look at me. He was English, too. "See the girl with the red dress on," he sang, sounding more like Prince Charles than Ray Charles.

"She knows how to shake that thang." Cosmo One pushed his glasses down the bridge of his nose and focused bleary eyes on my cleavage.

I turned my back on them.

"Here you go." Tina returned with a tall, ice-filled glass of Coke. It had a red swizzle stick in it instead of a straw. She slid it across the bar to me. "What can I get you boys?" she asked the smarmy Brits.

"That bird's number," one of them giggled. "Or yours, darling. And two Cosmos."

I took a swallow of Coke.

It went down like lighter fluid, burning my throat, taking my breath away. Instinctively, I spit it out. Horrified and choking, I wanted to apologize, but a coughing fit prevented it.

Tina shoved a stack of cocktail napkins at me. "Easy does it," she said. "What happened?"

"What'd you give her, darling, Drano?" one of the Britwits asked.

"I gave her what she ordered," I heard Tina say defensively. "Rum and Coke. I even repeated it. I said, 'Rum and Coke,' didn't I?"

"Oh, no," I managed to answer, black-mascara tears streaming down my cheeks. "I thought you said, 'Right, a Coke' not 'Rum and Coke'!"

"Innkeeper!" The shaggy-headed, dentally challenged guy slapped the bar. "Bring the wench another brew."

"No thank you," I said emphatically. I turned to go.

A hand clamped my upper arm. "No, no, no, no, no," Tinted Glasses insisted, "you can't just spew and run. Look what you've done to my blazer."

"I'm sorry. Honestly," I said. "It was an accident —"

He held on to my arm, tried to turn me toward him.

"Least she can do is have a drink with us," his friend said. "Learn how to drink properly."

"Let go of me . . . please," I added. It was amazing that even while being abused I felt I had to be nice.

"Just have a drink with us. Here, darling. Have a sip of my Cosmo —"

"No, thank you."

The snaggle-toothed guy held the martini glass to my lips, which I pursed the way Dylan would have if I'd attempted to force oatmeal into his mouth. I tried to look around, wondering why no one was noticing what was happening, why no one had come to my rescue. Tina was down the bar, her back to us; everyone around us was drinking and hollering to be heard over the earsplitting rap the DJ was spinning.

Bad Teeth tilted his glass. A spurt of stinging liquor stole between my clamped lips and dribbled down my chin.

Suddenly Simon was there. Without a word, he pulled the guy off me and shoved him hard. The Cosmo flew. Bad Teeth stumbled backward into Tinted Glasses. The drunks went down like Dominos. As a couple of security guys rushed to the scene, Simon whisked me away from the bar.

"Can't leave you alone for a second," he scolded, trying to hold back a grin.

I felt grungier than the cocktail napkin into which I was blowing my nose. "It's not funny," I fumed.

"I know. I'm not laughing at you," Simon insisted. "It's just . . . Well, it's true, isn't it? I left you alone and look what happened. On Diet Coke." The grin broke loose. "What are you like on beer?"

"Ha-ha," I said, sounding like a five-year-old, even to myself. "I'm a mess."

I was grateful for the club's murky light, hoping it would hide my blushing embarrassment.

"Oh man." In the dimness, he noticed for the first time. "Your dress is ruined. Hey, I'm sorry, Ohio." He took my hand. "I shouldn't make fun of you. Those guys were morons."

"They were," I whimpered. I felt shaky and stupid. Destiny was where the cool people partied, and I'd turned it into a grim ordeal.

"Abby." Simon pulled me close and wrapped his arms around me. He was looking down into my face. His smile wasn't about laughter anymore. It was warm and familiar and full of . . . well, longing. At least, that's what I thought. Of course, I could have been projecting. I was getting warm and weak-kneed.

"You know I really like you. A lot," he said, his mouth against my ear again.

My already accelerated pulse went off the charts. I actually felt faint.

With one hand under my chin, he tilted my face up. He stared at me. That's all. He just studied me.

"No," I whispered, forgetting the noise around us, not knowing or caring whether he could hear me. "I can't."

But I felt myself swaying toward him, stretching, standing on tiptoes. He lowered his head. The shadow of his face fell on mine. I closed my eyes. And Simon kissed me. Softly. On the lips.

Our mouths fit. The gentleness, warmth, the slight movement and sweet moisture. It felt perfect.

"Oh God. No. I'm sorry, Simon. I can't." I couldn't believe the words were mine. Or that I took a deep breath, put my hands on his chest, and pushed away from him. "I . . . I like you, too," I said, barely able to look him in the eye.

He took a step back. "Yeah. I know," he said, with a forced grin. "Ethan, right?"

I nodded. Simon released me. "My loss. But you're going to stick around to hear the group, right? They're awesome," he said.

As if on cue the rap music stopped and the Killer B's took the stage. "Which one is your friend?" I asked.

"He's the guy with the blue guitar; the one in the white shirt," Simon told me.

The one in the white shirt was actually the one nearly out of the white shirt. His softly wrinkled Indian gauze shirt was unbuttoned all the way to his waist, framing milk-chocolate, washboard abs. He had dreads and a beautiful green-eyed face as carved as an African mask. "So that's Reef," I said. "Your roommate?"

"Used to be," Simon said.

Reef struck a chord on his guitar, and the room went dead still. He leaned into the mic. "I'd like to dedicate this song to the bro who inspired it. He's out there tonight. Maybe you've heard of him. Dude by the name of S. G. Wagner."

"He knows S. G. Wagner!" I said excitedly. I strained on tiptoes trying to find the author in the crowd — or someone who looked like an author since I had no idea what Wagner looked like, except that he'd be in his early twenties.

"Come on," Simon said, taking my hand and tugging me through the crowd. "It's quieter upstairs."

At the side of the stage was a staircase, which was roped off and guarded by another pumped giant. At the top of the narrow steps, there was a carpeted balcony with sofas and a little private bar in the back. There was also a big flat-screen TV on which the B's' live performance was being shown.

Simon pulled me down beside him onto a plush velvet loveseat. "What am I going to do with you?" he asked.

I could think of a couple of things. But I just laughed. Nervously.

"I can't do this," he teased, brushing his cheek against my hair. "Or this." He lowered his head and rubbed my face with his prickly stubble. Very softly. "Because of someone named Ethan," he said. "And kissing you is out of the question, right? Like this —"

He kissed me again. Lightly. Softly. And when I'd nearly fainted from holding my breath, he pried my lips open, very gently, with his tongue.

His hands were gripping my bare arms, pulling me toward him. Which was exactly the direction my whole body wanted to go. I was burning up. I almost melted into him. His cool leather jacket could have been toast.

"Simon." I wanted to sound stern. Serious. But his name came out wrapped in a moan. "Simon, please. Stop," I tried again. And, unfortunately, got through to him. He pulled back.

"I'm sorry," we said at the same time.

He laughed, but I couldn't. I was too confused. Ethan had kissed me hundreds of times and not one of his kisses had affected me the way Simon's did.

*   *   *

TO: Jamie_the_lionhearted@OH.com
FROM: ABS@OH.com

Jamie. Help! Simon the cater-waiter kissed me and I feel like I lost my virginity.

I also feel like I've totally betrayed Ethan. Who, after a week of not calling, chose tonight — right after my "non-date" with Simon — to finally get in touch!

He sounded kind of distant (no pun intended) and so not passionate. But, you know Ethan, he's just not big on expressing emotions. I mean, he was really sweet and apologetic. He said all the right things: *I'm sorry I haven't called; we had a crisis out here; it would be so cool if you were here with me; you'd love it.* But he sounded even less excited than usual. I told him I missed him — which I do. And that New York is exciting but a little overwhelming. What I didn't tell him was where I'd been tonight and with whom. I didn't feel like I had to hide it from him. It was more like I wanted to keep the experience and feelings pure — unspoken, unspoiled — like something special that only Simon and I could share.

Jamie, please tell me I'm someone who can keep a promise — like not DATING anyone but Ethan! Only, what's happening with Simon can't really be called dating. It's more like . . . oh God, I don't know.

Anyway, Simon wants me to go with him to a reading tomorrow night. It's at this downtown café in TriBeCa. (Flash: TriBeCa stands for the Triangle

Below Canal Street. Isn't that cool?) Of course I want to go. Tell me that I can. That I should. Tell me like you always used to: "Carpe diem." Seize the day! Or the night in this case. And tell me what's happening with you?

xoxo

Abs

Chapter Eight

Tara's Fat Dress

Jamie

"Rise 'n' shine, sleeping bloaty!"

My eyes flew open. Tara's ice-blue peepers were in my face. I'd gotten into the habit of spending Saturday afternoons lounging by the pool while Olivia was napping. This time, I must have fallen asleep. But for how long?

"Rumor has it you're on duty tonight, Nanny McPhee," Tara said, tapping a finger on her diamond-studded wristwatch. "You'll need all the time you can get to look presentable."

"And you've arrived to do reveille?" I rubbed the sleep from my eyes. "How thoughtful."

"Count this as my favor to you. There won't be many."

I propped myself up on my elbows. What gave her the right to flounce into my face as if she's mistress of the manor?

Oh, yeah, right. She is.

I'm the "help," as she'd pointed out the first day. *She* could do whatever she wanted. When I awoke fully, I grasped the snarkiness in her remark, about needing time to look "presentable" for tonight.

Topher hadn't mentioned a dress code when he

downloaded me about this evening. "It's just another silly event Nic is obliged to attend." Just one of so many red carpet moments in their lives. Olivia would arrive with them and stay "just for the beginning bit," as he put it. "Nic and I will walk Livvy down the red carpet so the photographers can get the 'family' snapshots. You'll be posted behind the ropes, not too far from where we'll end up. When it's done, I hand Livvy over to you, and Kip will be waiting to drive you home. Easy."

"So," Tara was now trilling. "You'll be needing something to wear."

"Why? Rumor has it my job is to take Olivia home. What's the difference what I wear?"

Tara actually cackled. "You are just *too* precious, you know?" Then she was all business. "You work for us. In public, that means you clean up."

I wanted to clean her clock but, as if guessing my intentions, Tara quickly took a step back.

"I'll lend you one of my old outfits. From my fat days." She turned on her heel and strode across the lawn back to the house.

Wait. Did Skin 'n' Bones just call me *fat*? I didn't care who she was; being verbally abused was not part of my job description. I sprang up and jetted into the house after her.

But Tara had disappeared. Indignant, I bolted upstairs, slammed the doors to my room, kicked my sneakers off, and sent them flying. They landed on the window seat, streaking the white linen cushion with grass stains from the lawn. I brushed away the guilt, telling myself I'd clean it up later.

I was still nursing a righteous rage when I entered my private bathroom. But by the time the Jacuzzi tub was filled up, the overhead lights were dimmed, the aromatherapy candles were lit, and the soothing sounds of the latest Norah Jones CD wafted through the speakers, it was hard to stay pissed off. Lowering myself into the hot water, I surrendered to the warm jets pulsing pressure on my back and shoulders and flipped around, so every part of my body got massaged.

When I turned off the jets, and began to soap myself with the designer bath gel that smelled like apricots, I felt much calmer about Tara. Like Abby said, she's probably dealing with her own issues and acting out on the newcomer. Whatever. In the rain forest of life, she's a mere gnat. Why let her even distract me, let alone get under my skin? I threw my head back and soaked in the tub, feeling peaceful, approaching zen.

Then I chanced to look down at my naked self. What a buzz kill.

No wait, that's unfair. I have a *normal* body — for a regular person. Big boobs, okay, but I always wear loose-fitting tops, so no one notices. My thumb and forefinger felt for belly flab. So what if I could "pinch more than an inch"? Better to carry a little extra weight and be healthy than be a skinny marink like Tara.

If I wanted to drop ten or fifteen pounds, I totally could. But I'd do it for myself, not because of some screwed-up idea that, to be attractive to guys, you have to be borderline anorexic. LA guys maybe. But a boyfriend is not on my priority list right now — and an LA dude? As if. From what I've seen so far, they're boy-versions of Tara.

My suite was not as I'd left it. In the time it had taken me to bathe and shampoo, someone had slipped in and cleaned up the mess I'd left — including the grass stains on the window seat. And, laid out neatly on the bed, a pair of black pumps beneath it, was Tara's "fat" dress.

It was neither low cut nor slutty. It was almost prim, by Hollywood standards. The skirt was solid black, done in gathered pleats — flattering, I might point out, if you're a matchstick. The top was a scoop-neck, cap-sleeve number, in a sheer beige fabric. Strands of coffee-colored beading and sequins were woven into a matrix design to cover the bosom area.

The dress seemed fine — until I tried it on. It was not bra-friendly. My straps showed, and there wasn't enough beading to cover up my "fuller-figured" underwire bra. It looked ridiculous.

I'd never gone braless before, but I'd be in this dress a total of one hour. Sixty minutes where I'll be stashed anonymously among throngs of fans who only had eyes for the red carpet set. Who'd be paying the least bit of attention to me? As I dressed, I tried to picture what skimpy getup Tara would construct for the night. And what about The Shadow? Would Tripp emerge from his cave tonight? And then it hit me: When Topher talked about the "family shot," he hadn't mentioned

Tara or Tripp at all. Were they not going? Were they not considered part of the Hastings-Taylor family?

So this is the red carpet. As Abby would say, "It's déjà vu all over again." Just add *lots* more bejeweled and tuxedoed stars, and thick ropes cordoning off the masses from the Botoxed and bling-blinged, and you had my Julia Roberts-on-the-moving-walkway experience.

On the ride over, Kip filled in the details. What Topher had termed a "silly event" was actually the annual Family Values Awards, where TV shows and movies proffering "good moral values" are honored. This year, *Nikki's Way* had won the big prize, hence the star of the show — also its executive producer — was the star of the night. Befittingly, Nicole had spent the entire day being styled, primped, and pampered.

My post was behind the ropes, among the rabid fans who'd waited hours to stake out the choice spots. It was also where camera crews and reporters from the entertainment shows had set up camp. The klieg lights were so bright, I wished I'd brought shades.

The stars, actors and actresses, outshone the lights, and no one more so than my employer. Nicole was luminous; she sparkled. You could not take your eyes off her. I had no clue "who" she was wearing, but the dress was killer. A body-hugging, spaghetti-strapped, snow-white confection constructed entirely of sequins — except for the flirty fringe tickling her upper thighs. Need I mention it was mini?

The ensemble bared a lot of skin, but not all. The rest was draped in diamonds and pearls. Chandelier earrings, a dozen strands of precious stones worn choker-style around her neck, with bracelets, bicep cuffs, and rings to match.

Two thoughts collided in my brain. One: the tidy fortune adorning Nicole's buffed bod? Imagine what kind of research it could fund to find a cure for say, Juliana's sickness. And two: Was this what Tara imagined she had to live up to?

I thought about my mom. We had our issues, but she never made me feel like I had to be someone I wasn't, act or dress a certain way to please her — or worse, to be accepted by her.

"Nicole, *darling!*" The nasal voice of Joan Rivers infiltrated my daydreaming. "We're all so proud of you tonight! Who are you wearing?"

Nicole was "on." Graciously, she indulged all — photographers, press, and fans — with dazzling smiles, sound bites, autographs. Then it was time for the family photo ops. Nicole hoisted Olivia up, and leaned into her face, leaving a lipstick print on her cheek. The star posed holding hands with Livvy, kneeling next to Livvy, perching her chin on Livvy's head. Then it was Topher's turn. They held the baby between them, making an Olivia sandwich.

She was a prop. That was Olivia's purpose, to play a part in a well-choreographed routine. She was alphabet- *and* potty-challenged, but the kid knew her stuff: How to "turn this way!" And "give Mommy a kiss!" And twirl her curls around her finger while looking adoringly into Nicole's eyes.

One obnoxious TV reporter shoved a microphone in her angelic face. "Olivia," he drawled. "What does Mommy always say on *Nikki's Way*?"

She gave him a blank stare, but her smile held.

He prompted, "At the end of every show? What's that last bit she says?"

The answer: "Where there's a will, there's Nikki's way."

Only, Olivia didn't know that. This part wasn't in the script. She craned her neck to find Topher, but he was already off schmoozing with some TV host. Nicole, waving to another camera, was oblivious to Olivia's nonverbal SOS.

The insensitive twit persisted. "Come on, I know you know it. Talk into the microphone and tell us Mommy's motto."

Olivia was on her own. She leaned into the mic and blurted, "You *bang*!"

The reporter burst out laughing. "That's a good one!" He signaled his photographer to zoom in for a kid close-up. Other shutterbugs, afraid of missing something, rushed at her, too. My heart seized. *They'll blind her! Stop them!*

Topher had wandered too far away for me to get his attention. Nicole apparently thought the sudden rush at Olivia was cute.

It was up to me. I had to save her. I ducked under the rope, only to instantly feel the vice grip of a security guard on my arm. I had a choice, he told me quietly. Get back behind the rope, or get arrested.

Finally, Topher returned, whisked Olivia out of the

spotlight, and handed the now teary child over to me. I had not noticed the pack of photographers following him. But the minute Olivia was in my arms, the clicking, whirring and flashing started. Hadn't they gotten enough pictures of her?

"Nanny! Nanny! Look here!" one shouted.

They wanted me? Nicole's nanny? This town was cuckoo. Hadn't Kip said I'd better get used to it? I just didn't want Olivia near those damn lights anymore. I shifted her onto my hip, and twisted my torso so no one could flash her face. Then, I turned to the cameras and gave them what I hoped was an incandescent smile.

An instant later, Kip was by my side, rushing us into the car. Olivia was all-out sobbing now.

"It's okay, sweetie," I cooed, as Kip closed and locked the door of the limo. "It's all over. No more silly pictures."

She cried harder.

I tried harder. "We're going home now. We can read a book."

My thigh felt warm. And wet. Oh, no, Olivia was having another accident. What does it say about me that my first thought was Tara's dress that was being ruined?

I searched for a way to soothe the toddler. "Guess what?" I asked, stroking her back. "I know how to make the yummiest cookies ever. We can bake them together. Would you like that?"

The sobs quieted. She looked up at me hopefully, her tear-streaked face a mess. I took that as a yes. "That's it, then," I said cheerfully. "We'll change into dry" — I cleared my throat — "comfy jammies, we'll raid the kitchen, and bake organic chocolate chip cookies. How does that sound?"

Olivia hiccuped, but at least she'd stopped crying.

"And then," I said, trying to sound teasing. "Guess what we'll do?"

A tiny voice piped up, "Eat them?"

"You are such a smart girl!" I praised her. "Exactly."

Through her tears, a smile. Then, a thumb in her mouth, her head on my chest, and, as the limo rolled far away from the red carpet, the regular breathing of sleep.

When I was sure I wouldn't wake her, I leaned over the front seat and whispered, "Kip? Is this normal?"

"The crying jag? Yeah," he admitted, then added, "You're handling it amazingly well. She's lucky to have you."

"No, I meant the photographers coming at me. Why do they need shots of the nanny?"

Kip shook his head. "Never seen that before. It's almost as if someone tipped them off that a picture of you and Olivia would be important somehow."

When the phone rings in the dead of night, it's always bad news. Eyes still shut, I reached the receiver before a second ring.

"My God, Jamie! What *happened*!?"

My entire body tensed. It was Abby. I bolted upright. It had to be news from back home.

"Jamie, this isn't you! Did they drug you?" My best friend was upset, freaked, borderline berserk.

I exhaled, and flopped back down. The 911 was not about Juliana.

Abs jabbered on. "Did you know? It's all over the morning news! They're calling you an exhibitionist!"

The morning news? It's morning? I squinted at the window. A tangerine glow tinted the curtains. "What time is it?"

"Time to get up! James!" Abby commanded. "Focus."

"Okay, okay, I'm up, I'm up. Stop shrieking. Just tell me."

When she did, an electric current shot through my body. I fumbled with the remote until I found the E! News channel. A picture appeared behind the shoulder of the anchorman. The girl in the photo was exceedingly familiar. She looked like . . . me? Then I saw the rest of her — her breasts were showing! They had this pixilated box over them, but the girl was totally topless.

"How must it feel," the host was saying, "to be a nobody in this town, and upstage Nicole Hastings-Taylor at her own red carpet event?"

I was too stunned to feel anything.

"You're on every channel," Abby was saying, "CNN, FOX . . ."

I surfed. Each network had invented a "clever" pun. "Nicole's Naughty Nanny!" "Nanny Plays Peek-a-Boob!" "The Babysitter's Boob-Boo!"

I dropped the phone and walked right up to the flat-screen. It *was* me. Not at all flat.

It was the dress, of course.

To the naked eye, it looked normal enough.

To the camera's eye, it looked naked enough.

In the act of twisting my body to protect Olivia, the photographers had caught me full frontal. The dress was see-through. Under the klieg lights, in the intense burst of flashes, the beading simply blended with the sheer material of the top, rendering the whole top transparent. Adding insult to injury, I was smiling proudly. Like I was showing off.

I shrank away from the TV, and heard Abby's disembodied voice coming from the floor. "Jamie? Are you there? There are worse shots on the web," she was warning.

I sank onto the carpet and picked up the phone. "They're saying you did it on purpose," my best friend was reporting, "that you told the photographers they'd get the best shot of the night if they waited until you had Olivia."

Suddenly, the line went silent. Abby finally realized I had not said one word. She whispered. "Oh, Jamie. You didn't know, did you? I'm so, so sorry! I knew that wasn't your dress. I just assumed you'd bought it — or, they'd given it to you."

Oh, they'd "given it to me" all right. Tara had gone from nasty irritator to vile humiliator. But why? What had I done to her? And just when I was on the brink of feeling sorry for her, poor little rich girl, left out of the red-carpet family portrait. Just when I was thinking I shouldn't judge her so harshly.

Shaking with rage, I hung up and flung open my door, ready to burst into Tara's room and pummel her. The pile of tabloids stacked up outside my door stopped me. I knew I shouldn't — it'd be like seeing your own mangled body in a car wreck — but I picked up the papers, and backed into my room.

The headlines were the same: NANNY "NIPS" at NIC'S HEELS. NANNY BOOBY-TRAP. BABYSITTER MOCKS FAMILY VALUES AWARDS.

My anger exploded into wracking sobs, and a torrent of tears blurred the articles. I covered my face with the papers, ink and tears ran together.

I'd been so stupid. Why didn't I just ignore the cameras, turn away? I'm the least vain person in the world. What happened to me? And how was I going to explain it to my parents, my friends, Juliana? If they didn't know by now — they would momentarily.

The intercom buzzed. Topher's voice, when it came through, was clipped. "Jamie? Could you come down to the kitchen please? We have a situation."

I splashed water on my blotchy face and wrapped myself tightly in a long terrycloth robe. I'd taken one step down the staircase when I heard Nicole, shrill and enraged: "I don't care how it happened! The little slut! She'd better get her butt on the fastest plane out of here!"

The little . . . *what* did she call me?

"We haven't heard her side of it." Topher, in peacemaker mode.

Another voice I recognized as Nicole's live-in personal assistant, Leee. "We could sue her."

"Could we, Toph?" Nicole was asking hopefully.

I stomped down the stairs. Topher took one look at me, and moved to intercept the incoming, unpretty confrontation.

He wasn't fast enough. The star, dramatic and enraged, was in my face, smoke coming out of her cigarette and her ears. "How dare you! Making a mockery of —"

"It was Tara's dress."

As if she hadn't heard me, Nicole ranted, "Do you realize what you've done? This is my show! My show recognized for Family Values, f'chrissake!"

I cringed. It's not like I believed Nicole really liked me, but . . . how did I go from "delicious" to poisonous, without even the benefit of the doubt?

I had to set things right.

Backing away from Nicole, the charging chimney, I channeled my inner bullhorn. "Tara made me wear the dress!"

Snap! Insta-silence. A smoke ring hung in the air between us. Then Nicole burst out laughing. "She tied you down and forced you to wear it?"

Nicole, Topher, and the three-e'd Leee stared at me incredulously. Bravely, I explained how Tara insisted I "clean up," by wearing this particular dress. "From her fat days," I tossed in so they could see how I was the total victim here. I ended with an accusation. "Tara knew it was see-through. She tipped off the photographers —"

I'd been doing well until that last bit. It sent Nicole back into a flying rage. "You're accusing my daughter of —"

"Tricking me. It's the truth." I held my ground, praying the tears wouldn't come.

Nicole turned away and put her hand out. Leee placed another cigarette in it, leaning in to light it.

Topher regarded me quizzically. Finally, the lawyer emerged. "What motive would she have for doing that? What does Tara have to gain?"

I had to concede that I had no idea.

As if on cue — is everything staged in this family? — Tara-the-treacherous materialized in the doorway. Yawning! As if she was totally innocent.

"What's the commotion? You all woke me up."

Leee, in his mocking drawl, filled Tara in — like she hadn't masterminded this entire debacle. I'll give her this: Tara's a better actress than her mom. She did a spot-on indignant. "You come into this house and, first thing, ruin my mom's event? And you blame *me*?" Her voice had gone up an octave with each fake question. "I wasn't even there."

Was *that* the motive, then? She got left out, so I paid the price? I'd read about the chain reaction of bullying. The boss berates his employee, the employee takes it out on his wife, she punishes the child, the child kicks the dog. Was I the dog here?

Tara was getting into it now. "Do you have a police record for being an exhibitionist?"

"That's enough," Topher cautioned her.

But she was on a roll. "All I did was lend you a dress. Which — by the way — wasn't see-through when I wore it. You're just too much for it."

Shame choked my retort and threatened to bring fresh tears. But no way would they see me cry.

I hadn't heard the doorbell, nor footsteps heading toward

us, but apparently, the script called for supporting players to appear. Nicole's posse: publicist, manager, and agent. Team Spin-Control.

I was banished from the kitchen. It was little comfort that Tara was, too. I took the stairs two at a time. Screw them all. I was so outta there. I would miss Olivia, yeah, but that was all. I wouldn't even wait for a cab. I didn't care if I walked to the airport, I just wanted to go home. Tossing off the robe, I pulled on my jeans and Great Strides T-shirt, grabbed the few things I'd brought in my suitcase, tossed my books and iPod into my backpack, flung open the door, and walked out.

That's when I saw him.

Long-haired and lanky, he stood between me and the steps, blocking my way. His jeans were ripped. A gray T-shirt with a Modest Mouse logo hung loosely, barely covering ropy biceps.

The Shadow. He lives.

"Hey," he said.

My response was to sidestep him and continue toward the stairs.

His was, "I know a way out so they won't see you leaving."

Chapter Nine

Simon Uncovered

Abby

Sunday night, I blew it. Big-time.

I managed to turn my second non-date with Simon into this soap opera of suspicion, jealousy, and regret.

The night began with me waiting in front of the Port Authority Bus Terminal for Simon to pick me up and take me to the reading in TriBeCa.

I was "dressed down" as he'd suggested — jeans (I picked my tightest, boot-cut hip-huggers) and a burgundy, form-fitting sweater. My hair was long and loose, conditioned to a dark, gleaming shine. All in all, my last glance in the mirror had said, "Not bad."

It was cold and getting dark. Yellow cabs careened to the curb, picking up and dropping off passengers, but I was on the lookout for Mike's black Town Car. So when a Harley rumbled to a halt in front of me, I ignored it.

Until the rider shouted my name over the hectic traffic sounds.

"Simon?"

He lifted the visor of his helmet and gave me this

heart-stopping grin. "Climb on, Ohio," he ordered, handing me a helmet. "We're late."

Wrapping my arms around him seemed as right as any move I'd ever made. It didn't matter that he couldn't hear me shouting, "Oh, God. When you mentioned your bike I was thinking bicycle, not Harley." Or that my carefully brushed hair was going to be a sweaty muddled mess when I took off the helmet.

Weaving in and out of traffic, we wound up way downtown, below Greenwich Village and Little Italy and Chinatown. The neighborhood we finally stopped in looked a lot like the scarier parts of Williamsburg — narrow streets with trendy shops that were closed and covered by metal gates, old factories and warehouses with loading platforms in front of them.

Simon stopped at a café, the only shop open for blocks around. Its warm light was a beacon of safety. He got off the Harley and stretched, then locked his helmet to the back of the bike and reached for mine. I gave it to him, then shook out my hair. "Do I look janky?" I asked him.

"Janky?" He studied me as if he were trying to decide, but it was obvious he didn't know what the word meant.

"Janky. Substandard," I translated.

"Oh. Very." He didn't crack a smile. "Big-time janky."

I shoved him. "Get out!"

He caught my hand and held it against his chest. And used his other hand to draw me toward him. I made an embarrassingly lame attempt to pull away when he kind of nipped my lower lip, took it very gently in his teeth.

Which sounds weird, I know, but was just about the sexiest thing in the world. It didn't hurt and it didn't last long. It just made me want to push more tightly against him.

I could have backed away, but I stayed in his arms. "You sure you're in the mood for a reading?" he asked hoarsely. "My loft's just around the corner."

It took a beat. Then I heard someone say, "I can't." After another beat, I realized it was me who'd said it — despite the fact that listening to someone read was the furthest thing from my mind just then. "We'd better go inside," I finally replied.

The place was packed. It took less than a second to realize why. Curt Gordevan sat on a stool at the front of the café, reading from a stack of pages he was holding. Mike, the ponytailed driver, was at one of the little tables close to Gordevan, and a slender blonde sat alongside him, her back to us. On the other side of the room, I saw Lila. Even though I knew she was Curt Gordevan's publisher, I was surprised to see my fashionable employer in the cramped café, lounging against a wall near the espresso machine. There was a guy next to her, a J.Crew catalog kind of guy, wearing a turtleneck sweater, khaki chinos, and that sailing, surfing, rugged grin.

Gordevan's audience ranged from pierced college kids to thirty-plus groupies — all completely captivated by him.

Until a minute after we walked in.

"Oh, my God, it's S. G. Wagner," someone exclaimed.

"S. G. Wagner." The whispered name swept through the crowd. My entire body flushed with a realization.

"Simon," I asked hesitantly, "are you . . . I mean, does the S in S. G. Wagner stand for Simon? Are you S. G. Wagner?"

He ignored the question. With his arm around my waist he coaxed me toward Lila, who was waving us over. I noticed everyone in the crowd staring at us, confirming my suspicions.

I stopped short. Dug in my heels. "Are you?" I insisted.

He nodded yes.

Oh!

My!

God! I thought.

Sweet Simon, the poverty-stricken cater-waiter, was S. G. Wagner, the oh-so-hip camera-shy author of *Lost in Brooklyn*.

"Why didn't you tell me?" I gasped. "Why did you let me make a fool of myself?"

He didn't have a chance to answer. Lila latched onto him and threw a couple of air-kisses his way. "You're late," she said. "Curt kept asking for you."

Simon smiled sheepishly at me and said, "I'm Curt's official lucky charm."

"You are his *protégé*," Lila corrected him. "Without his support and his review in the *Times*, *Lost in Brooklyn* might not have gotten the attention it deserved."

"Simon." The J.Crew guy dipped his head in Simon's direction but kept his eyes on me. "Aren't you going to introduce me to your friend?"

Lila was looking from me to Simon and back. You could tell she was surprised, but not enough to lose her cool. "Matt, this is Abby, my nanny. Abby, Matt," Lila introed us. "I didn't realize that you and Simon were such good friends."

Good friends? Simon and me? I didn't even know the guy, I felt like saying. I was in shock, stunned.

My feelings were totally scrambled. I was wild about Simon. And I loved S. G. Wagner's writing. I just couldn't put the two of them together. My Simon — the one I guess I'd invented — was poor, but also proud, funny, sweet, and sexy. But S. G. Wagner was brilliant, successful, a guy — if Garrick was right — with a reputation for always being at the right party with the right blonde.

Mindlessly, I touched my hair — my dark, plain, non-blonde hair.

I needed to regroup. "Excuse me," I said, looking toward a long narrow corridor. "Is the ladies' room down there?"

"Yes, dear," Lila said. "Have you got a comb with you?"

I walked quickly down the hallway. My heart was beating very fast. I had that pre-dizzy feeling like air was rushing up my nose. I thought I might faint. I thought: *I have been kissed and held and had my bottom lip nipped by S. G. Wagner.* I thought: *Maybe he really likes me; maybe he wasn't just* amused *by someone who doesn't know how to dress or drink.*

I should have been thrilled. I should have called Jamie.

But seventh grade habits die hard. Instead of feeling special, flattered, and fabulous, I was catapulted back to my geek days, to the year I was the tallest, skinniest, least popular girl in the class. When nobody wanted to be seen with me — except Jamie, who had to remind me, over and over again, of the story of the ugly duckling and tell me I was her swan.

I splashed water on my face and looked up.

The ugly duckling looked back.

The mirror in the bathroom was not as kind as the one at Aunt Molly's. I looked exactly how I felt: a mess. The helmet had flattened the top of my hair; the rest, which had been out in the wind, was a tangled frizz fest. My face was pale, all except for my eyes, which — also thanks to the wind — were dark with streaming mascara.

Wasn't I just the hot girl a guy like S. G. Wagner would fall for?

I tried to be positive. After all, I told myself, one of New York's "most eligible bachelors" had shown me Brooklyn last night, had asked me to this reading. So I tidied up as best I could. Combed my hair, glossed my lips, and hit the door.

Lila was still standing at the back of the café. Alone. She gestured for me to join her. "Have you heard any of the reading?" she whispered. "It's from Curt's new book. What do you think of it? I'm trying to get a fresh view."

Any other time, I would have been wildly flattered to have Lila ask me my opinion of Curt Gordevan's work. But, at that moment, I was obsessively focused on another of her famous writers.

Who, true to his reputation, was cozying up to a blonde! The one who had been sitting with Mike the driver only minutes before. The blonde had one slender arm draped across Simon's shoulder and one high cheekbone crushed against his stubbly jaw.

There was something familiar about the girl. But I didn't recognize her right away. "Simon, really, the nanny?" I heard her say. She wasn't even whispering. "Darling, she's a schoolgirl."

"Come on, Jacqueline." Simon chuckled. "Don't be like that —"

Jacqueline! The blonde, the older woman who'd whisked Simon out of Dylan's playroom the night of Lila's party.

What an idiot I'd been. How could I have believed that someone like Simon would really be into me? He obviously had a girlfriend. He'd played me.

"Well, have you?" Lila repeated.

I said, "What? Oh, Gordevan's book. No, I didn't hear him."

I felt ill as I made my way to the door. Lila's "friend," Matt, was suddenly at my side. "Taking off so soon? Where're you going?" he asked.

"Home," I said. Matt held the door for me, then followed me outside.

"You okay?"

"Perfect," I lied.

"Can I give you a lift somewhere?"

"God, no," I blurted.

Matt looked surprised. Then he laughed. "Tell me how you *really* feel," he teased. "I mean, don't hold back."

"I'm sorry," I mumbled. "I just need to be alone."

He shrugged and took off. I watched him until he was totally out of sight. Then I turned toward the street. Seeing Simon's parked Harley was like a body blow. I had to stop and take a couple of deep breaths before I could move on.

How many bad moves could I make in one night? Whatever the number, add one more for telling Lila's pal that I wanted to be alone.

Alone was what I was now.

Just what I need, I thought miserably. To wander the dark streets of TriBeCa alone. A block from the café, the sound of my shoes clacking on the cobblestones echoed eerily between deserted buildings.

I had my cell phone. But who could I call? Jamie was a continent away; she couldn't come rescue me. After I'd run through those dearest but not nearest to me, I thought about Garrick. I wished I had his number. . . .

Suddenly, there was a car driving slowly alongside me. Shaken, I tried to ignore it, walking faster, feeling sicker. I was about to break into a run when the horn sounded. I jumped and turned toward the noise. The car was a black Lincoln. Mike was driving it. He leaned over to the passenger's side and pushed open the door. "Hey, where you going? You need a lift? Come on, hop in. I'll drive you home."

In the creepy dark of night, Mike's smiling face looked sinister, his ponytail the coif of a serial strangler. "That's okay," I assured him. "I'm fine. I mean, don't you want to hear the rest of the reading?"

"Nah," Mike said. "I was only there because I was driving Jackie. She's with Simon now; she won't be ready to leave for a while —"

Simon. Jackie. My stomach heaved.

Suddenly my cell phone rang. *Simon,* I thought like a jerk. *He's calling to apologize, to explain, to tell me he really meant what he said about liking me. . . .*

Mike waited while I answered my phone.

It was Ethan.

"Abby? Hey."

"Oh, Ethan." Just the sound of his voice, slow and deep, moved me practically to tears. "I'm so glad you called."

"Yeah," he said. "Me, too. Abby, listen . . . I've been . . . um, thinking."

I waited. Ethan had this absentminded way of speaking: as if he thought of each word separately, and coming up with a complete sentence took major concentration. He wound up sounding kind of laid-back and lazy — but he wasn't either one. He was actually amazingly bright, interested in everything from the environment to psychology to politics. He was also really cute. He had shaggy hair and thick eyebrows, and big, beautiful brown eyes, eyes the color of coffee with just a drop of milk in it. He was tall and solid and athletic. And when he held me I felt totally protected. Ethan was — how can I explain it? — Ethan was safe, and sweet, and home.

When he didn't say anything else, I jumped in with what I thought was a witty remark. "Sounds dangerous — you thinking, I mean."

"Yeah. Maybe," he said. "Abby, I'm . . . not sure."

"Not sure of what?" I prompted.

"I'm confused. It's different out here. It's different from what I thought."

"It's California, Ethan. Sure it's different." I remembered Jamie's e-mails.

"I'm just . . . I'm feeling kind of . . . pressured. Like when you were calling me all the time. I need space, Abby."

Space?

Space was the code word for breaking up.

It was too much. Seeing Simon cuddling with someone else followed by Ethan asking for space. My mouth went salty with my own tears.

"I'm confused, Abby. That's all. Just give me some time. Okay? So" — he took a breath, then said, as if we'd been making small talk all along — "how's New York?"

After that, I didn't care whether Mike was a murderer or not. I hung up on Ethan and I got into the car — and Mike drove me all the way home to Aunt Molly's house in New Jersey. He didn't ask if I'd had a nice time. My heaving shoulders and the sound of my blubbering made the question unnecessary. Mostly, he just clucked sadly and kept saying things like, "It'll be all right. It's not the end of the world. Whatever happened, it can't be that bad."

Dumped by two guys in one night.

It *was* that bad!

Chapter Ten

Taking a Tripp

Jamie

Seething and mortified, I had two words on my mind. Airport. Home.

Getting stealthed by Tripp, aka The Shadow, had confused and startled me. His offer of a clandestine way out of the house was too tempting to pass up. We'd slipped down a back staircase, which led to the corridor connecting to the staff wing, and to a side door.

Tripp had made for a tall row of shrubs several yards away, and pushed through them: a shortcut to the motor port. Tripp bypassed the Lexus I used, Tara's Range Rover, Topher's Bentley, and Nicole's limo for his own ride, a sleek black hatchback with tinted windows and sparkling silver wheel covers. The car blew me away. It's the one I would totally buy, if I could. A Toyota Prius: the hybrid that runs on electricity as well as gas. It's won all sorts of environmental awards.

Shadow Boy is just full of secrets, isn't he?

He slid in behind the wheel and, finally, cocked his head in my direction. "The getaway car." His upper lip curled in a subversive smile. "C'mon."

Trust him? Or hit the road solo, as planned? True, he *had* delivered on the promised quick and silent exit. Also true: He holed up in his room probably surfing the net 24/7, which gave him an all-access pass to my boobs.

So what was Tripp? A player? A treacherous trickster like his stepsister? Or the unexpected ally I needed right now?

I pivoted and headed toward the lane that led to the road. To freedom.

Tripp started the car and pulled up beside me. "You can't walk to the airport."

Watch me, I thought, quickening my pace.

"No one walks in LA. It's suspicious. Perverse." He eased his foot off the brake, attempting to coast alongside me. "If a cop sees you, you'll get stopped."

The headlines came at me: NIPPLE-NANNY ESCAPES! I pictured my mug shot: HAVE YOU SEEN THESE BREASTS?

I got in the car.

As Tripp navigated his way through the narrow, winding streets of Holmby Hills, we kept our eyes straight ahead. At least I hoped that's where Tripp's were, but who could tell with the dark shades? I tried not to think about the fact that I'd just abandoned Olivia.

"Mind if I put a CD on?" Tripp asked.

I shrugged.

I didn't recognize the band, but I knew that kind of music. It was meant to be blasted. Red-meat rock, a crash of guitars and drums, the deliberate clash of the singer's howl. But Tripp kept the volume low, so all that came through was the thrum of the beat and a low whine of vocals. I leaned over to turn it way up, accidentally brushing his bare bicep.

When we hit the broad Sunset Boulevard, Tripp picked up speed, taking the curves without slowing down. In spite of what had brought me into this car, next to this stranger, it was good to be out, to be moving, to roll the sunroof back and let the wind have its way with my thick hair. Out of the corner of my eye, I snuck a peek at Tripp, whose long hair was off his face. Dark and angular with high cheekbones, he gave off a soulful vibe. A peace-symbol stud adorned his right ear. He looked nothing like Topher.

I leaned back on the headrest, tipped up my chin, and stared out the sunroof. The tall, slinky palm trees waving in the breeze resembled a chorus line of dancing feather dusters.

Over the music, Tripp announced, "You missed the early flights out. Next one isn't for a few hours. Wanna grab some breakfast? I know a cool place."

I stiffened. "How do you know the airline schedule?"

"I checked online. Unless you want to make three stops on the way to Cincinnati — closest city, right? — you've got time to kill until the next flight."

Under other circumstances, I would have liked A 'Shroom of One's Own. The brick-walled café was cozy and pretension-free. The chalkboard menu offered the usual half-cafs, lattes, and designer chais, but you could also get muffins, bagels, eggs, or egg beaters, any way you wanted them.

The smoking policy was liberal.

Or so I deduced, as we slid into a dimly lit booth, and Tripp dug into his jeans pockets. From one, he extracted a small leather pouch. From the other, a cigarette wrapper. You didn't have to be a pothead to know what was in the pouch. No one swooped down to stop him. A waitress did come over, a young, short-shorts–wearing Cali-blonde with blindingly white teeth. "Hey, Tripp. The usual?"

So he doesn't spend all his time in his room after all. He nodded and motioned to me. "Jamie . . . ?"

It was the first time he'd used my name. I shook my head. "I'm not hungry."

Tripp overruled me. "She'll have a decaf chai and a carrot muffin, lightly toasted."

I wanted to protest, but I knew the combo of calming tea and warm comfort carbs would, as my grandmother used to say, "hit the spot."

We were in a corner booth, and Tripp was facing inside the nearly empty café. I had little else to look at, but him. He'd finally removed the sunglasses, so I actually could. As he busied himself sprinkling the marijuana leaves into the cigarette wrapper, I assessed. He'd finger-combed the hair out of his eyes, which were almond-shaped and a deep, dark, rich chocolate. He pursed his lips as he rolled the joint. Too full for his narrow, hollow-cheeked face, they softened — or ruined, if that's what he was going for — the bad-boy look. Absorbed in his task, Tripp didn't notice me staring at him. He raised the joint to his lips, and with the tip of his tongue licked it closed. I was mesmerized.

Suddenly, he met my eyes, measuring my interest. "Join me in an appe-toke-r?"

I shook my head. I'd never smoked up, and I wasn't about to start now. Best to be clearheaded when I made my escape.

"So you come here to get high?" I guessed as he lit up.

"Nah." Pinching the joint between his thumb and forefinger, he took a long drag, then slowly exhaled, filling our booth with a grass-sweet, distinct aroma. "I mostly smoke in my room."

Neither of us said, *Of course. It's not like anyone ever goes in there.*

Topher and Nicole were clueless. Tara was a backstabbing slut, Tripp a pothead slacker, and Olivia a trophy child. Yeah, that qualifies for a Family Values Award.

I studied Tripp's hands. Smooth, long, way too big for his body, like a puppy with huge paws. He bit his nails, but his fingers were clean, unstained.

Our order arrived. Tripp tucked into a three-egg omelette, hash browns, bacon, and a large coke. I sipped my tea, and savored the surprisingly good muffin. "Organic?" I guessed.

He nodded, and motioned to his joint. "Like this."

I've heard potheads brag about this supposed "moment of clarity" you get when you're high — when everything in your life is suddenly crystal clear. Maybe it was a contact high, but as I watched a plume of smoke snake from the corner of Tripp's mouth, understanding dawned on me. The Shadow, this hermit, knew my name, knew where I lived, knew I took my food organic . . . and most certainly knew exactly what had gone down last night and this morning.

About him? I knew pretty much zilch. Not that I cared — I was leaving — but unanswered questions nagged. About Tara. About Olivia, Topher, Nicole . . . and the elephantine one at the table: Why did they do this to me?

So the question that came out first was a total dark horse. "How come you're called Tripp?" Some druggie nickname, I assumed.

He gave me a strange look. Sheepishly, I added, "Unless it's your real name?"

"It's short for 'the Third.'"

"The third what?" I asked.

"Christopher Taylor."

Trip. Triple. The third one. Duh. "So Topher —" I started.

"— is Christopher Taylor, Jr.," he explained. "Grandpops, Judge Christopher Wylie Taylor, started the first law firm exclusively for the entertainment industry in the Southland. Movie contracts, high profile divorces, custody, and drug battles of the rich and famous. Made a ton of bricks."

So the uber-wealth wasn't Nicole's. Interesting.

"And your dad is following in his footsteps?" I guessed.

"Runs the firm — along with his brother and sister. My cousins are expected to be the next generation of attorneys."

"But it's not what you want to do?"

"Not so much."

"So what *do* you —"

He snickered. "Want to do with my life? Or, more glob-ally, what do I actually do?" He paused. "Besides chill and get high?" It seemed he was teasing me.

I squirmed. I had to change the subject. After a long awk-ward moment, I blurted, "I just don't get what I ever did to her! Why would Tara play such a foul trick on me?"

Tripp leaned back, and shrugged. "You're here. That's all it takes."

"What's that supposed to mean?"

He was quiet for a while, then said, "Think of Tara as the human body. Anything — any *one* — unfamiliar is treated like an invading germ. The body's first instinct is to expel it. It's her nature."

The image of vapor-thin Tara as the human body was too much. I burst out laughing. "Dude," I said when I caught my breath. "Your family is beyond weird."

"You don't know the half of it," he said, reaching for the ashtray, and stubbing out the joint. "Don't let her get to you."

It's a little late for that, I thought.

"Hey, Jamie?" he said softly now. "Don't leave because of Tara."

I looked up at him, but all I could see in those intense dark eyes was my own reflection. "What's it to you if I stay or go?" I challenged.

Tripp uncoiled his lean body from the booth, and stretched. "Olivia likes you, for one. You're doing an amazing job with her. Besides, this whole thing that you're running from? They've employed the Hastings-Taylor militia. They'll find a way to make the whole thing go away. Guaranteed."

Guaranteed, indeed. By the evening news on the east coast, the entire story had been twisted, rewoven, spun. Nicole's people were pros. They'd done an immediate and "thorough" investigation, and — *ta da!* — trotted out "proof" that the photos had been doctored! Someone else's bare body had been computer-imposed under my face. The dress I wore was not see-through, those bare breasts did not belong to the new nanny, who — for the record — was an innocent victim of some nut's grudge against Nicole. Some creep intent on sabotaging the Family Values Awards, who would be hunted down and prosecuted to the fullest extent of the law, it was alleged.

"Such are the hazards of working for someone in the public eye," cluck-clucked Nicole-in-the-news. "I feel so awfully bad for her. I'm sure we'll find a way to make it up to Junie."

She didn't even remember my name.

Her team had composed a "statement" attributed to me! "I am so sorry for Mrs. Hastings-Taylor," I supposedly said. "I've grown so attached to this whole wonderful family. I would never do anything to hurt them."

I sounded like I *had* left my brains at the airport.

The real shocker? Everyone bought it! Save a few photographers, totally paid off to keep quiet, America thought it was true. I got sympathetic e-mails — which I was asked not to respond to — requests for interviews, politely turned down by Team Spin-Control, and even empathy gifts, swiftly returned.

My own reaction surprised me. Relief trumped rage. It didn't matter that I was exonerated for something I hadn't done. Lesson learned: Wealth is power, and it comes in very handy at moments like these. I almost forgot that my parents hadn't called, or arrived to bring me home. That had to be a Topher call to Nannies Without Values, who had in turn reassured my 'rents.

That night marked the first time I helped myself to another luxury, courtesy of the Hastings-Taylors. I hit the bar in my room, and made myself a drink.

Suitably calmed, I decided to check in with Abby.

It was late in New York, but Abby was wide awake and miserable. She told me about her studly cater-waiter turning out to be none other than S. C. Wagner! I was blown away, until she explained Simon's blonde addiction and how the boy wonder had blown her off . . . and so, she was sure, had Ethan.

Ragging on her was not an option. She was feeling crappy enough. My job was to bolster what was left of her sinking self-confidence. So I reminded Ab-Fab that today's angst is tomorrow's bestseller material. "Remember how you feel now, and put it into a book later. As for males, the only one worthy of you right now is three feet tall and five years old. For that matter, the only family member *I* trust here is Olivia."

Abby sucked up her personal drama and immediately went into support mode. "I bet Nicole and Topher believe you, that it was all Tara —"

"Abs, I have no idea."

"I'm sure they do. They know how she operates. I bet Tara's good and pissed. She wanted you out. Only, now, you're the golden girl, the victim. You've got the spotlight, only not the one Tara intended."

The vicious vixen, I informed her, had split for her father's house. Great best-friend minds think alike. At the same time, we said, "She'll be back. Tara Hastings is so not through with —

"— You."

"— Me."

A week had passed. A quiet seven days, since Nicole was off on a press junket, promoting an upcoming "very special episode" of her TV series. Topher came home early every night to have dinner with Olivia, Tara had gone completely AWOL, and Tripp had faded back into the shadows. My rage was slowly ebbing, but I was still wary.

And so, when Nicole returned and I was summoned for an audience with Her Royal Heinous, my guard was up higher than the sentry post at the front gate. I didn't know which Nicole Hastings-Taylor I'd be confronted with — the sweet mom or the monster?

Actually, a new Nicole presented herself: all business, all

the time. This one waved me into her office and cut to the chase.

"Tara," Nicole had pasted a phony smile on, "although she had nothing to do with the incident, is *so* sorry for the misunderstanding."

Then why isn't she apologizing herself?

Tara's only sorry the scheme backfired on her.

So that's what they call dirty tricks in LA? A misunderstanding.

So many retorts, so little time. I bit my lip and said nothing. Which was fine with Nicole, because she'd planned this speech as a solo act. "Tara wants to make it up to you."

I shook my head, "Not necess —"

"She's invited you to join her tonight," Nicole continued. "She's going out with a friend to a very private club. I think it's very generous of her to invite you."

I think I'd rather dive into a vat of my own vomit.

I opened my mouth to protest, but Nicole's icy stare forced it shut.

"You've been here a month and Topher tells me you haven't been out at all. You should have some fun. Be ready at nine." Nicole turned to Leee. "Get Les Moonves on the phone —"

"I don't need to go out," I assured her. *Especially not with your evil spawn.*

But Nicole was dismissing me. "I insist. End of story."

Actually, it was just the beginning.

Chapter Eleven

Blonde Number Two

Abby

I hadn't heard from Simon since Gordevan's reading and I'd only gotten one e-mail from Ethan — the one repeating his need for space.

Ethan. Simon. They were the only two channels my mind would play. I switched between them obsessively, trying and failing to turn off the set.

Get over it, I kept telling myself. And finally, one windy November day, I began to. For starters, Dylan had been on the losing end of a few more skirmishes — a playground episode on the jungle gym, another with a girl who'd stolen his mid-morning snack at Mademoiselle Félice's, and a third involving DC at Party Place. I started home from the last defeat with a furious child howling and hanging from my hand, cursing me out for not taking on his tormentor. That was when I decided to focus on The Rock-ization of Dylan Matheson. I was determined to turn him into a lean, mean, fight-your-own-battles machine — get the bull's-eye off his back; get him to stand up, literally, for himself.

"The more you act like that — screaming and crying and wanting me to do what you think you can't," I told him in the elevator to the penthouse, "the more you're going to be picked on."

Raul, the elderly elevator operator, nodded his agreement.

"We have a choice," I said, kneeling to wipe Dyl's nose with a tissue. "You can stay scared of everything or you can learn how to take care of yourself." *Look who's talking,* the meany cockabeany voice in my head was saying. *Abby, the punching bag.* "You can kick DC's butt —"

He was too miserable to pretend. "I can't," he whimpered.

"You can, too," I said more impatiently than I'd meant to. "You're getting really good at karate. And maybe —"

He shook his little head as if the weight of the world was on it. "I stink at karate," he hiccuped. "I stink like cat poop."

I took a deep breath. "No, you don't. We'll work on it together," I promised. "You just need practice." And gymnastics, I thought. If I could spring him from the Elysée, where he'd been permanently tagged a crybaby, and get him into a more physical routine, it might build his confidence. . . .

"Listen to me, Dyl. It's not going to be that hard. Like let's say someone wants your sand truck and you don't feel like sharing. What would you say to them? Like if they said, 'Give me your truck'?"

"I'd say . . . 'no'?" Dylan answered.

"I can't hear you."

"No," he peeped.

"Uh-uh. I want to hear it!" I insisted, giving him my best you-can-do-it smile.

"No." He upped the volume.

"Say it loud, 'I'm the Dyl-inator and I'm proud!'"

He giggled and got into it. "NO!" he roared.

Raul jumped, clutching his heart. Then, grinning at Dylan, he gave us a solid thumbs-up.

That afternoon, I tried to get Lila to transfer Dyl out of the posh day camp and into a twice-a-week gymnastics class. She nixed that, but agreed to trade swimming for gymnastics, which, she decided, would look better on Dylan's applications for kindergarten — which, in New York, was more viciously competitive than soccer in Brazil.

The little guy was a natural. A tumbling fool. And it turned out that his talent for cartwheels and calisthenics improved his balance and confidence at karate. One afternoon, when Dylan was watching TV in his room after an amazing karate class, where he'd crushed two other kids in the Peewee Division, I wandered into the kitchen. Edith wasn't around but, on the gleaming steel countertop, there was a thick manuscript that Lila must have been reading before she left for her facial and sesame body buff at Bliss.

The pile of pages looked to be a new novel by Curt Gordevan. I felt a jolt of excitement — the first I'd had since my last date with Simon. So I grabbed a spoon and a yogurt from the fridge and started paging through the manuscript while I ate.

Dylan was still in his room and I was still reading when Lila got home. I'd assumed that she'd be all clean and glowing from the spa trip; instead her face looked red and sore, as if it had been sandpapered. She nudged her crimson chin toward the manuscript.

"Isn't it fabulous?" she gushed, flinging her Kate Spade bag and DKNY cashmere shawl onto the French country hutch. "I think it's Curt's best in years. Don't you think so?"

"Mmmm," I said tactfully. From what I'd read, I didn't really think it was as good as *The War Park,* the book we'd read in English class last year. Lila looked distressed, so I added, "It's pretty good."

"*Pretty* good?" Now she was stunned. "Excuse me? That's like saying Shakespeare is pretty good. Curt Gordevan is . . ." She paused for the right adjective: "Fabulous!"

I considered doing what I usually did with my parents when they'd whine to me about each other: nod sympathetically and look like I agreed with whatever they said. But, with no permission from my brain, my mouth went off. "It's good and all. It's just not as good as *The War Park.*"

Lila gasped. "Oh my God, that's exactly what I thought. I tried to tell Curt."

Her sudden turnaround threw me. "What did he say?"

"You don't really want to know. He just got defensive. He's such a stubborn man. So unfashionably macho. He doesn't listen to anyone."

Dylan waddled into the kitchen, rubbing his eyes. Lila didn't notice him. I started toward him.

"Wait!" Lila blocked my path. "I mean, please wait. I want to talk with you about Curt's book —"

"Mommy, I threw Josh and Brice today!" Dylan proudly announced.

"That's nice, dear." Lila had her own agenda, and it didn't include her son. "Would you give Curt's manuscript a thorough read and let me have your comments? I have an appointment with him on Wednesday. You could get something to me by Wednesday morning, couldn't you?"

Tomorrow's my day off, I didn't say. *I want to get going on my own book,* I didn't say.

"Sure," I said.

Lila might have emotionally shortchanged Dylan, but I was determined to make a big deal out of his karate triumph. I suggested we take a pass on the Young People's session at Lincoln Center and celebrate his win at this terribly trendy gelato joint across the park.

We sashayed out into the chilly autumn afternoon, holding hands. It was one of the first times Dylan had ever reached for my hand — or allowed me to take his without doing the flop and lug. He was yakking away, talking at a proud and loud pitch. His chatter rang off the tiled floor of the ice-cream parlor.

I opted for lemon gelato and Dyl chose chocolate. We sat on old-fashioned, ice-cream parlor chairs at a round, little, marble-topped table. We were deep into reviewing Dylan's progress at gymnastics when a scent wafted past, a fragrance that would have made me weak in the knees if I hadn't already been sitting down.

Without thinking, I smiled and looked up — right into Simon's stony face. His glacial blue eyes swept over me and coldly moved on. As my expectant smile froze, he exited the shop with a blonde who wasn't Jacqueline on his arm.

My heart started drumming frantically. My hands went clammy. My face paled enough for Dylan to stop his cheerful chatter and study me curiously. "Abby, whatsa matter?" he asked.

He didn't smile. He didn't say, "Hello." He probably didn't even recognize me. I'm just some anonymous jerk he picked up at a party and dropped at a café.

"Nothing," I lied to Dylan. "I'm okay."

Wednesday morning, I missed my bus to the city and got to the penthouse an hour late. Edith reminded me that Mademoiselle Félice didn't like stragglers crashing the Elysée, so I phoned to say Dylan wouldn't be coming in, left my notes with Gordevan's manuscript on the kitchen counter where I'd found it, and decided to take Dyl crosstown to the Children's Zoo. It was a beautiful day and I thought fresh air and a walk across the park would do us both good.

We were passing the playground when Garrick bounded over and positioned himself in our path.

"You look terrible," he announced. "Are you feeling okay?"

I didn't feel like doing my Little Miss Sunshine thing. "If you really want to know," I told him, "I'm south of crappy. Not enough sleep and too much on my mind. How about you?"

"Fine, fine." Garrick brushed aside my question. "But what's up with you?"

My impulse, of course, was to smile and just assure Garrick that nothing was wrong. Instead I gave him the Cliff Notes version: Abby finds out that Simon is S. G. Wagner; the minute she leaves his side, he's canoodling with a blonde.

"Wonderboy and I are over," I concluded.

"Good for you," Garrick said. "The guy's a known creep. Be glad you dropped him."

"He dumped *me*," I pointed out.

"No way." Garrick's green eyes widened with disbelief, carrot-colored curls bobbling endearingly. "What's wrong with that guy? I thought he was supposed to be smart."

Garrick. Why couldn't I have fallen for him instead of Simon? "I thought about calling you, but I didn't have your number," I told him.

"Well, you got it now." He rattled off his digits, then waited while I put them in my phone book. "Call anytime. It doesn't have to be an emergency. If you just feel like . . . talking or . . . you know, anything."

"Thanks, Gar," I said, managing a smile. "You're the best." He *was* such a sweetie, I realized.

"Does that mean I've got a chance?" he asked.

The question startled me and, clearly, embarrassed him.

He held his hands up and stepped back. "Just kidding," he said.

But a little voice in my head went, *Hmmm.* He was kind and considerate and concerned about me. And he was cute, too, though redheaded cute wasn't my type. No, I went for the tall, dark, relationship-allergic guys.

Dylan was watching the playground, zoning in on DC, who was swinging on the monkey bars. "DC's a cow poop," he grumbled.

I followed his gaze and saw the steely Ms. Farber, arms crossed, standing guard at the jungle gym as her charge, Hannah, climbed cautiously beneath DC.

Dylan tugged impatiently at my hand. "Right?" he was asking. "Isn't DC a cow poop?"

"You can do better than that," I reminded him. We'd been rehearsing comebacks to use on DC.

"Do you like movies?" Garrick asked me.

I did. In fact going to the movies had been one of Ethan's and my favorite things to do. There was this old movie house in Shafton that had been divided into two small theaters. It was where Ethan and I had kissed for the first time while watching a horror flick. Just as everyone in the place started to shriek when the masked teen murderer pulled an ax on the self-centered cheerleader, I grabbed Ethan and hid my face in his chest. He'd lifted my head and whispered in his reassuring rumbling voice, "Don't be afraid. I've got you," and then he kissed me. And then I wasn't afraid. I was kissing him back, oblivious to the screams around us.

"Would you like to go sometime?" Garrick continued, cutting into my Shafton reverie.

"You mean with you?" I blurted like a jerk.

Garrick smiled and shrugged and said, "Yup. With me."

I wasn't sure. *Right now,* I thought, *I need a friend more than I need a date.*

"How about some Friday?" he suggested.

I told him that Lila usually asked me to stay late on Fridays.

"No problem," Garrick said. "Bring Dylan along. We can catch an early show right after DC's mom comes home."

Cool. With Dylan "chaperoning" us, it would be a no-sweat deal. No moves to worry about; no awkward scenes. Just Dylan and me, and manny makes three. "That would be great," I said, and I meant it, thinking that it would be the first step in my new program — which I'd made up that minute — of only hanging out with guys who seemed one hundred percent trustworthy.

"Why don't you check the listings and I'll —" The rest of Garrick's sentence was cut short by Ms. Farber's booming cry.

"You leaf my girl alone or I vill drag you home by the ear!" Naturally, it was DC she was screaming at.

"We'll talk," Garrick said, racing back into the playground. Dylan stared saucer-eyed at Ms. Farber as she shrilly threatened DC. I tightened my grip on his hand and led him away from the scene.

To calm Dyl, I continued as if nothing had happened. "So

if DC isn't a cow poop, what is he?" I challenged as we made our way east.

"He is . . . uh . . . um . . . a big fat bully!" Dylan declared.

"Skip the 'fat,'" I suggested. "What else?"

"He is not nice. He is . . ."

"Dis —" I hinted.

"Dith-reth-pectful to others!" he asserted.

"Big-time," I agreed. "And you, Dylan Matheson, are a buff and brilliant boy. Okay." I stopped and stooped before him. "What are we going to say if DC makes a grab for your bike or a toy or anything else of yours that you don't feel like giving him?"

Dylan hardened his face. His juicy lips became an angry crease; his eyes squinted menacingly. "Go ahead, DC," he growled. "Make my day."

Chapter Twelve

Betrayals & Lox

Jamie

"Our ride is here, chop-chop."

This is what "she wants to make it up to you" sounds like. Tara, on the intercom, nearly an hour late, was summoning me.

After more time deliberating than I'd admit to anyone except Abby, I settled on the one outfit meant to have been worn in New York: jeans that I'd cut to capris and decorated with embroidery, a gauzy button-down top that looked best knotted in the front. I shucked my Birkenstocks for my favorite handwoven espadrille sandals. And for the first time since I'd gotten there, I put on makeup and gathered my wavy hair in a loose bun. At the last minute, for luck, I slipped on my purple chain-link Sixty-Five Roses bracelet.

The minute I saw Tara at the front door, I wanted to bolt back upstairs and change. Preferably into someone else.

Tara wore a smug smile. And little else.

I must have looked stunned. Tara struck a pose and pointed to her flashy silver-belted micromini. "It's Dior," she advised me. "You need long legs to carry it off."

My own legs suddenly felt like tree stumps.

She stuck her foot out. The ankle strap of her slinky

sandals was designed like a necklace, a cascade of diamond drops in the front. "Jimmy Choo's."

I calculated. In my no-heel, gem-less espadrilles, I'd look like a poor midget next to her.

The *pièce de résistance* was a jewel-encrusted strapless top made of mesh. It looked like a harness.

"It's called a bustier," Tara enlightened me. "It's Roberto Cavalli."

I took this diva display in the spirit intended: mean. I was not to forget anything: I was the help. Tara was to the manor born. She could hurt me.

But I just could not help myself. Mimicking her pose and her attitude, I rattled off my own no-label attire. "Thrift shop jeans, shirt from the sale rack at T.J. Maxx, and sandals hand-woven by South American women who were paid a fair wage for them."

Tara's mouth was stuck half-open.

"Oh," I added, "and the makeup? It's MAC. They don't test on animals."

Still, Einstein had no comeback. Which left me another opening: "If this doesn't work for you — I assume we're going to be in public — maybe you have something to lend me?"

I wanted to add, "from your fat days," but Tara had already turned her back, headed for the door.

A red Hummer was out front. Without a word or a glance back in my direction, Tara climbed into the passenger seat.

I tried to look nonchalant as I hoisted myself into the back. The girl at the wheel was a mass of curls and feathers, from her golden hair to her ostrich jacket. I couldn't tell where the hair ended and the jacket began.

Her name was Skyy, "With two y's," she said.

"Like the vodka," Tara clarified.

Skyy chuckled, "My parents downed a bottle when I was conceived."

"Lucky it wasn't Grey Goose," I deadpanned.

Skyy shot a sideways glance at Tara. Their secret code, I'd bet, for "I feel your pain."

Then she gunned it.

Tara and Skyy chatted in best-friend shorthand, left-coast style.

"Boho," said Tara admiringly.

"Retro," replied Skyy, pleased with the compliment.

"Beaded," noted Tara. "Herrera?"

"Baby Phat."

"Got it."

It didn't take a showbrats-to-English dictionary to know this was a fashion-exchange. It was the only language they spoke. They were raised on it, just as Olivia was being brainwashed to think that's all anyone cares about.

I horned in. "So what's this VIP club we're going to?" I had visions of the New York club Abby described in her e-mail.

"No one does clubs anymore," Tara flatly informed me. "They're played."

"What does anyone *do*, then?" I asked sarcastically. "The malt shoppe?"

Skyy started to laugh — then caught herself, on the brink of breaching the snob rules. Laughing is what one does *at* the nanny — not *with* the nanny. She switched to condescending. "Clubs are too lookyloo. We do scenes. We find them, we get there: It's a scene."

The building we pulled up to, a concrete eyesore on a deserted side street, looked like someone had stolen its CONDEMNED sign. There were no lookyloos, no inferior masses straining to get past the velvet rope. Too many *Law & Order* reruns had me considering the possibility that our "scene" was a "let's lose the nanny" — for good — mission. I felt for my cell phone.

I was relieved when a valet emerged from the pitch-darkness, even more so when a brute bouncer, straight out of central casting, nodded at Tara and Skyy, opened the giant metal door, and ushered us in.

To pure blackness. By turning her back on me, Tara inadvertently gave me something to focus on: The gems on her top were like beams of light. *And a little bustier shall lead them,* I chortled to myself. We walked through a set of heavy velvet curtains to another door. Another bouncer. Another wink and a nod. Finally, we were there.

"Welcome to Lox, ladies."

My breath caught. This was something different all right. A space as cavernous as an airplane hangar, yet designed for intimacy. Dim lighting, soft jazzy-bluesy background music, and dark corners everywhere. Smoke wafted from different directions, none overbearing, not all tobacco.

"It's the ultimate in exclusive and private," Tara pointed out. "If you're famous, you can come here and not be bothered."

By those pushy fans who made you rich and famous in the first place?

"Or photographed," Skyy put in.

By those pesky paparazzi who keep you in the news?

Tara added, "There's no list, and if you don't want a credit card trail, you can pay cash, or have a tab set up in a different name."

So it's the perfect place to cheat, I mused. Do what you wouldn't normally do in public. That's what Holly-wealth buys you.

"You can totally be yourself here —" Tara started.

"Or whoever you'd rather be — or be with!" Skyy elbowed Tara. "Three o'clock," she whispered.

Some teen boy star, I couldn't say which, was swapping saliva with a same-sex friend, apparently a worthy news flash.

Tara and Skyy filed the juicy tidbit, then deigned to show me around. There was something for everyone, for every taste and whim. Cocktail tables, couches, loveseats, booths, even beds on which the coolest of cliques sat, watching big-screen TVs, sipping designer brews, and popping munchies.

Each area boasted its own bar, but scores of waiters and waitresses ensured you never actually had to get up to fetch your own anything. The menu was all about finger food: sushi, sashimi, caviar and crackers, dim sum. Nothing so low-brow as cheese sticks or chicken wings. There were no prices listed, which reminded me of the saying, "If you have to ask, you can't afford it."

This was real decadence. It was also hypnotic.

"Everyone who's anyone is here," Skyy crowed.

Anyone, I translated, who'd fall into the junior glitterati category. Aside from skin tones and ring tones, they all looked and sounded alike: Skinny, slinky, cell-phoned, Blackberry-ed, and iPod-ed-out. Skyy rattled off names of actors I didn't know, from TV shows I don't watch, like *The O.C.*, *Chapelle's Show*, *Alias*, VH1's *I Love Any Decade I Remember*.

I was woefully under-equipped, underdressed, and epically out of place. What seemed like a cute outfit only an hour ago felt dowdy and dumb. Saving grace: No one noticed me. The self-absorption level was off the charts.

"That's where Jessica and Nick sit," Skyy whispered, motioning to the far left corner of the room. "When they're together."

We approached a spiral staircase, which led to the mezzanine, the VIP room. "You have to meet certain standards to get in," Tara bragged in a tone that meant she and Skyy did. And we'd come to the place in the script where they ditched the nanny.

Without even a "See ya, wouldn't wanna be ya," Tara climbed the stairs. Skyy was set to follow, but something stopped her — probably the urge to show off more. "Wanna come?"

Tara flipped around, scowling.

Aha! Skyy's invite was impulsive, an ad lib!

The VIP area was ash-paneled and illuminated by red lights. Up here, the bar was more elaborate and, as we swung by, I noticed substances other than alcohol being served on it.

This was the rarefied air fit only for the most major stars du jour — Beyoncé, Cameron, Justin, Usher, Paris — to breathe. A few waved/winked at Tara and Skyy, but the duo dove for a semicircle banquette on which several young hotties were already settled.

Their turf, their peers, their table, situated right up against the floor-to-ceiling glass window. So you could look down on, and feel superior to, the people below. In the real world, this was like the best table in the lunchroom, if your school cafeteria had a loft from which you could spy on your classmates.

The three guys and two girls who were already there were, I'd bet, celebrity spawn, older versions of Olivia's lunch bunch. There was only room left on the circular banquette for two more. Skyy slipped in first, and Tara "generously" insisted I sit next to her friend. She perched on the end, her long legs facing out.

No one seemed surprised to see me; polite introductions were made.

As soon as a waiter materialized, Skyy ordered a dirty martini and flung her arm around the doe-eyed hottie she'd scrunched next to — Liam, I think. She pulled him in even closer and — was she licking his ear? *Ew.*

Tara winked at the waiter, and said she'd have "the usual."

I was about to order, but Tara had suddenly commanded the attention of the entire room by crossing her legs. Her micromini, already approaching indecency, hitched up. Was she even wearing a thong? Every guy within drooling distance angled to get to her. The winner had slicked-back dark hair, an olive complexion, and wore shades. "Tara, my love," he said in a faux-Italian accent, moving his chair over to her. "How exciting to see you."

Her eyes wandered south, to his lap. "Yes, I can see that, Antonio." She laughed.

After some inane chitchat, their drinks arrived. An excellent time to excuse myself, pretend to head to the bar, and leave. But Skyy and Tara were mid-performance, and it was train-wreck charisma. I could not pull myself away.

Skyy downed her martini as if it were a shot of tequila, ordered another, and began "canoodling" with Liam.

Canoodling: a G-rated word for R-rated action. Eyes closed, mouths open, their sucking sounds were loud enough for the whole group to hear. Their hands were in constant motion over each other's bodies. Then the contortions began. A leg swung over a lap, a palm slipped under a butt and a rhythmic dance began. My heart hammered. They weren't going to —? Not right here!

Tara tapped me on the shoulder. "What do you think of the scene so far, Nanny Jamie?" The platinum princess was grinning devilishly, sipping her "usual," which was colorless and on the rocks. Gin or vodka, I'd guess.

Antonio, meanwhile, was persistent, trying to woo Tara

from conversation to a lip lock. But Tara rebuffed him. She was all about the tease, crossing and uncrossing her legs, running her tongue over her lips, asking Antonio about some music video he was apparently directing. Every once in a while, she'd look at me and wink. Like we shared a secret or something.

Finally, I looked away, out the glass partition to the floor below. The view was excellent. The kids on the bed were having a rollicking and, comparatively, wholesome good time. The saliva-swapping dudes had switched partners.

I decided to scout for Jessica and Nick, an A-list star sighting I could report to my sister, Juliana. Training my eyes on the cozy twosomes in the darkest part of Lox, only one couple caught my attention.

This pair was at full canoodle. They were *not* Nick and Jessica.

They were Ethan — Abby's Ethan! And a girl! Who was not Abby. I did a double, then a triple, take. She was a golden-haired stunner wearing a white halter top that offset her deep tan and seriously toned biceps.

I bolted up, knocking a startled Tara right into Antonio's lap, and raced down the stairs. I came to a screeching halt right in front of the cheater's table. This, Abby always says, is one big difference between us. She's passive, nonconfrontational. You can practically hear those beeping sounds as she's backing up. Me? Bring it!

I stood over them. Ethan and Not Abby. They were too

involved to even notice me, until I loudly banged a stray beer bottle on the table.

"Hey! What the —" Ethan's face morphed from anger to horror in record time.

Ms. Tan 'n' Toned was shocked, but not stupid. "You must be Abby. I'm Samantha Harris."

"Worse," I snarled. "I'm Abby's best friend."

Ethan was propelled into motion. He rose guiltily. "J-J-Jamie," he stammered, "what are you doing here?"

"I get to ask the questions, Ethan."

Ethan had obviously informed his Cali-sweetie about Abby, yet he'd failed to download Abs about Sam. Samantha.

I exploded. "Why aren't you building houses? Why are you here? Who the hell is she? How could you do this to Abby?" By the last question, my voice had gone up an octave, attracting the attention of cheaters all around them.

"Please, can I talk to you for a moment?" Ethan drew a breath, took my arm. To Sam he said, "I'll be right back."

As he led me away from the table, I kept at him. "Do you know how guilty she feels even thinking about other guys? Why would you do this to her?"

Ethan whirled on me. I was ready for the usual lame-o excuses: "It's not what it looks like," or "It doesn't mean anything." I wasn't ready for:

"Maybe it's because I can get something from Sam that Abby won't —"

"I can't believe you, Ethan!" I cut him off loudly.

"You can't tell her," he said. "Let me. It's the best thing."

"The best thing for who?" I demanded, thinking that the best thing was that at least Abby had gone out with Simon. Even if the date had ended badly.

"For Abby," he pleaded. "All you can do is hurt her when you can't even be there for her. Please, Jamie. Just give me some time."

I glared at him.

"A day. Okay? I'll tell her tomorrow."

Now I knew why I'd never liked Ethan. I'd been right to trust my instincts.

"Besides," he went for the big finish. "This is my responsibility, my mess."

I folded my arms. The lowlife is taking the high road? I felt like spitting on him. Instead, I turned — and ran.

Between slutty Skyy, teasing Tara, and cheating Ethan, I was on emotional overload. I raced through Lox, weaving my way around the tables until I saw a clear shot to the EXIT sign. I put the real speed on.

Unfortunately, so did some random girl, coming from the left. When she slammed into me, I believe I was at my personal track-team best. As my legs slipped out from under me, I prayed that Tara wasn't looking down right now. I'd rather die of a cracked coccyx than embarrassment.

I never did hit the ground.

I hit a guy instead.

Clarification: I landed *on top of* a guy. Was he an innocent bystander caught in a domino effect, or a hero who'd run up to catch me? He had broken my fall. He'd also caught me in the kind of compromising position you see in the movies. Girl on top of boy, his muscled arms circling her. She lifts her head, he lifts his, they look into each other's eyes — kismet!

It didn't work like that. I'd landed with my nose pressed against his flat stomach. Pressing my palms to the floor, I started to get up — problemo. I wasn't positioned to roll off, I'd have to slide — down his body. Propped up on his elbows now, my hero seemed embarrassed. Whatever. I just went for it.

Meanwhile, people were cheering.

"Righteous save, dude!" someone shouted from the bar.

"You da man." Another saluted with his beer bottle.

"Thank you so much — you totally saved my butt," I said.

"You're very welcome," he responded with a smile. "I'm Chase O'Brien, by the way."

"Jamie Devine."

"Are you okay, Jamie? That girl smashed into you pretty hard."

Now that he mentioned it, my entire left side was aching, especially my arm. I'd be bruised, for sure. Chase stood up, and extended his hand. "Come on, let's go have a look."

I was wobbly, so he helped me over to his table, and examined my arm. My elbow was bloody, my upper arm scraped, but I didn't think anything was broken. Chase grabbed a cloth napkin and dipped it into a glass of water. Gamely, he applied it to my wound — and managed to soak my arm, my hip, and my left leg.

I laughed. His well-intentioned clumsiness was sweet. "Give me that," I said. "I can do it."

Just then, a club manager-type scurried over. "I am so sorry, miss, for your unfortunate accident, but you must agree that Lox is no way responsible." Perhaps, he added, my "compromised mental state" was at fault.

"I wasn't even drinking!" I protested. Meanwhile, Chase continued to play nurse. His attention felt nice, protective, like someone was on my side for a change.

The club manager changed tactics. "But you were running and not looking where you were going."

"So was that other girl," I pointed out, not sure why I now had to defend myself. I got his point: *You can't sue us.*

"Miss —? I'm sorry I don't recognize you." Translation: How did the likes of *you* get into my hip "scene" in the first place?

"I'm with Tara Hastings-Taylor," I said, motioning up to the VIP area. "You can check with her if you'd like."

Score. Club manager backed away quickly.

Chase was awestruck. "You're a friend of Tara's?"

"Do you know her?" *Please say no,* I prayed.

"Not personally, but isn't she Nicole Hastings-Taylor's daughter? The star of *Nikki's Way*?" Chase could not have been more impressed if I'd said I was with Chelsea Clinton or the Bush twins.

Best of all, he didn't connect me with the bare-breast

scandal of the previous week. He said, "So, look, the kids I came with met some friends — so I'm kinda by myself. I could use some company. You could probably use a drink."

I hesitated. His spiky hair was gold, with dark roots. A dye-guy. Did I even want to sit with him?

Chase grinned. "It's the least you can do for the guy who saved your life." His abandoned drink was still at his table. He summoned a waiter. "What'll it be? A cosmo? White wine? Champagne?"

"What are you having?" I asked, nodding at his glass.

"A mojito. I heard it's the 'in' drink. Figured I'd try it."

"And it's . . . ?"

"See for yourself." I took a sip. Definitely rum with lime, but I wasn't sure what else. I'd need my own drink to figure it out.

Chase's cell phone rang. "Text message from my bud Ty Pennington," he said after a quick glance. "Mind if I return it?"

He's buds with the guy from *Extreme Makeover*? Okay, that's kinda cool. As Chase rapped on the tiny keyboard, I observed: square jaw, chiseled cheekbones, ripped bod. In high school, he'd have been the football team captain/prom king. In college, chick-magnet frat boy. In LA? Surfer/slacker most likely. Or maybe "actor wannabe."

Reality check: Chase would be the anti-type, if I even had a type.

The rest of what I learned about him, as we sipped mojitos, seconded my first impression: He was taking a break from

Arizona State University, to see if he had "the right stuff," to make it as an actor. He was quick to say that Hollywood was "not his scene," but "this is where the work is, so what can you do?"

Not that he'd gotten any real acting work yet. But "you gotta be in it to win it," he said without irony, and raised his glass. I clinked and forced myself not to count the clichés.

"So where were you racing to?" Chase finally asked.

"It was more like who I was racing from." The liquor was doing what liquor does to me. Loosening me up. And I knew, in the way you know you're about to fall, but can't stop it, that I was going to tell the truth to a complete stranger.

The complete stranger cocked an eyebrow.

I took in his lips. They looked soft. His eyes were an astounding shade of glow-in-the-dark green, like a cat's. And so I told him about Ethan and Abby and Samantha. Chase listened sympathetically, and then we fell silent.

"That's pretty," Chase finally said with a nod to my Sixty-Five Roses bracelet. "A gift from your boyfriend?"

"No, I don't have a boyfriend, it's —" I started to explain, but just then, he slid his hands across the table and covered mine with his.

"Maybe," he said, "our accidental meeting will turn out to be the best thing that happens to both of us in LA."

Chapter Thirteen

Lovesick

Abby

Lila was at home. She barely looked up when we came in. She was pacing back and forth in front of the wraparound sofa, wringing her slender Kiehl-creamed hands. She stopped suddenly and in a quavering voice that I barely recognized, said, "So, what do you think?"

That was when I noticed a pair of Western-style riding boots (Tom Ford for Gucci — around eight hundred smackeroos, I learned later). The urban cowboy turned out to be Curt Gordevan. The burly author, splayed out on the silk brocade couch. He was sitting back and reading . . . my notes!

"Mommy!" Dylan gave us away.

"Darling," Lila said. "Come in here a moment. Meet Curt."

Dylan raced in, all expectation and excitement, until he realized that his mother had been talking to me. "I'll just make him his afternoon snack," I said, grabbing Dylan's hand, hoping he wouldn't pitch a fit and fall to the floor. He didn't. He held on to me as if I were the last life preserver on the *Titanic*. I felt a rush of love for the chunky monkey, love and empathy. After all, I knew a thing or two about crushed expectations.

"I'll be right back," I promised Lila, who was rolling her eyes at Gordevan as if to say, *What can I do? This is how hired help behaves these days.*

I walked Dylan into the kitchen where Edith was slicing the crusts off little sandwiches obviously intended for Lila and Curt. The iced crystal goblet on a tray, beside a frosty bottle of ale, was a dead giveaway. There were also two Martinis. Gordevan's response to my notes must have made Lila incredibly thirsty.

I was going to fix Dyl a peanut-butter-and-jelly, but something in me snapped and I snatched two of Edith's carefully pruned sandwiches instead.

Startled, she raised her eyebrows at me.

"Who's more important around here?" I asked rhetorically. "Dylan or Curt Gordevan?"

"To me or to Mrs. Matheson?" Edith responded dryly.

"Give them peanut-butter-and-jelly," I suggested, leading Dylan to his room. "Remember, we're in training," I told him. "Five push-ups, then five minutes to cool off, before snacks."

I suffered a major attack of self-doubt on my way back to the living room. I hadn't expected Curt Gordevan himself to read my notes. I'd thought Lila would go over them, and then talk to Gordevan. I hadn't shaped my book review to fit a bloated ego.

"Oh there you are." Lila stopped her convo as I walked into the room. "Ask her yourself, darling," she told Gordevan, looking very relieved. "Abby, this is Curt." She took a martini from the tray Edith had left and sucked it down. "He has some problems with your analysis."

My pulse quickened; my stomach dropped. I had ticked off one of the best-known writers in America — in the world, actually. A living legend. A Pulitzer Prize–winner.

"Okay, you pinpointed a couple of spots where I might have gone overboard," Gordevan growled. "I'll give you that. But, basically, pardon my French, kiddo, you don't know shit from shinola. How old are you?" It wasn't a question, it was a challenge. "Nineteen, twenty?"

"Seventeen," I croaked, my throat dry.

"Jesus!" he grumbled in disgust. "Well, come on. I've got to be at Columbia in fifteen minutes."

He studied me through shrewd, bloodshot eyes. Lila cocked her carefully coiffed blonde head in my direction. The room became extremely quiet. To soothe my throat and give my clammy hands something to do, I grabbed the second martini and did an excellent imitation of Lila.

The drink burned going down. My eyes watered. But I clamped my lips shut and willed myself not to cough. After a minute, the burn and the breathlessness became tolerable. Even . . . nice.

Gordevan watched. His shaggy eyebrows knit together above his lumpy nose — a nose mapped with tiny red veins that suggested the big man had knocked back more than his share of martinis and ale.

"We've gotta talk," he decided. "But not here, not now.

I'm doing a reading at Columbia this afternoon." He checked the gleaming Rolex cutting into his fleshy wrist. "Christ, I'm going to be late. I'd say the hell with it, but I asked Wagner to meet me there."

Wagner? As in Simon Wagner? I'd forgotten that Gordevan was Simon's mentor.

"You." Gordevan pointed his glass at me. "You'll come with us," he commanded, downing the dregs of his ale.

Oh God. Was I going to see Simon again? And have him snub me?

I picked up the martini and took another swallow — a big one. Same thing, second sip: fire searing from throat to gut, and then the burn cooling to a comforting warmth.

"Sure," I said.

Like twin caterpillars, Gordevan's woolly eyebrows lifted as he turned to Lila.

"Of course she'll go," she said. "I've got to get back to the office, but Edith's here till seven. She can see about Dylan. And Abby can explain what she meant in the cab uptown."

One more sip for courage finished my filched martini.

"Let's go, kiddo." Gordevan's calloused hand encircled my arm in an iron grip. I felt a little lightheaded and strangely grateful. I needed someone to steady me. I grabbed my backpack on the way out of the apartment and floated alongside him contentedly.

I have no idea what, if anything, Curt Gordevan and I discussed in the cab. I remember being very happy to climb out — with Gordevan's help — to get away from the car freshener-and-tobacco stench of the taxi. I was so happy that I was beaming.

I was still wearing that tipsy grin when I saw Simon.

He was hunkered down behind a book at the back of the lecture hall where about two hundred kids and a handful of press people were waiting for Gordevan. The students started applauding the moment Gordevan came into view. They went wild again as Simon trotted down the aisle toward us.

He stopped midway. His expression went from "Aw, shucks" to "Oh no," as he spotted me.

For some reason his horrified surprise made me giggle. Gordevan leaned me against a wall near the door, then grabbed hold of Simon. "Christ, the kid's blasted out of her gourd. Take her outside and walk her around, would you?"

Simon led me out onto the campus. "I've got a headache," I told him. Squinting, I took in his amazing face, the piercing blue eyes, the full lips. I could almost taste them. . . .

"I've got some Tylenol," he said coldly. "Or would you rather have crack cocaine?"

I didn't get it. Not at first. Slowly, I remembered that the night we'd gone to Destiny, I'd made the lame joke about him doing drugs. I straightened myself up and, in as snooty a voice as I could manage without slurring, said, "Give it to your girlfriend."

Simon studied me. "How'd you get so trashed? I thought you were a Diet Coke girl."

"Well that just goes to show how little you know about me." I tried to sneer but it was hard to control my lips.

"If you hadn't skipped out on me, I might have had a chance to know you better." With a withering look, Simon succeeded where I had failed. He won gold in the sneer Olympics.

"I ran out on you?" I huffed. "Correction. I knew where I wasn't wanted. You looked totally comfortable with what's-her-name, that blonde octopus, hanging all over you . . . Jackie, Jack-o-Lantern, whatever."

"Jacqueline," he snapped.

"Yeah right, Jacqueline." Suddenly, I felt like I was going to throw up. For real. One martini was even too much for lightweight me.

"Oh, Simon," I whispered. "I'm so sorry."

"That you split on me?"

"No. That I'm going to hurl —"

And I did. In the middle of the Columbia University quad, with students walking briskly by, giving Simon these pitying, I-feel-your-pain looks. Seeing his helplessness, one girl tossed him a little cellophane wrapped tissue pack. He, in turn, handed it to me and I mopped myself up as best as I could.

"Come on," he ordered curtly.

I followed him out of the courtyard and along Broadway into a Starbucks, where two pricey cups of caffeine later, the fog in my head began to lift — making space for shame and humiliation to move in. My stomach was still churning and my fleece vest — picked up at Overstock.com for a mere eighteen bucks — was still stained when Simon led me back to Columbia.

He waited outside a ladies' room while I swabbed at myself with wet towels. Then I trooped shakily behind him back to the lecture hall to catch the tail end of Gordevan's Q and A.

By the time the session was over, I was a little more sober and a lot more embarrassed. I slipped out into the corridor and waited as animated students and equipment-lugging news people filed out. When neither Curt nor Simon had exited, I peeked into the vast room. They were together, up front, at the podium, deep in conversation. Probably, I thought, rehashing Gordevan's performance.

Well, what was I waiting for? Did I need Curt Gordevan to get me a cab, share a ride, drop me off at the bus terminal? Simon turned toward the door and I ducked out of view. I leaned flat against the hall wall, shaking. My hands and the nape of my neck were clammy — which might explain why there was no moisture left for my lips. My tongue felt thick and furry. I'd either been stricken by a deadly virus or I was experiencing my first — and hopefully my last — hangover.

Still woozy, I wheeled on my heels and headed for daylight.

As if walking underwater, I made my way through the press of Upper West Side pedestrians — students, young mothers with toddlers in hand and infants in carrying pouches, musicians toting instrument cases, academics in wrinkled tweed. I passed three Starbucks, three Korean fruit markets, one Chinese take-out place, two Puerto Rican bodegas, four pizza parlors, and one Dominican restaurant hawking "comidas y crioles" and "café con leche."

Instead of living the adventure, enjoying the real New York, I felt as if I were in a cartoon I'd seen. A deer is looking at his friend who has a target on his chest; he's saying, "Bummer of a birthmark, Hal."

I slogged along as if I were Hal. But at the subway entrance, a saying of Jamie's came to mind: *There are no victims, only volunteers.*

You'd think that would have perked me up. Instead, as if to test the accuracy of Jamie's adage, I volunteered. I did what Jamie would term "Dialing Pain." Which means I phoned Ethan.

He actually picked up. "Hey," I said, feeling unnerved and a little desperate.

"Abby?" At least he remembered my name. "What's going on? You okay?"

"Perfect," I lied. "I was just thinking of you. What're you up to?"

"Um . . . you know . . . uh . . . working. We just got a new assignment . . . checking out worker living conditions in Orange County. Um . . . you know, undocumented workers . . . they're abused and exploited every day. Hired for slave wages as gardeners, housekeepers, cooks, nannies . . . So Sam and I are . . . um . . . heading south . . . to document the situation. I'm sorry, Abs . . . I really don't have time for you . . . I mean, I don't have time *to talk* to you right now . . . I just . . . well, you know."

162

I knew. He was trying to get off the phone as fast as possible. So that he could go save exploited and abused Orange County nannies. Hooray for Ethan. Shame on me. How could I, who had everything going for me (except boy-savvy and self-esteem), dare distract Ethan from his urgent do-good mission?

But "I don't have time for you"? The words landed like a punch to my gut. I actually slumped forward, grabbing the subway stair railing to keep me from sinking to the cigarette-butts-and-candy-wrapper-littered street.

"Sounds important," I acknowledged, when I could catch my breath. "But . . . I don't know. I just miss you." It slipped out, sounding whiny and wounded.

"Yeah," he said dismissively. "But I really think . . . like taking a break from each other . . . I mean, that's the best thing for now."

"But what about —?" Our agreement, I was going to say. Our pledge to be true to each other —

Busy Boy cut me off. "Listen, Sam just drove up. I gotta go."

I clicked off, threw my phone into my backpack, and headed down the grungy subway stairs — which were as dark and rank as my mood.

Two weeks after Simon had seen me throw up, and a few days before Dyl and I were slated to see a movie with Garrick, Lila came home early.

"It's all set. We're booked at the Chateau Marmont. You're going with Curt and me. We're leaving from LaGuardia on Friday!" she announced, as if I'd won a billion-dollar Lotto jackpot. "We'll be talking to some movie people about Curt's new book. You can hang out at the pool and work on your tan. After that, we'll all be free to meet and go over your notes."

This weekend! My reaction was immediate. I'd promised Dylan, my crouching tiger in training, that I'd rent us some inspirational DVDs, like *Rocky, Seabiscuit,* and *Miracle* — all tales of underdogs who triumphed against the odds. And I'd already gotten tickets to the Brooklyn Academy of Music Kids Film Festival, which Dylan, who'd never been to the outer boroughs, was totally psyched about. Garrick would be joining us.

"Friday?" I asked. "I've got plans. I mean, Dylan and I —"

"Don't you have a friend out there? Junie, the Boo-Boob Nanny?"

"Jamie," I corrected her. "And she was tricked into wearing that dress."

Out there? It registered slowly. Out there, where she and Gordevan would be talking to movie people. Out there, where I could work on my tan? Out there was LA! And LA was Jamie-world! I mentally smacked my forehead. I was being asked to take a free trip across the country to see my best friend!

There was only one problem. A pudgy five-year-old one.

"I'd love to go. I'm very flattered. But what about Dylan?"

"Nancy Harris-Frieberg's nanny has agreed to pinch-hit

164

for you. Her daughter, Hannah, will be in the Bahamas with her father and his new wife — and they've got a nanny down there for her. So Ms. Farber is free."

The hair on the back of my neck stood up. Farber? There couldn't be two Frau Farbers nannying for two different Hannahs. It had to be Central Park's own Queen of Mean, DC's bullying adult alter ego.

"What about Speed?" I asked. "I mean, Dylan's dad? Couldn't Dyl come with us and stay with him — ?"

"Speed is in Hong Kong on business, then he's off to the Dominican Republic to restore his tan at Oscar and Annette de la Renta's place."

Before I could come up with another scenario, Lila said, "I'm afraid this trip is not optional, Abby. Curt is one of my most important authors. The only way I could tell him you weren't coming with us would be to tell him you'd quit — or been fired."

Her meaning couldn't have been clearer. This was not an invitation, it was a command. And Ms. Farber was a nonnegotiable part of the deal. "Right," I said. "I'll just say good-bye to Dylan, then go home and pack."

I knew I had to tell him and I knew he wasn't going to like it. In the recent past, he'd called Farber a *peenith faith, cow doody,* and a *poo-poo head.* All of which, I had to agree, were totally on the mark. And I doubted very much whether she'd sit through *Rocky* with him.

Dylan was predictably shaken by the news. He threw himself onto his bed, sinking into his pricey patchwork quilt, and had a kick-and-bawl relapse. "I hate Ms. Farber. She's a meany cockabeany. And I hate you, too!"

I tried to pick him up. I wanted to hold him in my arms and tell him that the trip wasn't my idea. But his plump little legs were flailing and I couldn't get near enough to grab him.

"Dylan, stop it now." I begged more than scolded. "It's only for a few days. I'll be back soon. And . . ." And what? "And I'll give you my cell phone number so you can call me every day, any time you want to, morning, noon, or night! We can talk whenever you want, okay?"

His weeping gave way to hiccups; his thrashing legs slowed down. "Dylan, listen to me. I love you." He rolled onto his tummy and hid his face. "Get up. I want a hug good-bye. I'm not leaving till you give me my hug."

"No!" he shouted into the quilt. It was a righteous *no*, full-lunged and emphatic.

"Wow," I told him. "You're getting really good at saying that —"

He turned over. "No!" he hollered at me, his face red. "No!!!" he screamed even louder. And at my startled expression, the hint of a proud smile curled his juicy lips.

I opened my arms, and Dylan scrambled to his feet on the bed and flung himself at me. "Oh, what a great hug!" I told him, my throat thickening with tears. "Dylan Matheson, you're my hero, my champ!"

I speed-dialed Jamie on my cell the minute I was outside. Her voice mail picked up. "James!" I shouted over the blaring taxicab horns and the pneumatic drill tearing up the sidewalk a block away. "I'm coming to LA! Friday!! I'll be staying at the Chateau something or other! Call me back! Can't wait to see you!" I decided to IM her later, once I knew all the details.

The next call I made was to Garrick. I explained what had happened and we agreed to postpone our movie-going until I got back from LA. Which was all good, until he added, in a kind of sexy voice, "You're worth waiting for."

I put my phone away and started wondering if Garrick liked me more than I liked him, if he thought my agreeing to go to the movies with him was a sign that it was mutual, if he thought I wanted a . . . relationship.

Which I so did not.

I still thought of Garrick as a friend. I had no romantic thing going on, and I really hoped that he didn't, either.

My hope was totally selfish.

Although I hadn't had to say *no* to boys a lot, the idea of doing it made me very nervous. I was always afraid I'd hurt their feelings; I was afraid they'd get mad at me. Or worse, what if I was wrong and mistook their friendship for something more? How embarrassing.

Get over yourself, I thought. *How can you even think that Garrick is interested in you as anything but a fellow nanny? I mean, look at your track record, Abby. Two out of two guys you had the hots for avoid you whenever possible.*

My cell phone rang. "Hello," I said, after fumbling the phone out of my backpack.

"Hello . . . ?" a cautious, hesitant child's voice said.

"Dylan?"

"Hi, Abby. Where are you?"

"Dylan, hey. I'm practically across the street from you." I shielded my eyes from the sun and squinted toward Lila's building. "Is something wrong?" I couldn't make out their apartment. I waved anyway.

"Mmmm, no. When are you coming back?"

Despite my dismay and confusion, I was smiling. The little guy's voice was so heartbreakingly sweet. "I'll call you from California, okay, Dyl?"

"Okay, Abby," he said.

"Okay, Dyl, I'm going to hang up now. Okay?"

"Okay."

"Good-bye, Dylan."

"Okay, Abby."

"Say good-bye," I prompted.

"'Bye," Dylan said.

Now there was a guy who really loved me.

Chapter Fourteen

Chasing the Waves

Jamie

Sex.

In high school, I acted like I was too cool to be obsessed with sex. That I was above it all, in no hurry. That I'd rather wait for Mr. Right than experiment with Mr. Right Now.

It was a good line. But it was bull.

I wasn't waiting for anything. Or anyone. I was a virgin because the big "it" wasn't something I was into then. I had other priorities, like Juliana and my family, like going to college and maybe med school. I didn't have time for a serious boyfriend.

Abby was the only one allowed to question me about it. As recently as last week, she IMed, What happens if you meet someone? You're in LA, all by yourself? What happens if you get serious and, you know, want to —

I guessed she was referring to Simon. And herself. But I countered quickly and defensively, C'mon, Abs. No way could that happen. For me, to get serious means I'd have to meet someone who understands what my life is like. Who understands *me*. What are the chances of even meeting a guy like that here?

Now, things were different.

TO: ABS@OH.com
From: Jamie_the_lionhearted@OH.com

He's not even my type! Captain Peroxide — we couldn't take those dye-guys seriously in high school!

And Chase. I told you his name, right? Okay, it's pretentious. Maybe even made up. But I've been out here almost six weeks. Having no friends over the age of three sucks. And in the land of Sedonas, Siennas, double-y'd Skyys and three-e'd Leees, he seems normal. He programmed himself in my cell phone. How cute is that?

Don't worry! I'm not scribbling Jamie Devine-O'Brien in my notebook, but in the plus column, he doesn't even drive a car, here on planet What I Drive Is What I Am. He's not into spending just for status —

The jingle of my cell phone halted my e-mail.

"Hey you." Chase sounded pumped. "I called to see how you're doing. Aches? Pains?"

"A little hungover," I admitted. "*Mas Mojitos* equals one achy breaky hangover. You?"

"Nothing a day spent in the LA sunshine wouldn't cure. Wanna hang out?"

So he's asking me out? On a date? Or asking me outdoors?

"You have off, right? They don't make you work on Sundays . . ."

"How'd you get here so fast?" I asked, greeting a tan, toned, duffel-bag-bearing Chase at the main gate a half hour later.

"Got a lift from a friend," he answered casually, his sparkling green eyes taking in the grandeur of Casa Verde. "This crib rocks!" he raved.

Wearing low-riding surfer shorts and a tank top that revealed bulging biceps, Chase looked more amazing in the daylight than in the dim club lights.

"Bitchin' ride!" Chase commented, ogling the Lexus sports car designated for my use. "Okay if I drive? I asked you out, after all." He winked and slipped into the driver's seat.

So it *was* a date. Instantly, I regretted the cutoffs, T-shirt, and sneakers I'd chosen, wishing I had something girlier.

"Smooth." Chase caressed the steering wheel of the Lexus, as he pulled out of the driveway. "Someday, I'm going to own one of these babies."

To my amazement, I found myself leaning over and pointing out the luxury car's accoutrements. I felt like a saleswoman, detailing the navigation system, and video player in the back for games and DVDs.

"By the way, where are we going?" I asked as Chase circled the neighborhood.

"Okay if we just cruise for a while?" He slowed to point out a French-style chateau behind a set of gates even more elaborate than the Hastings-Taylors'. "Know who lives there?" he asked.

I had no clue.

"Your neighbors just happen to be Michael Douglas and Catherine Zeta-Jones. Hey," he said. "Maybe they need a nanny."

I frowned. "Thanks, but I have my hands full with Olivia." I wanted to tell him about the exquisite, healthy child who gets ignored or used as a prop. But Chase was into the scenery. "That spread over there? You can't see much beyond the shrubs, but that's the Playboy Mansion."

I hoped I wasn't supposed to be impressed. No problem. Chase was enough for the two of us. "The host of *Access Hollywood* lives there," he said. "And —"

"Hey," I stopped him. "How do you know all this stuff?"

He shrugged. "Everyone in this town knows who lives where."

"Where do you live?"

He stole a glance at me. "I'm between places right now, so I'm crashing with friends. But it's cool, one of my roommates is Leo's cousin. And that guy who text messaged me last night? Ty Pennington? He's really cool. Anyway, we've been scoring concert tickets, getting into clubs and stuff."

Stuff like getting past the VIP guard at Lox, I suddenly realized.

"So how 'bout the beach?" Chase asked after we'd been driving for about twenty minutes. "We're not far from Santa Monica."

I hadn't brought a bathing suit, and was debating whether to mention this when he turned a corner and the Pacific Ocean came into view.

Wow. I'd been on the West Coast for six weeks, yet had not seen the ocean. The sun glinting on the rippled aqua water was amazing. As we got closer and pulled into a parking lot, I saw that the pristine white sand was a football field wide. On a breezy Sunday, it was dotted with families, gaggles of teenage girls, and kissy couples.

We found a spot sandwiched between a family and a posse of high school kids. Chase withdrew a blanket and couple of towels from his duffel and spread them out for us. He peeled his tank top off. Mmmm. Those broad shoulders came with six-pack abs.

"No bathing suit?" Chase deduced.

"Didn't bring one," I admitted.

"No problem." He pointed down the beach to an area lined with outdoor clothing stands and kiosks. "They've got suits, sunglasses, T-shirts, tanning lotion, whatever you need. Cheap."

By the time I got back, Chase had already been in the water, and was waiting for me on the blanket. Dripping wet in his surf shorts, he was hotter than ever.

Chase grinned as he watched me walk over. "Nice choice."

There hadn't been much choice at all. Not when you were looking for a one-piece with a built-in bra roomy enough for me. As it was, I was sort of spilling over the top. Where Chase's eyes were now glued.

Reflexively, I sat down and crossed my arms over my chest. I scanned the beach. "This is so beautiful," I said lamely. He sidled up close to me. Droplets of ocean water transferred from his thighs to mine. He tasted, I'd bet, of salt. Chase took my hand, turned me around, and looked into my eyes. "Ever done it in the ocean?"

Okay, maybe he said, "Ever *been* in the ocean?" or "Ever *swum* in the ocean?" But in a court of law, I'd swear that's what I heard.

The answer to all of the above was no.

"That tickles!" I giggled, as little white foamy waves lapped around my ankles. The water was warm and clear, the mud beneath my feet squishy. It wasn't unpleasant, just weird. I wasn't sure I wanted to go farther.

Chase had no such hesitation, stomping straight in, parting the waves to his strong-armed will. He was up to his waist when he turned and waved me forward. "Come on! You can't do it a toe at a time. You gotta dive right in." He demonstrated, and came up grinning big. He shook his head and brushed his hair, matted to his forehead, out of his eyes. "Don't worry, I won't let you drown!" he yelled, before beginning a crawl stroke.

I took a deep breath, and stepped farther in. I could do

casual and confident thanks to those swim lessons at the YMCA. Only, I couldn't stop laughing. Big difference between a chlorine-water pool and Mother Nature's version: the waves! They crashed onto my knees, uneven and relentless. I'd just recovered from the splash of one before another was upon me. The undertow wasn't strong this time of day, but one wave hadn't gotten the memo. It took me by surprise, and knocked my feet out from under me. I went down butt first.

Now it was Chase's turn to laugh. "That's one interpretation of diving right in."

"That's exactly what I was going for," I assured him, surreptitiously pulling on the bathing suit top to be sure nothing more got uncovered.

"Pretty great," he said, as we matched crawl strokes, swimming side-by-side.

If he was referring to the day, the sand, the surf, the ocean, and being together, he took the words right out of my mouth.

After, we lay side by side on the blanket, letting the sun dry us. All thoughts of safe sunbathing and ozone layers melted away. The warm rays felt like a caress. Chase rested his head on his palms, and tipped his face to the sun. Eyes closed, he looked like a native, bronzed and completely blissful.

I teased him, "Arizona-desert boy takes to the ocean like camel to sand?"

He turned to me, smiling. "The beach isn't hard to take," he agreed. "They call this area SoCal, by the way. That's short for Southern California."

An Abby quip zipped up to me: *It's not the heat, it's the*

stupidity. I pushed it away and rummaged for a Jamie line. "I could never get used to living here. The scene is so over-the-top, so many people not caring about the rest of the world. You could probably get a college degree in Self-Absorption."

Chase ran the tip of his finger along my cheekbone. "Are you always so serious?"

"When there's stuff to be serious about, yeah," I said unconvincingly, acutely aware of his touch.

His finger hadn't left my face, and now he twisted his body toward me, and traced my neck, shoulder, along the side of my body down to my waist, and over my hip. "I like your curves," he murmured, starting at the top of my thigh, and retracing his route up my body. I didn't stop him.

Chase moved closer to me, and gently brushed my hair from my face. And moved even closer, letting his arm fall across my body until his hand reached the exposed small of my back. He was strong enough to pull me toward him, especially since I wasn't resisting.

I inhaled. The combo of salt and sweat made me dizzy. I closed my eyes, lifted my chin, and waited for what I knew would be soft, salty kisses.

I heard a quick *whoosh*, a spraying sound. My eyes flew open. Breath spray. Just about to kiss me, Chase had stopped to use breath spray?

How little it took to drive a stake through the heart of the moment, I thought. Only then his lips were on mine, and then his tongue was in my mouth, and I didn't taste breath spray at all, just the sweet salty pleasure of being wrapped up in his strong arms.

"I'll have s'more of that," I murmured after the first go-round. He was only too happy to oblige.

The next day, I felt bold enough to do what I'd wanted to since beginning my nannyship. It was up to me to save Olivia from a life of designer clothes, luxury cars, and self-obsession — or put another way, of growing up to be Tara.

Project SOS, Saving Olivia's Soul, was officially launched.

We made a secret pact to "tweak" her schedule. Neither Topher, who was caught up in some messy merger and coming home late these days, nor Nicole, who was predictably caught up in herself, was going to check on us. It was Olivia's first lesson in "Don't ask, don't tell."

Back when Abby and I had planned our New York trip, we'd decided to take our charges each week to Books of Wonder, a famous kids-only bookstore in Chelsea, and read to them there.

Was it remotely possible LA had anything like it? My Google search turned up Storyopolis. It was located on a chi-chi street in a designer-deluged neighborhood. But that's where the LA-ness of it ended. Storyopolis was a wonderland of tomes for tykes within an actual art gallery, where staffers weren't just trying to sell books, but, through art and storytelling, encouraging the little ones to stretch their imaginations.

Livvy loved it from the moment we walked in. Seren-dipitously, we'd arrived in time for story hour, and the book being read was called *Olivia,* about a very special, and a bit obsessive, piglet. My Livvy sat in a circle with other kids, wide-eyed. When story hour ended, the kids were encouraged to draw pictures. Olivia proudly drew hers, exulting, "I can send this to Juliana!"

I treated Olivia to her own hardcover copy of the book, and while at the register, overheard two nannies talking about a shopping spree to the Beverly Center. "A vertical mall," one said, "with great shops, and a lot on sale," agreed the other.

I hadn't planned it — but when Storyopolis turned out to be close to the Beverly Center, it didn't seem like a bad idea to check it out. No harm in Livvy lunching at a real-people food court, I rationalized.

I wasn't totally deceiving myself. I knew the reason for the sudden interest in the mall.

Chase.

No, I told Abby, I wasn't smitten. He was a beach bum, a dye-guy who, as far as I could tell, didn't have an apartment or a job.

But spending the day with him was the most fun I'd had since arriving at Casa Dysfunctional. So what if he's a few twists behind the current plot? Brains can be overrated.

Chase had called that morning, suggesting we go out tonight. And I wanted something, not slutty, just date-appropriate. My pay envelopes had been generous. I'd dutifully started a college savings account and aside from weekly gifts to Juliana, everything I earned went into it. It wouldn't be the end of the world if I charged a few items of clothing, would it?

So what if the Lucky jeans were cut lower than I ever thought I'd be caught dead in? They were totally closer to classy than trashy. A lively little loop for the cell phone came with. I couldn't decide between the stonewashed and deep indigo, so I bought both. At the Gap, I sprang for a batch of colorful T's, and found adorable flowered flip-flops at Nine West. I liked a V-neck at Banana Republic, and a ruffled sleeveless striped top at Ann Taylor Loft.

Each time I tried something on that Olivia liked, she'd clap her hands and squeal, "Who are you wearing? Jamie is scrumpdeli-ish-us!"

Before leaving, I snared a Fossil wristwatch for Juliana and an "Olivia the piglet" doll for my l'il Livvy.

I was actually whistling and swinging shopping bags, picturing myself in my low-cut jeans and fitted tank top, when Livvy and I got back. We were headed toward the staircase when Tara and Skyy appeared. I stopped mid-whistle. Had the devious duo been waiting? Paranoia could, and should, not be underrated.

Olivia lit up. "Look! Tara, I got shoppin' bags!"

Tara kneeled to Olivia's level. "You do? Can I see?"

Proudly, Olivia presented her book and doll. "I heard a story. Wanna hear it?"

Tara stood up and put her finger to her lips. "A story. Let's see, would that have been at soccer? Or are they doing storytime at Yogalates?"

Busted.

She snickered, "Or, is it possible we might have changed Olivia's schedule today?"

"Don't fret, little nanny," Skyy put in. "We won't tell."

"We wouldn't want to ruin your perfect day," Tara said slyly, nudging Skyy, who pointed up the stairs and said, "There's something waiting in your room. A gift from an admirer, I think."

No one had ever sent me flowers before. These were lush, a bouquet of red long-stemmed roses and white calla lilies. The card read, "To Jamie, the coolest chick in town! Chase."

I was never big on flowers. In a hospital environment, they suck up the oxygen. Juliana can't have flowers, so I've never really wanted them. But then again, I've never received a bouquet from a guy before. Who thinks I'm the coolest chick in town.

Exactly at eight P.M., the intercom from the front gate buzzed and the guard announced, "Miss Devine, a Chase O'Brien is here to see you. Are you expecting him?"

I wanted to run out and greet him, to let him know how much I loved the flowers. I totally expected him to notice my girlier look. Only I had to look around to actually find him.

Chase had been circling the house, awestruck. "Wow," he pointed up to the arched two-story windows. "Is that Nicole's room?"

Hands on my hips, I cleared my throat. "Um, hi, Chase. Great to see you, too."

He turned to me. "Hey, hi, Jamie. You look . . . wow! Awesome! I heard there are servants' quarters, and a guest-house."

"Want a tour before we go out?"

It was kind of fun watching his reaction as I led him around the grounds.

"This place is so amazing. I can't imagine what'd it be like inside." He looked at me hopefully.

"Maybe you don't have to imagine," I caught myself saying. *What am I doing? Am I even allowed to bring a guy inside?* I tried to remember if the confidentiality agreement I'd signed had any rules about that.

Chase looked so grateful and astounded, like a kid on Christmas who's been told, "Come to the North Pole. Take anything you want."

Experiencing Casa Verde through Chase's eyes was a whole new trip. The huge kitchen with the slate countertops, espresso machine, and designer fridge. The ornate dining room with the crystal chandelier; the living room boasting art by Picasso and Van Gogh, though dominated by a portrait of Nicole. I walked him around to the library and the Great Room. Deliberately, I skipped Nicole's office. Once in there was enough for me.

Chase didn't realize the omission. He kept repeating, "When I get my break, I'm gonna buy that," and, "As soon as I make it big, I'll have two of those."

"So I guess, what, you call the valet or something to send the car around?" he asked after we'd finished our tour. "I know an amazing sushi place, and then I thought we could go to Avalon. Ty's bodyguard can get us in."

I weighed the options for a moment. A trendy sushi place, a dark and crowded club, juxtaposed with what I knew Chef Roberto had prepared: Free-range chicken, fresh organic veggies, homemade pasta.

It's not that I didn't want to go out with Chase. But I'd gotten used to room service.

Chase lit up. "Here? Eat here? Can you do that?"

I took him upstairs, and we narrowly missed bumping into Tripp, who was sullenly leaving his room. I hadn't really encountered him since the day of our getaway, so I felt momentarily awkward — but he barely greeted me.

"Man — what a gig! This is the suite they gave you to live in?" Chase inspected everything in my room — the cushy chairs, the flat-screen TV, the balcony, the bar. And the bed.

Suddenly nervous, I began to pace. "What do you want to eat? I can just intercom the chef and —"

Chase came up behind me, and massaged my shoulders.

"— they'll prepare anything you want. Chicken and . . ." I was babbling.

He leaned in, nuzzling my neck. "You . . . smell so sweet."

He was going too fast. I'd been ready back on the beach. Now, at the place of my employment, I wasn't so sure.

Chase encircled me in his arms, and pressed the full of his

body into my back. I felt myself melting. I turned, and tipped my head up. And then came those kisses.

When he pulled away, his eyes were bright. "I can't believe my luck, meeting you. You're incredible. Smart, funny, hot —"

"Not." I blushed.

He shook his head. "Amazing. You're an amazing girl."

Amazing. No boy had ever called me that before. Chase headed to the bar. "You think it's okay?"

"I can call for the ingredients to a mojito," I suggested. "If they don't have —"

He shook his head. "I have what I need to make you, Ms. Jamie Devine, a drink that is just . . . Devine. One divine cosmopolitan for the most divine girl I know."

I'd heard every play on my name in the universe and had long ago stopped finding them amusing. Devine intervention. Devine being. Even "de fruit of devine." Now, I giggled. From Chase it was kinda cute.

I'd been perched on the bed. He joined me.

The cosmopolitan was kinda strong. As was the next. On an empty stomach, it approached dangerous. Chase took my drink and set it on the end table next to his.

He slid the strap of my tank top down, and traced my shoulder blade with his forefinger. Gently, he guided me down on the bed, and positioned himself on top of me.

I ran my fingers through Chase's hair, and stroked his back, while arching my own. His kisses became more fervent. And longer. This was getting intense.

Suddenly, a familiar jingling sound rang out. An IM?

"What's that?" Chase murmured.

"I must have left the computer on."

"Can you turn it off?" he asked. I rolled out from under him and headed for my desk.

"I'll be right —"

I shrieked when I saw what was on the computer screen. "Oh my God! It's Abby! She's coming to LA!"

Chapter Fifteen

Abby in Wonderland

Abby

On the flight to LA, I was seat-belted in steerage, while Lila and Curt belted back complimentary champagne in first class. I was wedged between a white-haired grandmotherly type with a death rattle snore, and an obese man whose hammy arm took up more than his fair share of the armrest.

There was plenty of time to think. Too much. Excitement at the prospect of seeing Jamie alternated with shame at what an idiot I'd been about Simon.

I found myself flashing back to him cheek to cheek with his blonde du jour, chuckling about his conquest of a nanny.

"Your mind is a dangerous neighborhood, Abs," Jamie used to tell me. "Don't go there alone. You'll get mugged."

So when Lila appeared, lurching down the aisle from first class, I was grateful for the distraction. She was clearly smashed. "Hi," I said.

"That bitch," she replied.

The overweight guy looked from her to me, waiting for my response, I guess. But I was dumbstruck.

"Jackie," she went on. "That arrogant bitch."

"Jackie," I repeated, nodding as if I knew exactly who and what she meant.

"Jackie! Jackie!" she hollered at me. "You know. Curt's goddamn agent! She wants to see your notes before she'll let us make any changes to the book. Says she'll take them both to another publisher — Curt *and* Simon!"

"Curt and Simon? You mean she's — Simon's agent, too? His girlfriend *and* his agent?"

"Girlfriend? Puh-leez!" Lila rolled her eyes. "What would a gorgeous twenty-year-old like Simon want with Jacqueline Harris? She's twice his age and a goddamn botox pincushion. One more shot and her lips won't move at all. Which would save everyone a lot of trouble!"

"You're talking about Jacqueline, right?" I asked. "The blonde at your party, the woman who was all over Simon at the reading in TriBeCa?"

"All over Simon — and Curt, and almost every other decent writer in this town —"

The plane hit an air pocket, and Lila stumbled backward, bumping against the seat behind her. "I've got to sit down," she announced. "Oh my God, you don't even have an aisle seat!" She gave my traveling companions the once over. "You've got to be kidding," she grumbled.

"These seats get smaller every year," the heavy guy to my left said apologetically.

"Get up," Lila ordered him. "Go. Go on up front. You can have my seat. It's roomier. Up, up, up!" She clapped.

When the man, confused but accommodating, hauled

himself up and moved down the aisle, Lila fell into his vacant seat.

She was totally looped and clearly intended to nod off. But I wouldn't let her. "So you're saying that Jacqueline —"

"That bitch," she muttered drowsily.

"Yes, that's the one, that bitch," I agreed, "so she's *not* Simon's girlfriend?"

Lila's eyebrows arched. "Certainly not. I thought you were."

"You thought I was Simon's girlfriend?"

"Until you walked out of Curt's reading with Matt Savage," she said. "One of my other authors — a mediocre one, I might add."

"Matt Savage?" Oh, *Matt*. J.Crew, I remembered. He'd followed me out of the café, asked if I wanted a lift.

"Filthy thing to do," Lila continued, her eyes drifting shut again. "I found it shocking, actually. And I think Simon did, too. He was very hurt."

"Simon was hurt?"

Her eyes sprung open. "Why are you repeating everything I say?" she demanded. "That is very annoying! As was your cruel, insensitive behavior toward Simon Wagner, who is one of the most decent men I know and deserved far better than he got."

"I'm sorry," I said, my mind reeling. "I didn't know. I . . ."

"Wake me in twenty minutes," she snapped, and promptly slid off to sleep.

Oh. My. God!

Lila thought I'd dumped Simon. She thought I'd picked up someone else and split. And, apparently, Simon thought so, too.

I felt sick. I felt elated. I felt extremely confused.

The Chateau Marmont looked like a cluster of little castles nestled in the hills above Sunset Strip. The brochures in my small room said that the Marmont had been home to stars of Hollywood's golden age as well as today's celebs. The whole place was supposed to "perfectly replicate an eighteenth-century French Chateau."

The room I'd gotten was dark and cool. A ceiling fan creaked overhead, and closed shutters kept the beautiful sunny day at bay. But the quiet, shady room was a relief from the limo drive along Sunset Boulevard. There, hundreds of billboards, hyping TV series and upcoming movies, showcased gargantuan stars whose eyes seemed to follow you. The billboards flipped like sideways Venetian blinds, to display a second and sometimes a third ad. Between billboards, motels, hotels, and tourist attractions competed for attention. It was like Times Square squared! A brassy, shameless display of check-me-out.

Lila and Gordevan were going to dinner with one of the three film executives who wanted to turn Curt's new book into a movie — without even reading it! Tomorrow morning, they had an appointment with a completely different honcho who also wanted film rights for the novel.

Which gave me tonight and all tomorrow morning to hang with Jamie.

She'd left a message to call her the minute I got in. So I did. And we screamed and laughed and said how we couldn't wait to see each other — and then Jamie got another call and put me on hold. She was back in a flash.

The caller, she said, was Chase O'Brien — the "sensitive," wannabe actor she'd e-mailed me about. "Abs, can you hang on for just another sec? I'll be right back, I promise. Or do you want me to call you back?"

"I'll hold," I said.

I felt disappointed. But petty. I *should* have been happy for James. She'd finally found a guy she liked, even if he sounded like some cliché Cali slacker. But that she liked enough to put me on hold?

Sounded serious.

Sounded so not like Jamie.

Jamie knocked on my door about an hour later. We flew into each other's arms and jumped up and down, squealing.

"You look fabulous!" I told her when we finally went from hugging to arms' length. "I love your belly!" I blurted. I'd meant to say "your shirt." She was wearing an Indian print crop top and hip-hugger capris, which left a span of tanned tummy on display.

Jamie cracked up and reddened. "I know I really need to lose weight, but I went shopping with Olivia, and it was so fun and . . ." She shrugged. "I'm a blimp, right?"

"Never!" I said. "You look great. You look *fabulous,*" I said again, somewhat taken aback that Jamie gave a damn about her weight. She never had before.

"Excuse me?" Jamie gave me a look. "Fabulous? When did 'fabulous' infect your vocab?"

My turn to blush. "It's a Lila-ism," I confessed. "How's *wonderful? Gorgeous?* Jamie, you just look great. All tanned and . . . even your hair is sun-streaked. And I'm so glad you're here. I've got so much to tell —"

"Oh God, me too!" It wasn't like Jamie to cut me off. "I can't wait until you meet Chase. I can't wait for you to *see* him. Abs, he's just eye candy and so sweet and . . . sexy."

Sexy? "You didn't, did you?" I asked.

Jamie looked away, toward the sunlight now streaming through the shutters I'd opened five minutes ago. "Well . . . no. Not yet," she said, without looking at me.

"James! You're going to . . . lose it with this guy?"

She blushed again. "He's just . . . I don't know how to describe it. He's buff and beautiful and he gets me and likes me. I mean, he *really* likes me."

Buff and beautiful? I'd never heard Jamie describe anyone by looks. Even Adam Elsmere, the physics geek in our ninth-grade homeroom who had this unfortunate growth on his jaw; while everyone else called him Bumpy Adam — to distinguish him from Tall Adam Greenberg and Ripped Adam McAdams — James always called him Science Club Adam.

"Of course, he likes you," I replied. "Who wouldn't?"

Jamie grinned. "Only you'd say something like that. God, Abs, I've really missed you. Why don't you get dressed and we'll get out of here —"

I looked down. I was wearing jeans, Adidas, and a plain white tank.

"Change?" I asked. "What's wrong with what I'm wearing?"

"Nothing," she said quickly. "I just thought . . . I mean, I was going to take you over to the casa and show you how the 'fabulous' other half lives."

"Can't I go like this?" I waited while my best friend did silent battle with herself. At least that's what it looked like from the outside, as if Jamie was trying to come up with the correct answer to some deeply complex question. Finally, she smiled and said, "Sure. Grab your backpack and let's blow this joint. You know, John Belushi died here."

She was driving a Lexus, gleaming and big.

"What's S. G. like, up close and personal?" she asked, as we tore out of the driveway. "Is he a total hunk?"

A total hunk? There it was again. Jamie all focused on looks. Was this my real deal best or a Stepford replica? *My* Jamie couldn't have cared less whether Simon — or Chase, for that matter — was studly or not. My Jamie would only have cared about how the boy treated me.

Then I remembered!

"James, oh God. I forgot to tell you. Simon didn't dump

me, I dumped him! I mean, that's what *he* thinks. He thought I'd left the reading with this other author of Lila's, Matt something or other."

"Cool," Jamie said distractedly.

"All this time," I tried again, "I thought Simon hated me, that he had the hots for this older woman Jacqueline. Turns out she's his agent and he thought I split on him and *he* was hurt. Hurt!"

Jamie glanced at me. "Who was hurt?"

"Simon," I said, frustrated. "Studly Simon," I added sarcastically. "Anyway, James, I was wrong. And, I think he does like me. Or else he wouldn't be feeling hurt, would he? I can't believe I thought of him as this total cheater."

"And speaking of," Jamie said, suddenly, "what about Ethan?"

Where did that *segue come from?* I wondered.

"What about him? I haven't heard word one since he told me he was heading south with his trusty companion, Sam —"

"Sam." Jamie made a face. "Oh, that's right. They're supposed to be saving humanity, right?"

She hadn't seemed interested in what I'd told her about Simon. And now she sounded more annoyed than usual with Ethan. Jamie always claimed her "radar" told her something was off about my boyfriend — ex or not. That he wasn't the Boy Scout he pretended to be. Still I wasn't ready to concede that Ethan was a total creep. I opted for a quick, if shallow, change of subject:

"Did I mention this other guy I met? Garrick. He's 'a manny.' A male nanny. Isn't that fabulous?"

Jamie did an exaggerated eye roll.

Whoops. I'd fabuloused again. "Okay," I backed up. "He's . . . really nice. His charge is the wildest kid in Central Park, but he's totally patient and sweet —"

"And hot?" Jamie wanted to know.

There it was again: the new Jamie.

"Never mind about me," I said. "What about you? Have you seen the stealthy Shadow again? Tripp, that's his name, right? And how's Terror?"

"Don't get me started. . . ." Jamie moaned.

Chapter Sixteen

Pimp My Ride

Jamie

Abby had won the nanny lottery. She'd been magically transported from mind-numbing Shafton to sizzling New York City. She was rubbing elbows with the glitterati of the literati, and had two boys clearly vying for her attention.

So why did she seem so small-town and bewildered?

Not only was she wearing a plain tank and grubby jeans, her whole vibe was wary, contrary. Judgmental.

Oh well. Nothing a little dazzling couldn't cure. I pulled up to the imposing double gates of Casa Verde, and gave a casual tap on the horn, just for effect. "Alakazaam!" I said, as the gates opened. Abby must've been struck speechless, 'cause she said absolutely nothing.

"So?" I nudged. "Something else, huh?"

"Something way else." Abby agreed, wide-eyed. "Too bad it's wasted on such a dysfunctional family, right?"

I bristled. "Not entirely. Topher's really nice, and Olivia's just a baby. . . ."

"But what about Nicole?" Abby said. "You made her sound like a two-faced monster. And Tara tricked you into wearing that dress —"

I shrugged. A weird thought hit me. Abby had gone over Curt Gordevan's manuscript and spent, in my view, way too much of her free time looking for what was wrong with it. Was she doing the same thing to me? Judging and editing everything I said or felt about California?

Maybe she thought I was showing off? Was that why she was being so negative?

When we entered the house, I decided to bring her up to my room to *really* talk. But halfway up the stairs, we ran into an obstacle. Times two. Tara and Skyy. Who were way too enthusiastic at the sight of us — fresh meat, prey.

Tara pointed at Abby. "You must be the chum! I could just tell."

Skyy took her cue. "How cute you bumpkins look together!"

"This is Abigail Burrows. Curt Gordevan — not that *you'd* know who he is — flew her in on his private jet."

Please don't contradict me, Abby, I prayed. She never got the chance.

Tara put in, "Gordevan? I've heard they're shopping that new novel of his all over Hollywood. Word has it that it's not nearly as good as *The War Park.*"

Abby's mouth opened. "How . . . ? It's not even pub —"

Tara waved Abby's questions away. "Nothing goes down in this town that *I* don't know about."

I'd had enough. "Whatever. See you gals later."

I tried to go around her, but Tara gripped my elbow. She was stronger than she looked. "Say! I've got a neat-o idea.

Why don't you give . . . Abigail is it? . . . a tour of the real LA scene. Do Sunset in West Hollywood at night."

"Abby and I have other plans."

"She's here for like, what, forty-eight hours? No, this is a must. I'll set it up with Kip. You'll take the white limo. I insist. End of story."

Nicole had used the exact same expression the night she'd forced me to go out with Tara. Signifying: No way out.

"You gals get all gussied up now," Tara teased. "I'll have Kip call for you around eight. How's that? Not too late, I hope. Bye-ee."

An hour later, Abby was still reeling from Tara's inside-stuff gossip. "I can't believe it," she kept repeating, pacing my suite. "I should call Lila."

"Ix-nay on that, Abs, at least for now. We've earned quality catch-up time. Can we put the angst on pause?"

Like the U2 song, Abby was "stuck in a moment she could not get out of." "But how could they know?" she ruminated, running her fingers through her hair. "Only Lila and I know —" She whirled on me, gasping. "I told *you*. I e-mailed you all about it."

I shook my head. "You think I told her? Are you nuts? We're not exactly girlfriends, as *my* e-mails might have pointed out. Besides, why would I discuss a legendary author with subliterate Tara?"

I exhaled and fell back on the bed. I didn't want to think

about Tara. *Or* argue with Abs. I wanted to have a rocking good time.

Maybe that was why, when I called Kip, I nixed the everyday white stretch, and asked for the brand-new Hummer limo for our night out on the town. And maybe that's why I called Chase and asked him to meet up with us. I even told him what corner to be on, and when.

Maybe I should have rethought things.

The H2 Hummer stretch waiting for us in the driveway was the size — ginormous — and color (screaming yellow) of a school bus. Which is where the comparison ended.

Kip held the door open for us.

Abby refused to move.

"Go on, get in," I urged.

Over her shoulder, she shot me the strangest look. For the first time in our friendship, I could not interpret it. Finally, she allowed Kip to grasp her elbow, and help her up. I jumped in behind her — and immediately channeled Chase. *This* was truly, madly, deeply, "Bitchin'!"

When the door closed, we were cocooned in another time and place. Mirrored disco balls spun from the black, star-spangled roof. A black leather couch wound around in an L-shape. Plasma TVs, DVD players, and Internet connections were at our remote-controlled fingertips. The bar was all glass, mirrors, and crystal stemware, stocked with an array of imbibables, including champagne on ice.

It was all supersized.

It matched Abby's super-snit. She perched on the end of the buttery leather couch, hands clasped primly on her knees, lips pursued in disapproval. What a buzz kill.

"Okay, I know you think it's over the top," I allowed.

"Try plain grotesque," Abby retorted.

"This is a hoot," I cajoled. "Besides, this is you and me."

"Half credit, James," she stared hard. "This is me. But this is *so* not you."

Fine. Whatever. I let her vent.

"This . . . this . . . road hog," she grumbled, "is too ugly, too big."

"Sometimes," I tried to joke, "size does matter."

Finally, Abby cracked up. I tossed a soft leather pillow at her.

When she grabbed a bigger one and aimed at me, I knew I had her.

Score! Fun *would* be had tonight — even if Abby had to be dragged into it kicking and screaming.

We tossed pillows back and forth, then launched ourselves into a totally third-grade bouncing competition to see who could propel herself higher off the couch and hit the dangling disco ball first.

When we were laughed-out, I reached over to the bar, and unscrewed a bottle of Bacardi rum.

"What are you doing?" Abby was still out of breath.

"Toasting the winner, of course," I responded with a devilish grin, and proceeded to mix us two amazing mojitos.

"You sure this is a good idea?" Abby joked. "You know my reputation with liquor."

"Relax," I said, savoring my first sweet sip. "Not a problem. Throw up all you want. Ain't *my* limo!"

I put on the music, which sealed our deal. We sang some vintage Avril, bemoaning how "complicated" relationships can be, segued into some hip-shaking Beyoncé, and the classic "Toxic" by Britney.

The "Abby and Jamie Show" was back! Interrupted by — her cell phone. How LA! Could it be Ethan, I wondered, making good on his promise? Maybe Simon (secretly, I was rooting for him)? Or Lila the user?

But when Abby was all, "Dylan, sweetie pie!" I lost interest.

By the time Abby got off the phone with Dylan, we'd stopped to pick up Chase, who was waiting exactly where I told him to be.

He bounded up the steps of the Hummer, in all his broad-shouldered, hottie glory. Wearing a ribbed tank top, Hawaiian print, knee-length shorts and red flip-flops, he looked smokin' enough to hang ten, or whatever number you hang with.

Running his tongue along his full lower lip, he joked, "Hey sexy mamas. Need company?"

I threw my arms around him, and greeted him with a kiss. "I'm so happy to see you!" I shouted above the music. I turned to Abby. "You guys have to meet."

Chase smiled big at Abby, revealing excessively white teeth.

Abby smiled tightly at Chase, revealing excessive disapproval.

"Check this out," Chase said, whipping a silver handheld device from the pocket of his shorts. "My excellent new Sidekick — a little Sundance swag," he bragged, flipping it open. "Tobey didn't want his. And, Ashton gave me the extra iPod he got. He was there with Keanu and Maggie Gyllenhaal. Dude, it was an amazing scene — freebie city!"

I felt like a showbiz-to-Shafton translator for Abby, as Chase name-checked every hot young star who'd been at the Sundance Film Festival. Abby gamely tried to look interested.

We crossed Doheny Boulevard, the official dividing line between Beverly Hills and Los Angeles. The difference between the stately Sunset Boulevard, and the wild Sunset Strip was like comparing Victoria's Secret to Frederick's of Hollywood.

The Boulevard was peaceful, winding, and wide. The sights along the way were grand mansions, gated domiciles, the venerated Beverly Hills Hotel, slinky palm trees. It whispered wealth.

The Strip was a supersized assault on the senses. Kong-sized billboards for mega-movies faced off with 3-D marquees flashing upcoming appearances by rockers and hip-hoppers. I pointed out some icons of the nabe: Tower Records, the Comedy Club, the Palm restaurant.

Impulsively, I hit the button to slide the moonroof open. The outside world blasted in. A cacophony of car horns made me think there'd been an accident, until I hoisted myself up and stuck my head out. The scene, three hundred sixty degrees around, was jaw-dropping.

"Get up here," I told Abby and Chase. "You're not gonna believe this."

A hundred cars were on the road, not one actually moving. SUVs, Hummers, convertibles. All were custom jobs, loud and proud, in safari stripes, turquoise, hot pink, screaming green. Hip-hop and metal battled for airwave space.

Abigail was speechless.

I was not. The liquor, as usual, had loosed my tongue. "Pimp my ride!" I shouted into the smog-clogged air.

"Look at that one!" Abby, finding her voice, pointed to a Hummer with a string of neon lights lining the bottom.

"Check out the ride in front of us," I cried, indicating a monster truck bouncing up and down.

Abby and I ducked down into the limo. Chase was busy chugging mojitos. Kip winked at us. "It's like Mardi Gras in LA. We don't even have to get anywhere. We can inch along for hours if that's your pleasure."

It kind of was. For now.

Kip got it. "Binoculars are located beneath the bar."

I grabbed my second-or-third mojito, Abs went for the zoom lens, and we climbed back up to our front-row view. "Is this for spying on people making out in the backseats?" Abby asked, suddenly unsure she wanted to use the binoculars.

Making out. How . . . Ohio. "You mean hooking up," I clarified, as we took in the scene.

It was a smoggy LA night, yet all the windows were down. Guys in cars sidled up to girls in cars — and vice versa — checking each other out. We weren't the only thru-the-moonroof girls, or boys, on the scene. The SUV and limo kids littered the road, arms aloft, waving, shrieking, smoking, drinking, and yelling insults. I didn't know why, but I was lovin' it. And I wanted to share it with Chase.

I slid back into the limo beside Chase, who was getting drunker. We started kissing, and barely looked up when Abby rejoined us. Then, as the three of us started chatting, I desperately searched for some common ground between my two best friends. Geography — the LA-NY-Arizona-Ohio convo — led to a dead end. I tried comparative club-hopping — New York's Destiny vs. LA's Lox. Mojitos vs. cosmos, surfing the net vs. surfing the waves. I poured us more drinks. I laughed louder than was called for. I hugged Abby. I hugged Chase.

But no matter what I tried to affect détente, or at least to get Abby to see how amazing Chase was, or to get Chase to approximate conversation with her, no go. Not happening.

Finally, Abby erupted. "I'm out of here."

Translation: Either we lose Chase, or she really would bolt.

I ran my hand up his back, beneath his T-shirt, then handed him the binoculars. "View's interesting from the moonroof. Go see for yourself."

Two things happened then. Chase lunged for the

moonroof, Abby for the door. He hoisted himself straight up. She bolted out into the night.

I wasn't all that drunk. Or that stupid. With a shout to Kip, and one to Chase that I doubt he heard, I flew out after Abby. She was hoofing blindly down Sunset Strip, about to be swallowed up by the crowds of raucous revelers — by the time I caught up with her, she'd dashed across the street.

Panting, I grabbed her elbow. "Abs! Come on. Don't be like that."

She whirled, heated. "Don't be like what? This is our big one night together after three months. And you drag *him* along? How could you do that?"

My jaw dropped. "You don't even know him! Why do you hate him?"

Abby caught her breath. "I'm sorry, James. I was looking forward to being just the two of us. We have so much to catch up on."

"I just wanted you to meet him," I mumbled, caught at the intersection of guilt and fury. She had a point. But Chase was important to me.

"Look," Abby said. "Is there somewhere we can go? To just talk?"

I'd heard of The House of Blues, but had never been inside. It served Cajun food, like voodoo shrimp and Creole jambalaya, and had live music — but most important, it was situated just a few feet from where we were standing in the middle of Sunset Strip. I didn't give a second thought to leaving Chase in the limo, so Abby and I headed in.

We had to thread through the maze of performance spaces, restaurant sections, the company store, and the private club area, before we found our way to the bar. Abby ordered a Diet Coke; I asked for a mojito. I did a quick celeb check, just to see if anyone hot was in the vicinity — but we were surrounded by the usual assortment of blinged-out kids.

The band in the adjacent performance space was rocking out. We practically had to shout to be heard.

"So," I said, taking a sip of my drink, "tell me what you think of Chase." I hoped she'd now calmed down.

"He's . . . um," she hesitated. "He's great-looking. But I wouldn't have guessed he was your type."

From the stage in the next room, I heard a familiar male voice. "Hey, we're Cornucopia!" He sounded like . . . Tripp. I strained to hear more, but the room erupted in cheers and hoots.

"He's nice, you know," Abby was saying. "But I thought you'd go for . . . well, like a brainy do-gooder."

I heard myself saying, "But Chase makes me feel . . . amazing."

Abby tapped the bar with her finger. "I don't doubt it, but —"

"Wait, can you *listen* first?" I took a deep breath. "I'm sorry if you think I ruined our night, but you're my best friend, and well, I want you to know: I want Chase to be my first. I'm I'm going to do it. With him."

I couldn't believe I'd just said that. I felt fuzzy, but somehow, right.

"Sleep with Chase? Bad plan," Abby said flatly.

"How can you say that? Chase is special and if you can't see that, well, maybe you're jealous, or something."

She shook her head. "You really have changed, Jamie."

Okay, I was good and pissed off now. I banged my drink on the wooden bar top, and growled, "Stop beating around the bush. Whatever you have to say — go for it, right here, right now."

Abby looked wounded. "About Chase, I just . . ." She trailed off.

"You just what?" I badgered. "You disapprove of Chase. You've made that clear without actually saying it. Which is your modus operandi. You like Simon, but you can't tell him. Even when you found out, by accident, that he didn't dump you, did you rush to call him? The only calls you've had since you got here are from a needy five-year-old! When is Abby going to stand up for herself, stand up for something?"

Abby's face tightened. "I didn't come here to be psychoanalyzed. Especially not by my so-called best friend, who's wasted out of her mind."

"Just because I'm drunk doesn't mean I'm wrong. And I'm not finished, either."

Abby folded her arms. "Knock yourself out."

I did. It wasn't pretty. My Ab-attack went something like this: "You're a self-centered wimp. You live in your head, not your heart — always thinking of what you should do or say or not do. When was the last time you said what you really meant? Hell, when was the first time? You're all about being there for others — your mom, Dylan, even Curt Gordevan — because then no one will notice that you haven't got the guts to stand up for yourself."

Abby reddened, and raised her hand. In my compromised state, I thought she was about to slap me, but when she brought it down, it landed hard on the bar. "You want me to say what I really mean? Sure you can handle it?"

Fear factored in. What can of worms had I just opened?

"Something's rotten in the state of . . . Hollywood!" she sputtered, waving her hand around the House of Blues for emphasis.

"Props for the Shakespeare shout-out, Ms. Burrows. Can you give me an example of said rottenness?"

Abby frowned. "Look, Jamie, I don't know how I know, but I just do. That boy is not what he seems."

"Really?" I challenged. "Do tell."

"He's a user. A leech. A name-dropping Hollywood slacker. A hanger-on! I don't know why you can't see it."

"When it comes to being used, you're the expert." I barked back at her. "You let Lila walk all over you, just like your parents do!"

I'd added fuel to a wildfire. "Use your head!" Abby snapped. "This clod tells you exactly what you want to hear — he's anti-Hollywood, he wants to give money to charity — but in fact, he's nothing, a loser, a complete lame-brain. He's worse than Sean Axton!"

I could not breathe, let alone retort.

She demanded, "What happened to you? The Jamie I know would be able to see right through that. Call that school in Arizona where he says he's a student. See if that's even true. Google him!"

Google him? Check up on him? She'd gone too far. I was furious. And I came out swinging with the one truth I hadn't ever planned to tell her. "If you're such an expert on guys, riddle me this, Abigail. You. Ethan. Sam. What's wrong with this picture?"

"This isn't about me. I'm trying to tell you something."

"Right back atcha, girlfriend," I said stubbornly. I dug my cell phone out. "Call Ethan. Now."

"Why?"

"Ask him if Sam has a penis."

Chapter Seventeen

The Morning After

Abby

The jangly ring of my cell phone coaxed me out of a restless sleep. I woke in a sweat, my feet tangled in bedsheets, my brain flipping through emotional flashcards: See Abby angry. See Abby sad. See Abby hating herself. And Jamie.

I didn't know whether I was awake or in the middle of a nightmare. My phone rang again. I finally opened my eyes to see a pale light threading through the shutters of an unfamiliar room. I glanced at the digital alarm clock. Four forty-five, it read, A.M.

Slowly I realized that I was at the Chateau Marmont in California and that if I'd drunk a dozen mojitos I couldn't have been more hungover. Emotionally.

My best friend, who'd always pushed me to tell the truth, lost it when I did. She'd become a material girl living in a material world — and was blindly besotted with a self-centered slacker.

My own former, so-called boyfriend was a liar and a cheat, caught publicly smooching-up a girl named Sam. Which, though it made me feel like a gullible jerk — and hurt way more than it should have — was also kind of freeing.

I wouldn't have to guilt trip every time I thought of Simon. And, if I could explain to him what happened that night in TriBeCa, he might even want to hold and kiss me again. But for the moment, the blue-eyed guy I was deeply crushed on thought I had blown him off and was majorly miffed at me.

Feeling like a sack of wet sand, I pulled myself to a sitting position, dropped my feet to the floor, and fumbled for my phone.

"Abby? Hello. Abby?" The nervous but unmistakably sweet voice of Dylan Matheson put my pity party on hold.

"Hey, Dyl! What are you doing up so early?" The time difference, I remembered. Still, it was only seven forty-five in New York. I usually tickled Dylan awake about eight thirty.

"Miss Farber makes me get up early. She won't let me sleep. She won't let me do anything! Are you gonna come back, Abby?" My baby was crying now, slurping back contagious tears.

"Of course, I'm coming back, Dyl. Hey, don't cry. You're making me cry. I'll be home soon."

"When?"

"Tell you what, I'll ask your mom when we're going back and I'll call and tell you, okay?"

Snuffle, snuffle. "Hokay." A heart-wrenching sigh. "Promise?"

"I'll call you in a couple of hours. Just as soon as I can talk to your mom. Promise." I sent him a bunch of long-distance kisses and hung up.

Sometime later, as I stepped out of the shower, the room

phone rang. Hope soared. *Jamie,* I thought. Habit, I guess. But no — hope dashed — it was Lila.

"Well, we've got a deal," she enthused, "now we need a really *fabulous* book. Oh my God, don't ever tell Curt I said that. You can talk with him this afternoon, on the flight home."

"Great," I said, not because I was eager to chat with Curt Gordevan, but because by "home" Lila meant New York City, which was thousands of miles from Los Angeles and Jamie.

Lila had upgraded my ticket to first class and exchanged luxurious leather seats with me. So she was across the aisle and two rows behind Curt Gordevan and me, chatting up this cowboy in a pin-striped suit, a white Stetson, and a tan to rival Speed Matheson's.

"Okay," Gordevan said, as we lifted off. "Let's do it."

I tried to smile but my mouth had gone Velcro. "Okay, well, um, first I'd like to say that I love your writing. I think," I added, groveling, "it helped me decide to become a writer —" Not entirely true, but I *had* loved *The War Park.*

"Spare me the shmear. Get to the new book," he ordered.

I was toying with a cuticle when Jamie's angry words came back to me: *You're a self-centered wimp. . . .*

Self-centered? Sure, I *was* thinking about myself. I was petrified that Gordevan would holler about how lame my suggestions were.

"Do you really want to know?" I found myself blurting. "I

mean, you don't have to agree with me, but if you want me to tell you what I think, then please don't yell at me."

"You drinking?" he asked. I thought he meant, *Are you drunk? No one would say that to me sober.* But then the booze wagon stopped in the aisle and I knew the question had been innocent, sort of. I shook my head. He held up two fingers and the stewardess gave us each a small bottle of bubbly and a champagne glass.

Gordevan quickly chugged his down and confiscated mine. "Okay, shoot, kid. Let me have it with both barrels. Don't hold back."

I cleared my throat and took my notepad out of my backpack. Gordevan tilted his head back and took a big gulp of the second drink.

"Um," I said.

He narrowed his eyes at me. "Jesus. Say something," he demanded.

When was the last time you said what you meant? Egged on by my (former) best friend, I willed my tears to freeze in my throat. "Could you please not drink until we're finished talking about the book?"

He stared menacingly, then slammed back the second champagne, set the empty glass onto his tray table. "This better be good," he warned.

I couldn't stop my voice from shaking. I was still afraid he'd think I was an idiot. But I did manage to begin.

"All right. Enough. I'll think about it." He cut me off a

minute later. "And I'll try to remember from whom these weighty literary opinions come."

I winced. I wasn't sure I could speak. But no problem, he wasn't through.

"Did you know I just got a seven-figure movie deal for this baby?" Gordevan growled. Since the manuscript wasn't handy, he tapped my notes hard, with a thick, blunt finger. "The one you think stinks?"

I cleared my throat again and squared my shoulders as best I could. "That's not fair," I managed. "I don't think it stinks. And if you were really listening to what I said, you'd know that." A voice in my head went, *Oh my God, are you insane?*

"You mean if I wasn't drunk, don't you?" Gordevan roared, coming out of left field. "So I had a couple of Bloody Marys this morning. What are you, some spy for AA? You gonna tell my sponsor?"

"If I knew who that was," I snapped, scaring myself. "I probably would. I didn't mean anything like that at all!" I was amazed at how self-assured I sounded. And felt. *If Jamie could see me now,* I found myself thinking, *she'd probably have the same reaction Curt Gordevan is having.*

Mouth flopped open, he was staring at me as though I was an alien who'd just landed in the seat next to him. He strained to look back at Lila — for help, I guessed, but she was comfortably snoozing.

"So," I said, when he turned back to me, looking kind of cowed, "you want to hear what I've got to say or not?"

He did. With a condition. "I can drink and think at the same time. Christ, I've been doing it for years." So while he chugged champagne, I delivered my review of his new book.

"Christ, you're a ballsy kid. Crazy, pushy, way off base, but ballsy, I'll give you that," Gordevan grumbled when I'd finished. Then he threw back the last half inch of booze in his glass and turned to look out the window.

If Jamie was right, progress is two steps forward, one step back. "You know, I really do love your writing," I said, looking down, unable to face him again. After the temporary triumph of saying what I meant, I was taking my step back. "And I'm sorry that I . . ." I began hemming and hawing. I got as far as, "I didn't mean . . . I mean, I'm not —"

His response was a violent snore, loud enough to make the empty glasses on his tray table tremble. I finally looked over at him. The Great One was out cold.

Gordevan had his own driver waiting at Kennedy Airport, so I had the privilege of being locked in a limo with Lila all the way to the city.

She spent the first twenty minutes on the phone, filling someone in on the A-list parties she'd been to in LA — who had looked fabulous and who had seemed pathetically faded, and which guests had cornered her with idiotic ideas for books. She sighed and cackled and finally, she flipped her phone shut, and asked me how it had gone with Curt.

Before I could answer, she reminded me that she'd published his last three books. That their friendship was precious to her. And that she hoped I hadn't done anything to piss him off.

With that lead in, I mumbled something like, "It was okay. I mean, I told him where I thought he might want to cut. But, I'm not sure he understood what I was saying —"

She raised an eyebrow. "I'm assuming you were speaking English."

"He was . . . kind of drunk," I told her.

"He's always drunk," Lila said, "except when he goes to his AA meetings. Well, did he say anything? Did he agree with you?"

"I don't know," I admitted. "He wasn't exactly thrilled —"

"Oh God. You pissed him off, didn't you?" she shrilled, as the limousine pulled up in front of her building. "I'll be lucky if he speaks to me again. Didn't I explain how important this was?"

She seemed startled and angry when I got out of the car with her at Fifth Avenue. "Um, I thought I'd say hi to Dylan," I said.

"Fine." She strode ahead of me, ranting. "I'm going to be on the phone for hours trying to make up for the damage you've caused. God. Curt Gordevan. Do you know what will happen to my business if he decides to publish with someone else?"

At least I'll get a hug from Dylan, I thought. He saw me and broke into tears. I knelt and opened my arms to him, but he hung back.

"You went away!" he snuffled. "I hate you! You're not my friend anymore!"

I phoned Garrick from the street outside the building. I told myself that he'd know how to deal with Dylan's upset. But honestly, I just wanted to be with someone who liked me. And I wanted a sympathetic sounding board for my misery. Gar was happy to oblige.

First he seemed genuinely glad to hear from me. And he was the perfect listener. He asked me if I'd had fun in LA, then let me rant without interruption until I finally got it all out. I told him everything: Jamie, Chase, Ethan, Curt Gordevan, Lila, and finally, Dylan. It felt like they were all against me.

Instead of laughing or being appalled, Garrick asked if I wanted to know what he thought.

"Oh yes, please," I answered gratefully. Because I knew that Garrick was a new but true friend. That he'd find me innocent, tell me I was right to be upset.

Which he did. And then he asked solicitously, "Are you wiped out?"

I was, but didn't say so.

"Do you want to grab a cup of coffee or something?"

I didn't.

But Garrick had listened to me and been so attentive, and I felt it would be rude to just tell him I was tired and wanted to go home. So I agreed to meet him at the diner on Amsterdam and Seventy-second Street.

I got there first and took a booth for two near the window. He saw me through the glass, and smiled so brightly and easily that again I asked myself, *Why not him?* Wasn't it just as easy to fall for someone nice as it was to be obsessed with someone neurotic?

Like Simon — someone who jumped to conclusions and acted on them without giving me the chance to explain what really happened. (It didn't occur to me then that I had also jumped to conclusions and acted on them without giving Simon a chance to say what really happened.)

Garrick came in and stood next to the table — looking cute in his same old Yankees jacket, T-shirt, and jeans. It had been nippy out and his cheeks were bright with color. He bent to give me a peck on the cheek but I turned and his lips brushed my ear instead. It felt amazingly good, and sent a shiver straight through me.

"So, you want my opinion?" he asked, sliding into the booth opposite me. "I think your chooser is broken."

"My what?" I asked, immediately feeling lighter, brighter, and wanting to laugh.

"Listen," he said, his green eyes lit with mischief. "The way you choose guys — me excluded, of course. You choose the wrong people, and then you're surprised when they can't give you what you want and need."

"And what would that be?" I challenged.

"Okay. Stop me if I'm wrong — I'm guessing loyalty —" That was an easy one since I'd told him about Ethan's betrayal.

"And a sense of humor —" Garrick illustrated what he meant by making a weird face. It made me laugh again.

"And brains," he said. "Very important. Someone at least as sharp as you. And last but not least, heat."

"Heat?"

"You know, someone who turns you on. Someone hot. Sexy."

Simon, I thought.

"Someone like me," Garrick said with a grin.

I laughed, and then he did, too. "I know, I know," he protested. "You think I'm trying to come on to you. But really, Abby, I've got enough drama in my life."

There was something about the way he said those last words that made me go *hmm. Oh my God,* I suddenly thought. Garrick — who I'd just been thinking was loving, caring and, oh-shallow-me, hot — batted for the other team. He was gay. *That's* what batting for the other team meant. I'd realized it the minute I met Kip, the Hastings-Taylors' chauffer.

Talk about a broken chooser.

Chapter Eighteen

New Best Friend

Jamie

Abby was wrong. About Chase.

I was right. To tell her about Ethan and Sam. *Samantha*.

I'd hurt her, but she'd struck first, and blindly. She'd met Chase *one time* and suddenly, she knew everything? I told her what I'd *seen*, for sure. Truth bites.

"Hey babe," Chase said, rolling over on his stomach. "Could you rub some sunblock on my back?"

Chase and I were out by the free-form pool, our cushy chaise longues set close enough to touch. In the week since Abby's visit, Chase and I had been together every minute I wasn't working, or he wasn't surfing or on call for an audition. We split our time between going out and staying at Casa Verde. We'd been to glitzy restaurants — we split the tab mostly — and celeb-spangled clubs where just getting in meant you could get a drink, regardless of your age. In one club called V, I noticed Mischa Barton (thanks to my Chase celeb-ucation, I knew she was from *The O.C.*) and in another, I went to the bathroom in the stall next to Scarlett Johannson. Kinda cool, in an "ew" sorta way. I thought briefly about an autograph for

Juliana — but nah. How weird would that be in the ladies' room?

I borrowed Chase's Blackberry to text message my sis instead. Turned out she'd have been more impressed with a Hilary Duff or JoJo sighting anyway.

The nights we stayed on the lush grounds of Casa Verde had their own rewards. Everything was available to us — tennis, swimming, first-run movies — including the yummiest munchies and libations.

Feeling frisky, I rolled onto Chase's chaise lounge, straddled him, and gave him an extra sensuous sunblock rubdown. I started at his waist, and zigzagged my way up, making circles around his backbones. Massaging his shoulders, I leaned in to tickle his neck with the tip of my tongue.

"Does Nicole ever come out here?"

Hardly what I expected him to say after my suggestive moves. "Who cares?" I murmured, continuing to stroke his back and shoulders.

"It's strange," he continued, resting his chin on his laced-together fingers. "We never see her."

It's a relief, I thought. "She's nothing like her TV image, you know. She's tough and business-y. I don't think you'd like her."

Chase twisted his neck around to me. "She has to be tough, she's a star. Power is what it's about, and you don't get that being a wuss."

I leaned in closer now and gave him little teasing pecks on

his ear, neck, and shoulder. He didn't respond, so I kissed him harder behind his ear.

"Whoa! Don't go leaving any marks," he warned.

I knew when I was being rebuffed. "If you don't like what I'm doing, just say so." I extracted myself from his lounge and walked over to the pool, where I dangled my feet.

He was by my side in an instant. "Sorry, I didn't mean that. It's just that I can't go to an audition with a great big hickey on my neck, that's all." He put his arm around me, and pulled me close.

From out of nowhere, I heard Abby: *He's a user. See how he mentioned Nicole? He cares about his audition, not your kisses.* I tried shoving her negativity away, but couldn't help pulling away from *him*.

"Don't be mad, babe, I loved what you were doing."

I sighed. "I've just . . . got a lot on my mind, that's all."

"Well, if you need someone to talk to, Dr. Chase is in the house."

My shoulders slumped. I was still angry at Abby — she'd completely spoiled the great time we were supposed to have. Guilt gnawed at me, too. Would I ever forget the horror-stricken look on her face when I drunkenly lashed out about Ethan?

And I was lonely. Eviscerating your best friend, even if you're telling the truth, still leaves you alone. Neither of us had tried to contact the other since.

"I didn't have a great visit with Abby," I finally said to Chase. "We weren't on the best terms when she left."

"Oh that? It'll blow over" — he sounded relieved — "whatever it was."

I exhaled. "I'm not so sure. Harsh things were said. I mean, it was all true, what I said anyway." I slid his sunglasses up onto his forehead, I wanted to see his eyes. In the bright sunlight, they looked mint green, light and sparkly. *So unlike Tripp's deep, dark, soulful chocolate.*

Whoa . . . where had *that* thought come from?

Chase nudged his shades back on. "You told Abby the truth and she couldn't handle it? Too bad, man." Then he grinned, "If you're looking for someone to fill the part of best friend . . . how do I audition?" He put a muscled arm around my shoulders and pulled me in tight.

"Your new best friend looks familiar."

I whirled around, gripping the banister to keep from toppling down the steps. Tripp, doing his stealth act, stood behind me at the top of the stairs. It was early Monday morning, and I was headed to the kitchen for a mug of green tea before waking Olivia.

"Hey!" I recovered, psyched to see him. "Have you even been around lately?"

"Not as much as you have."

Stung by his tone, I went into defense mode. "Is there a problem with me using the pool?"

Taken aback, Tripp said, "Of course not. What do I care?"

Ouch. Why was he talking to me like that? Even though

he looked like he'd slept in his wrinkled T-shirt, and even though *razor* and *face* had been out of contact for days, the effect didn't suck: It was more Orlando Bloom than hermit boy scuzz-fuzz. I eyed his guitar and remembered the band I'd heard at House of Blues.

"You play?"

He gripped the stem of the acoustic guitar tightly and shrugged. "Yeah." Which I heard as *None of your business.*

Not wanting him to get the last word, I challenged: "By my new best friend, I take it you mean Chase?"

He laughed. Not in a good way. "Chase. Perfect. If the name fits . . ."

"Tripp, what's going on? You're acting all pissed off. Have I done something wrong?"

He shook his head. "You're about to."

And then he was gone.

The bizarre encounter with Tripp made me crave my former best. I started counting the times I would have speed-dialed, IMed, e-mailed, FedExed, even sent Hedwig the owl, to connect with Abby. A dozen times I had to stop myself from doing what had come naturally all these years. Was she stopping herself, too?

When Chase came over Monday night after I'd put Olivia to bed, I suggested going out. "Unless we could hang here?" he countered.

But Tripp thinks we're here too much. Tripp doesn't like you.

"Change of scenery?" I offered.

"Speaking of change," Chase said suggestively, "why don't you change into that cute bathing suit and we do the Jacuzzi? I sure could use those pounding jets, I got totaled by a wave this afternoon."

Normally, I loved the hot tub — who wouldn't? But tonight, even though it was one of those rare LA nights when you could actually breathe, I couldn't relax. I brought my cell phone, in case Abby called. It stayed silent. This time, when Chase kissed me, I couldn't get into it. Someone else was in the hot tub with us, or might as well have been. Could Tripp see us?

Later in the week, things should have gotten better. One of Chase's NBF's (new best friends, in LA-speak) had to give up his reservation at Crustacean, an A-list restaurant, so Chase scored it. The food was amazing, but the scenery was off the charts — the restaurant boasted illuminated glassed-in koi ponds so customers could feel like they're walking on water! All that, plus a full star-sighting smorgasbord: Nick, Jessica, and Ashlee in a back booth, Lindsay Lohan, Tara Reid, and another starlet I should have recognized were chowing down and laughing. When the bill came, my half was like, $120. I purposely didn't add up the books that would have bought me at Ohio State.

The following night, after Chase played a round of Halo 2 on the Xbox in the media room, we cuddled up and watched *Batman Begins* in the screening room.

It was all good, as Chase kept reminding me. So how come

I couldn't shake Abby's cold shoulder or Tripp's chilly attitude?

A week later, on Saturday morning, I was surprised to bump into Topher. Sitting in the breakfast nook, he was the picture of contentment with the *LA Times* spread on the table, a steaming mug of coffee in one hand, a muffin in the other.

"Jamie!" He greeted me with a warm smile. "Join me?"

I checked my watch. Olivia wouldn't be up for a while. I slipped onto the bench across from him and gazed out the window. The breakfast nook overlooked a grove of orange trees, thriving even though it was November.

Topher bit into the muffin. "I hear these are your discovery. Organic orange-cranberry. Maybe we'll have our first ever all-organic Thanksgiving."

Thanksgiving. It was hard to wrap my brain around that, here in the land where the seasons never change.

The breakfast chef came over, and planted a mug of green tea and my own muffin in front of me. Ever since that day at the café with Tripp, it had become my "usual."

As if reading my mind, Topher continued, "Tripp's got us all eating them. Good call."

"Speaking of Tripp," a natural segue presented itself. "He kind of implied that I might be, I don't know, overstepping my bounds, having a friend over, using the pool and stuff . . . ?"

"Nah," he scoffed. "You must have misinterpreted my shy son. He adores having you around."

No, he adores sending mixed signals, keeping me off balance.

"Nic and I are thrilled you've made some friends and you're having fun," Topher added. "The whole paparazzi incident is long forgotten. I've been meaning to thank you for the wonderful job you're doing with Olivia. Our little baby seems like a changed child. She's upbeat, babbling away, having fewer accidents, and just so happy this fall. And for that, you can count on a nice bonus in your paycheck."

I lit up. Not because of the bonus. I'd fallen so in love with Livvy that to know she was thriving and making her parents happy, was more than reward enough.

He continued, "Between working with Olivia and getting us to go organic, I'd say things have fallen into a great place. Wouldn't you agree, T?"

I jumped. Tara, wrapped in a silk La Perla robe, and bejeweled flip-flops, was thwacking into the kitchen, stretching and yawning.

"Absolutely, Toph." She strode over and kissed him on the cheek. "Jamie's been . . . what? A godsend?" Topher had one bite of muffin left. Tara swiped it from his hand, winking. "Calories. Fat. Carbs. Net-net? Middle-aged man-gut."

Topher laughed genially and patted his flat stomach. "The calorie commando strikes again."

"A simple thank-you will do," Tara said breezily.

Topher closed the newspaper and slid out of the booth.

"*Gracias,* T, I know you're looking out for me. Well, as much as I'd love to chat and chew, the charity tennis tournament calls. Why not order up some low-carb something or other, and keep Jamie company?"

Tara was only too glad to. Emphasis on "to." Unsurprisingly, she'd "overheard" my convo with her stepdad and, like a heat-seeking missile, found her target.

"My Spidey sense tells me something's not right in lovey-dovey-ville. Worried I'm gonna steal Chase?" she teased.

"No, Tara. Despite your astronomic wealth and awesome beauty, I'm not that worried about it."

Tara chortled, "Your cluelessness is precious. So, what is it then?"

I never should have answered her, let alone honestly. But maybe it was lack-of-Abby, the diss by Tripp — or even the sweet exchange between Tara and Topher — that made me sort of confide. "I'm just not sure about him. We're so different."

When Tara narrowed her topaz eyes, I knew I'd messed up. And was about to suffer for it. "You mean like he's hot and you're not?"

I should so not have been shocked, let alone hurt. Yet I was both. When Skyy ambled in, Starbucks chai latte in hand, I got up.

"Don't go," Tara urged, scooting over to make room for her friend. "Let us help. We can, you know."

Skyy chimed in, "We're all about community service."

"Thanks," I snorted. "I'm not your IP."

"That's so quaint," Tara squealed, stealing a sip of Skyy's latte. "Improvement Project — so nineties. But here's the down-low. If you want to keep Chase . . ."

"Who says I do?" I bristled.

Tara smirked, "Oh please."

Skyy practically bounced off the bench. "We'll get you styled so fast, no one will ever wonder what he sees in you."

"No thanks." Again, I tried to slide off the bench and leave.

"You *like* having an inferiority complex?" Tara shot at me.

A *what*? She was pushing too hard: This had to be another trick. "What's in it for you?" I demanded. If I'd learned anything in the past months, it was the California-golden rule: DO UNTO OTHERS ONLY IF THEY CAN DO BETTER UNTO YOU.

Tara purred, "Don't be so jaded. I'm just a sucker for romance, and this one is so perfect: Nanny meets slacker, loser gets loser. I'm practically tearing up just thinking about it."

Skyy added, "Shopping is an art, and we happen to be extreme and passionate pro-sumers."

I looked at her blankly. Tara explained, "We're not your average consumers. We don't follow trends, we set them."

"Take Uggs," Skyy was describing. "We were first to realize they'd be over, so we discovered Chip & Pepper mocs, and made them the next big thing in footwear."

She turned to Tara, and they went into their patented shorthand.

"Rodeo."

"I'm thinking McCartney."

"Melrose?"

"Accessories only."

"But," Skyy cautioned, "we'll need Monique."

"And Guillermo."

It was like a tennis match, with me, the back-and-forth spectator. Eventually, I spoke. "I'm not *The Swan*, and I don't need a makeover, thank you."

The bffs broke out in tandem giggles. Finally, Skyy blurted, "This isn't a makeover. This is an Extreme Do-Over!"

After a while, I stopped asking myself why I'd put myself in their hands. They couldn't force me to buy anything sleazy or unflattering. Chase hung out with friends of sexy starlets — what was the harm if I looked more like one? Bonus: As Tara had offhandedly informed me, "You'll never see a bill. We'll pay for everything. Nicole will get great press for her generous treatment of the wronged nanny. It's all good."

Reluctantly, I gave the duo props for their efficiency. In short order, they'd enlisted Tripp to babysit Olivia for the weekend and called for the limo and summoned the family stylist, Monique, to "work her magic." A slender, one-facelift-away-from-Joan-Rivers-type, she treated me like I wasn't even there, insisting to Tara that we'd need to travel the "trompe l'oeil" road with me — buy stuff that masked my imperfections. Or as the verbally challenged Monique put it, "too much she has the blubber," and "too little she has the height."

All this so Chase and I would match in hot-worthiness.

Beverly Hills was our destination, but *not* — Tara looked down her slender nose — the Beverly Center.

Skyy dittoed distaste by scratching her arms as if she might catch cooties at the mention of "The-Mall-That-Must-Not-Be-Named."

We were headed for Rodeo Drive. "It's pronounced," Skyy informed me, "Ro-DAY-Oh."

"Well, Oh-KAY-oh," I cracked. "I'll be careful when I Oh-SAY-it."

"The stores represented," Tara told me, "are the most exclusive in the world. Dolce & Gabbana, Ferragamo, Cartier, Dior, Gucci, Tiffany, Prada . . ." She babbled on, but I got the picture. All designer, all the time. So, would there be a quiz afterwards? Should I be taking notes?

Kip pulled to a stop at Louis Vuitton.

"It's only one of 319 Vuitton stores in the world," Tara confided, "and it's one of only two places in LA where you can snag a Marc Jacobs."

"Good to know," I deadpanned.

Inside, Monique instructed me to "stand up, stand tall, arms at sides." She snapped her fingers and a fleet of salespeople materialized. Monique barked something in code — they returned with a slew of stylish frocks, bags, and shoes. "We" settled on a Marc Jacobs white halter top — a pleated cotton-and-linen number from the low-plunging department. "It minimizes your boobies," Monique offered.

Well, Oh-KAY-oh.

We accessorized with a signature bag, and tortoiseshell sunglasses.

For a millisecond, I thought-slash-hoped we were done.

Not so much.

If we were in a movie, this would be the montage scene — quick cuts of us flitting from overpriced store to luxury boutique, where I tried on and took off to a soundtrack mix of "Material Girl" and the hum of the credit-card swipe.

"We" agreed that the BeBe turquoise blue, off-the-shoulder tube top, when paired with white stretch capris, was totally flattering, and the Jimmy Choo strappy stilettos "slimmed" my ankles (who knew ankles could need slimming?). The platform Puccis added height without inflicting quite as much pain should I want to do something radical and actually walk in them.

I swallowed my guilt at the non-animal-friendly footwear, reasoning that the critters sacrificed for fashion were already dead when they got to the store.

I even opted for leather over pleather high-concept flip-flops — they were orange, with little zippers! How could I not? And yes, I did kinda "have" to have a candy-colored Chanel jacket with those big buttons. Because it really did go with everything, even my down-market Lucky jeans from "The-Mall-That-Must-Not-Be-Named."

Doing lunch was, according to slinky Tara, a necessary evil. We ended up at a Juice Bar, instead of The Persnickity Pasta: overpriced fruit juice instead of undercooked spaghetti. Post-lunch, it was off to Melrose Avenue to accessorize.

At an upscale celeb-haunt called Kitson, I got pedi-ready with Michael Kors's earthshoes. Here, I learned that even Birkenstock has gone Hollywood; a style called Gizah was a silver thonglike model. At Fred Segal, a department store designed like a series of mini boutiques, I picked up big round bejeweled earrings — if a Ferris wheel was an earring, and the spokes were diamond studded, that's what they'd look like — cinch belts, toe rings, and a Chloé leather cuff.

So much shopping — it was exhausting! I was one brain cell away from thinking, *How do Tara and Skyy keep up? This is hard work.*

Sunday night, I dragged myself into Olivia's room, where I found my little charge sitting on the floor, drawing.

I planted myself next to her. "Hey, Livvy-lu, whatcha drawing?"

"A pitcher of Sesame Place."

"Did you go there today?" I guessed.

"With Daddy. And Trippy."

Olivia held her picture up to show me. "I'm makin' it to show Juli-yana."

The mention of Jules sent my heart hammering and a sour taste surging up my throat. I hadn't given my sister a thought as I breezily shopped. I couldn't even call her now; it was way too late in Ohio.

"Look!" Livvy jumped up and ran over to her desk. She grabbed a printout. "Juli-yana sent me a new drawing today!"

Today? "That's so great, Oliv —"

My joy turned on me the minute I looked at the drawing. Jules had done a self-portrait. She'd drawn herself very small, caged in a huge hospital bed, hooked up to giant-sized IV's, with oxygen straws in her nostrils.

"She's *fine,* I promise you, Jamie." I'd gotten my dad on the phone, woken him up. He was doing his best to assure me that Juliana's trip to the hospital was just precautionary. She'd be home by tomorrow. I could talk to her then.

"You don't want me to come home?" I'd asked nervously.

"You'll be back before you know it," he'd said, "Christmas is only six weeks from now. And I can assure you, Juliana will be pink-cheeked and robust."

"Put Mom on," I'd demanded.

My mom was usually more forthright about my sister's health. But she, too, was reassuring. "A hiccup, that's all. You can talk to her yourself tomorrow."

I was shaking when I put down the phone. I started to pace around the suite, anxiety gripping me. I wished I could find a sedative, like Xanax, and thought briefly of breaking into Tara's room. I bet she had a stash.

You don't need that stuff, I could hear Abby saying. *It wears off anyway. You need to talk to someone, you need a friend.*

Ha! I thought miserably. I only had one friend who knew

the full Jules situation, who'd always been there for me, who'd force me to take deep breaths and talk things through.

I broke down and called her. But after four rings, I chickened out and didn't leave a message.

How sad was it that I didn't have anyone else to call? Then I thought of Chase. Okay, so maybe his mental elevator didn't go all the way to the top floor, but he was sweet in his own way. I got Chase's voice mail: "'Sup dude, can't hear the phone right now, leave a message. Rock on." I didn't leave a message. I didn't feel like rocking on.

"Bad news?"

I whirled. In my haste to get to the phone, I'd forgotten to shut my door. Now Tripp stood in it.

My guard went up. "Why should you care? I'm just the help, remember?"

He sighed. "Can I come in?"

"It's your mansion, do what you want," I muttered.

Tripp ambled in and perched awkwardly on the window seat. He conceded, "Okay, I deserved that. That was shitty of me. Can we cut to the scene where I say I'm sorry?" He looked at me hopefully with those large almond eyes. "The one where I really mean it?"

I stared at him. My lip trembled.

"Because I do mean it, Jamie. I overheard a little of what you were saying on the phone. I can be a pretty good listener."

I covered my teary eyes, but couldn't stop the sobs. "I just feel . . . so alone," I croaked.

Tripp closed the door. When he came back, he picked up my hand. "I recognize that bracelet."

That stopped me mid-sob. "You do?"

"It has to do with one of the charities Nic and my dad support."

I looked up at him. "Yeah. It's what the little kids say, the ones who can't pronounce their disease, Cystic Fibrosis. They say 'sixty-fi-rosis.' Sixty-Five Roses. It's become sort of the symbol for a cure."

And I told him about Juliana. And then about Abby.

I don't know what possessed me. I just kept on talking. About taking this job so I'd make money to go to school. About getting out of the Shafton-doldrums. About doing something with my life that was meaningful and helped other people.

Tripp was thoughtful. "I could hook you up with Angelina Jolie. She's all about humanitarian work — she's started some organization, I think."

I burst out laughing. Wasn't that exactly what some Hollywood scion would say? What was I expecting?

Tripp looked wounded.

I shook my head. "You just don't understand. You couldn't."

The next evening, as soon as I had a minute alone, I called home. Juliana herself picked up. She sounded tired, but otherwise okay. Relief washed over me.

I chastised myself for not calling sooner: Abby would have forced me to and I could have avoided an entire day of anxiety.

I checked my e-mail. Nothing from Abby. Except her voice ringing in my head.

I surfed the net. Before I realized what I was doing, I typed in "University of Arizona." This was my chance to find out if what Abby suspected was true — if Chase was a student there or if he was scamming me about everything. I cupped the mouse, just about to go for it, when I heard him.

"Hey, babe." He was posing in the doorway.

Startled, I shut down the computer. "How'd you —?"

Chase was aglow. "Guess who I just saw? Nicole!"

"Really?" I stammered. "I guess she does live here after all."

"I think she saw me." Chase was pumped. "She was getting into the limo, but I'm pretty sure eye contact was made."

I so doubted it. There wasn't much Nicole paid attention to, besides herself. *Her loss,* I mused. She'd missed Chase-at-his-hottest. He must have been outdoors all day, his body had a golden sun-kissed glow, his sleeves were rolled up, exposing his biceps. The fusion of my relief over Juliana and the sight of my hot boyfriend in my doorway overshadowed all other feelings.

Time to expose him to Jamie: The Do-Over version.

I opted for the blue tube top and white capris with my orange flip-flops. I put on makeup, and let my hair go long and loose.

His back was to me when I emerged from the dressing area. "What hot spot shall we hit tonight?"

He turned. "How about we stay in?"

"That could work, too," I said coyly. I should have felt glorious — instead, I heard Abby's voice again. *He's a user. How many times has he mentioned Nicole now?*

I took a deep breath. "Can I ask you something?"

"Anything," he licked his lips, scoping me out.

"This is lame. But . . . I mean, you're not hanging out with me just so you'll meet Nicole?"

"'Course not!" he scoffed.

If only he'd left it at that. He had to add, "Not that I'd mind. Nicole Hastings-Taylor is a huge star, babe. Anyone would want to meet her. That's the whole point of being in Hollywood."

That was the first profound thing he'd said — and he didn't even know it.

Chase sidled up close and put his arm around my waist. "Let's not think about Nicole now, okay?"

To prove where his mind really was, he took my hand, and led me to the bed, kissing me lightly at first, then more ardently. He lay down, and guided me on top of him. I began to slowly unbutton his shirt, massaging his chest first, then opening a few more buttons, giving him little kisses on the lips, on his cheek, and chest.

He closed his eyes. Then I got to his shorts. The top button took a little maneuvering, but the zipper slid right down. I ran my finger beneath the elastic of his boxers, tickling him ever so slightly. He squirmed a little.

I bent over to kiss him, murmuring, "Don't worry, I know the rules. No hickeys."

His laugh morphed into a low groan, and my heart pounded. I kissed him more passionately. He responded in kind, slipping his hand beneath my top and unhooking my strapless bra — a practiced one-handed move. With his other hand, he managed to get my tube top completely off.

It was the first time I'd willingly let anyone see me topless. There was no embarrassment, just the raw excitement of sharing myself with an extremely hot guy. Not Mr. Right? That was okay. This Mr. Right Now would do just fine.

Chase looked me over and his eyes popped. "What a rack! They *are* yours! The photos didn't do you justice."

What had he said? I crossed my arms to cover my chest. The excitement I'd felt a nanosecond ago dissolved into confusion. So, Chase *had* known all about Nanny Nipple-gate. And he'd been dumb enough to buy the whole "fixed photo" explanation.

"What's the matter, babe? Don't cover up, they're beautiful!"

They're beautiful. Not *I'm* beautiful.

I shook my head. "Chase, I'm not . . . I don't want to do this."

Deflated, but not dissuaded, Chase gamely tried to get us "back on track," as he so delicately put it. He stroked my arms, resolutely crossed over my chest, and shifted up on his elbows, bending to give me little kisses all over.

They were having no effect. Not in the way he meant them to. I tried to be rational, to give him the benefit of the doubt.

Of course he knew that if I was Nicole's nanny, I'd been the one in the photo. Which he'd never mentioned.

But why should he have? Maybe he thought it was rude to bring it up? But we'd been together for over a month. He should have disclosed.

Another thought struck me. Was Chase dating me because of my own sicko moment of quasi-fame? Because he could brag to his "friends" that he'd been with me?

I sent Chase home, told him I'd call him tomorrow. Then, I put on my new Juicy sweats, and went down to the family fitness center. I hit the elliptical machine hard. You'd think it would be impossible to exercise while sobbing intensely.

It isn't.

Chapter Seventeen

Busted

Abby

I saw Simon again shortly after I got back from Los Angeles. I was at the police station, my hands still blackened from having been finger printed, when he arrived to bail me out.

It's a long story.

It all started with Dylan. Even though I'd explained over and over that it wasn't my idea to leave him for a week, he had reverted to the worst of his old behavior. On Friday morning, I was trying to get him dressed for preschool at the Elysée. He struggled against all my efforts, yelling and flailing his arms and legs. So I stopped. And sat down on his bed, defeated. "Dyl, I don't know what to do," I admitted. "You've got to get dressed. So, what do you think I should do about that? You tell me and I'll try to do it, okay?"

"I don't want to go to crazy, poo-poo Madam Fleas's school anymore!" he asserted.

"Where would you like to go?" I asked innocently — not realizing I was signing, if not my death warrant, then my embarrassed-to-death warrant.

At first Dyl shrugged. "I don't know."

I started dressing him again. He was more cooperative as

he tried to come up with an answer to my question. "Statue of Liberty!" he decided, as his head popped through the top of his red-white-and-blue Tommy sweatshirt. Ever since we'd read a picture book about "The Lady in the Harbor," Dylan had been fascinated by the Statue. He'd tried to draw it and hadn't done too bad a job. You could tell it was something — either the Statue of Liberty or a loaf of bread holding up a salami.

I'd never been to the Statue either. "It's all the way downtown," I thought aloud. The morning rush hour was on. It would take forever in a cab. And the subways would be crowded. "Have you ever been on a subway?" I was just making conversation.

Dylan's eyes lit up. "My daddy promised we was gonna go on the subway. But then he went away. But I want to go. Please, please, please," he begged. "I'll be so good. Please, Abby. I'll be your best friend."

Who could turn down a deal like that? Not someone who had a gaping vacancy in the best friend department. "Okey-dokey," I decided. "It'll be fun."

A day off for Dyl. A mini vacation for the two of us. I thought about asking Edith to make us a couple of sandwiches; then I thought better of it. (Or worse, as it turned out!) I figured we could do the hot dog and pretzel lunch like real New York tourists.

Rush hour was in full swing when we hit the subway. I held onto Dyl's hand, as much for my comfort as for his, and we took our place on the platform at the back of the waiting crowd. It took three trains going by for us to get pushed to the front and into the brightly lit, thankfully heated car. The subway roared and swayed. Surrounded by grown-ups like a flower in a forest, Dylan stared up at me, his expression caught between delight and terror.

Shivering, we sailed to the Statue of Liberty on a boat overflowing with picture-snapping tourists. We climbed to the top, and had a grand time. We returned with tired, red-cheeked Midwesterners blowing warmth into their hands, wearing old sneakers, down jackets, and spiky, green Styrofoam Lady Liberty crowns.

It was on the way home from our adventure that everything went, as they say in mystery novels, terribly wrong. It was mid-afternoon so the subway wasn't particularly crowded. We got seats. Cold and tired, Dylan leaned against my shoulder. His hand in mine felt like a clammy, iced little fish. The swaying of the subway car lulled him to sleep. And then it was our stop. I shook him gently and led him off the train. He was barely awake when we climbed the steep stairway to the street.

Two policemen were waiting at the top of the stairs. One had a flyer in his hand. He looked at the flyer, then looked at Dylan, then nodded to his partner and said, "That's him. Get the nanny."

The next thing I knew, Dylan was shrieking in the policeman's arms. And I was spun around, my hands forced behind my back. The cop holding Dyl started reciting the "you-have-the-right" thing to me and wound up shouting it above Dylan's howls and screams as the other one snapped handcuffs over my wrists.

I was forced into the backseat of a squad car. An officer gallantly covered my head with his hand so I wouldn't bash my head getting in. The last I saw of Dylan, he was kicking and screaming and demanding to be let down all the way to the other cop's car.

You can't smell police stations on TV. The one I was taken to was a combo of cigarette stink, sweat, and a dash of urine.

It reeked. Literally.

And figuratively, so did my life. Especially when I found out that, because I was a minor, they'd have to call my parents. After being fingerprinted and relieved of my backpack and cell phone, I was taken to a dingy little office where a policeman, armed with a gun, a bulletproof vest, a pen, and some official-looking paper sat across a table from me and prepared to take my statement. I was still shaking, swiping at my tears. I had no idea what he expected me to say, so he asked some helpful questions: Why had I taken "the kid"? Did I intend asking for a ransom? Where was I going to keep him?

My statement consisted mainly of: "Are you crazy?" "No way." "This is a mistake."

I was marched to the back of the station and put into a "holding pen" while they checked to see whether I had a rap sheet — a record, a history of crime.

Grim? My mood *and* the holding pen — where a couple of disheveled women were continuing the argument that had landed them there, while I cringed against a wall, my arms wrapped around my knees.

Didn't I have the right to make a phone call? All the cop movies and TV shows I'd seen suggested that I did. Great. Now who to phone? The first person I thought of, of course, was Jamie — but aside from the fact that our friendship was on pause, what could she really do from the other side of the world?

Aunt Molly who would be no help either. Ditto my parents, who were getting called anyway. I could see my menopausal mom now, freaking, knocking back handfuls of Prozac, or whatever new drug her pill-pushing shrink was trying this week. No doubt about it, I'd wind up having to explain to her and my dad what I didn't know myself — why I was in a New York City jail, accused of a heinous if unspecified crime.

Garrick, then? I had his number — in the backpack the police had confiscated. Even if I could get it, I reasoned, what if he casually let slip to everyone that he'd bailed me out of the clink? Did I want the entire benched line-up of New York nannies to share my shame? My mind flashed to Margaritte; I had a hunch she was completely levelheaded and trustworthy. But I didn't have her number or know her last name.

The dim thought that had been cowering in the back of my mind suddenly became a bright idea: Simon.

I had planned to call him right after I got back from LA, but got stuck rehearsing what I would say . . . and how he'd react . . . and what I'd say then . . . and, in my mind, none of it worked. Now I had a real reason to reach out to him.

I called to the policewoman who was guarding the pen. After a short phone conversation with someone, she agreed I had the right to make a call. She gave me my address book and I followed her to a public phone.

Simon's voice mail picked up. "Um, uh . . . this is Abby," I said. "I'm in sort of a bind. I mean, I'm in jail . . . at the twentieth precinct, on West Eighty-second Street. I've been arrested — by mistake. Um, would you? I mean, could you, like, come down here? And, you know, help me. Oh I'm sorry, Simon —" Tears here. Big, blubbery tears and snuffles and sighs of wrenching misery. "I just don't know who else to call."

How pathetic! "Oh, God," I added, before hanging up. "Nevermind."

I followed the policewoman back to the cell, embarrassed, ashamed, crying.

Nobody came. Nobody called. Nobody cared.

It was dark out and I was deep into a quicksand of self-pity and despair, when Simon finally showed up. *My hero,* I thought, when I saw him sitting in a chair near the front desk. Head down, reading a novel, Simon Wagner had come to rescue me. The sight of him made my pulse race and my face flush with amazed happiness. The awful confusion and fear that had kept me company for nearly five hours vanished.

He stood when I came in.

"Oh God," I said. "Thank you. Thanks. I didn't think . . . I mean, I wasn't sure —"

Did I notice then that he wasn't smiling? That he didn't open his arms to me or whisk me off my feet and romantically spin me around right there in the police station? I guess not. Blinded by optimism, all I saw was tall, incredibly handsome, blue-eyed Simon . . . shaking his head at me. "Save it," he said. "You have to sign for your things over there."

Something was wrong. Definitely. Simon didn't know his lines, didn't say what someone kind and concerned was supposed to say. I retrieved my backpack and cell phone. "Okay, let's go," he said.

Outside daylight was a distant memory, but the neighborhood was neon bright; all-night delis and fruit stands were cheerfully lit, fashionable stores were opened fashionably late. The streets were bustling with strollers and shoppers. Simon raised his arm to hail a cab. "Can we walk?" I asked.

He thought it over and after a beat, he nodded.

"I'm sorry I got you involved in this mess," I murmured, doing what came naturally to me — apologizing. "There was no one else. I mean I couldn't think of anyone else to call —"

He glanced at me as if I was speaking some strange new language.

"The message I left on your voice mail," I reminded him.

"I didn't get it," he said. "I came because . . . Lila called me, freaked and hysterical, saying that you'd kidnapped Dylan —"

"Kidnapped?!" It was my turn to be freaked and hysterical. "Lila actually said that? She must've known better. Dylan must have told her where we were and what we were doing. How could she think I'd do anything to harm him?"

"The truth? She's been ticked at you," Simon said. "Curt's been brutal with her since the LA trip. He's been messing with her head, telling her that you know more about books than she ever did —"

Even in my misery, I felt a dash of pleasure thinking that Curt Gordevan thought I was smarter than Lila Matheson. But how had that led to my arrest? Being bright wasn't a felony.

Slowly and coldly, Simon filled me in. When Dylan didn't show up at preschool and no one had called the Elysée to say he'd be absent for the day, Madam Félice had phoned Edith. Edith, who had no idea where we'd gone — if only I'd asked her for the sandwiches! — phoned Lila. Conjuring up the worst possible scenario, Lila contacted the police and put out an all-points — complete with a quickly faxed picture of Dyl and a description of me!

Now she wanted to talk to me about dropping the charges, Simon said. So we were heading back to the apartment.

Good, I thought. I could see Dylan and explain what had happened: I could try to make up to him for the trouble and trauma my not notifying "Madam Fleas" had caused.

Meanwhile, Simon had clammed up again. I could feel myself getting jittery, stressed out at his silence.

"Are you mad at me?" I said or, rather, squeaked. Victim Girl had surfaced again, changing my voice from self-assured adult to pleading toddler. I cleared my throat. *When was the last time you said what you meant?* "I mean, *why* are you mad at me?" I amended.

Simon looked at me, studied my face. I couldn't wait.

"I didn't run out on you at Gordevan's reading, Simon. I ran out on me," I was surprised to hear myself say. "As soon as I found out who you really were, I started worrying, wondering if you could really be interested in me. Especially when I saw you with Jackie. It was like, *bingo,* there it is. I mean, people told me you went for blondes. This guy I know said you were always at the right party with the right blonde."

Whoops. Major blunder. Simon's face hardened, his stubbly jaw flexed angrily. "And you believed him, right?"

"I didn't know what to believe," I whimpered. "I was jealous of Jacqueline. I thought she was your girlfriend, not your agent —"

"You left with Matthew Savage," Simon said coldly.

"I didn't. That was just a coincidence —"

"You just took off. No good-bye. No explanation."

"I . . . I'm no good at confrontations," I said.

We walked along side by side after that, not touching, not talking.

Simon left me under the awning in front of the building. "Good luck, Ohio," he said, suddenly gentle again.

It was the last bit of gentleness for the day. Dylan was hysterical when I got upstairs. He was in his room, about half a football field away from the front entrance hall, but I could hear his muffled fit. Edith shook her head at me. "She's waiting in there," she said, waving an arm toward the living room. Lila was pacing back and forth on the plush white carpeting. I cleared my throat and said, "Hi." She whirled like a vampire, her face pale and hungry. I could almost hear black wings whooshing. "You're out," she hissed. "Get your things and get out of this house!"

Slow on the uptake, I said, "I'm fired?"

"Are you deaf as well as dumb?" she demanded. "I said, get out. Your services are no longer required. Dylan's got a new nanny. A woman who believes in discipline and order —"

"Not Ms. Farber?" I gasped.

Lila's eyes glistened with rage; she smiled her vampire smile. "Yes, Ms. Farber!"

Trying to contain my tears, I headed for the subway on Central Park West.

I was on my way down the steps when I bumped into Margaritte coming up. She greeted me with her wonderful, welcoming smile. "Is that you, Abigail?"

I nodded, tears streaming down my face.

"What's wrong?"

"Nothing. Everything," I told her as much as I could get out between slurps and sighs. "Nobody can stand me anymore —"

"Well, there's always Garrick," Margaritte teased. "He's very fond of you."

"He told you that?" I asked, amazed.

"Girl, he tells everybody everything," she replied. "Everything but the truth."

It occurred to me that Margaritte might just be saying that because Garrick had brushed *her* off. She'd liked him and he'd told her he wasn't interested in her. I thought I'd make her feel better. "You know, I think he's gay."

She cracked up.

We both heard the train pulling into the station below us. "Go on," she said, pulling a pack of tissues from her pocket and pressing it into my hands. "Go catch your train, Abby. Ya best go home now and get some rest."

Chapter Eighteen

The Top of the World

Jamie

"You're causing extreme water damage."

Through my tears, I looked up, confused. Tripp stood there, his hand on the elliptical machine. I'd been frantically pedaling, keeping pace with my self-pitying sobs.

"Do you know the damage a torrent of tears can do to these contraptions? They seep into all the uh . . . gadgety-things and get all waterlogged." Tripp smiled sheepishly. "C'mon, let's get you off this torture device."

What was he doing here? My tears were not for public consumption. And how'd he *know* I was even here? Bristling and sniffling, I challenged, "Are you following me?"

"No, Jamie, I'm not. I'm just worried about you."

This time, we went out a back door, even closer to the motor port.

As I slid into the Prius, Tripp leaned over to the backseat to fetch me a sweatshirt. "It can get chilly," he said by way of explanation. "Especially when you're soaked from sweat and tears."

Had I been bleeding, I realized, I would have hit the tri-fecta of misery, confusion, and self-pity.

I didn't care where we were going, though the night air felt good. I turned on the CD player, switching tracks until I got to one loud and angry enough to blast every woeful thought out of my head. Satisfied, I reclined the electric seat all the way back, folded my arms over my chest, and closed my eyes.

We were climbing uphill. Zipping around a series of sharp turns. I sensed this road wasn't built for zipping. It felt reckless. Perfect.

When Tripp slowed down, I was disappointed. I wanted to drive fast, take the road to the end, then dive off. My eyes still closed, I felt him pull over and park. "We're here," he announced, killing the music and the motor.

I sat upright. And gasped. He'd taken me to the top of the world.

"Mulholland Drive," Tripp explained. "We're officially in the Santa Monica Mountains Conservatory Zone. But most people just know it as the highest point in LA. You have to get out of the car to appreciate it."

No kidding! Tripp had pulled into a mini park, a scenic overlook. We walked to the edge of the mountain. From this vantage point, Los Angeles looked beautiful and pure, like a string of pearls twinkling against the night sky. "What you're looking at now is the Los Angeles basin — it includes Hollywood, Beverly Hills, Brentwood, Bel Air, and where we live in Holmby Hills."

We could see houses built on stilts, set deep into boulders in the rolling hills, and the neon sign of the Hollywood Bowl arena. Farther away, city skyscrapers, all spread out before us, intercut at various points by the wide, car-packed freeways. A telescope had been set up for tourists, but I wasn't interested in a zoom lens view.

"The city of angels," I mused. "From up here, you could almost buy that."

"Some famous person once said that this is how he likes Los Angeles best — at night, and from a distance," Tripp put in.

I laughed, in absolute agreement.

Tripp motioned to a bench behind us. Not your typical wooden bench, naturally. Being LA, this resembled a wrought iron swing — a cuddle stop for two pairs of tired feet. It featured a tall back for leaning against, arms to rest yours on, and a canopied top sculpted with flowers and vines. Sitting there, I hugged my knees and gazed out over the treetops, the sagebrush, and the canyon roads that cut into the mountains.

"If we walk up those steps," Tripp pointed to an higher vantage point, "you can see the San Fernando Valley, and the Hollywood sign."

"I can do without that," I assured him, feeling inexplicably peaceful.

"This used to be an oasis of calm," Tripp said, "a broad valley filled with orchards and vegetable fields. Not so much anymore."

We sat in comfortable silence for a while. Then, without explanation, Tripp trooped back to the car. I was pretty sure I knew why. Chances were this amazing view would look even better seen through the haze of a marijuana cigarette. I was ready this time.

So when he returned with a shopping bag from Whole Foods, I was surprised and disappointed.

"I figured maybe you worked up an appetite." On cue, my stomach growled. He'd packed a couple of wrap sandwiches, and a bottle of wine. I dug in to both.

"How'd you know I was so upset?" I asked after I'd refilled my plastic wine glass for the third time. "And how'd you know where I'd even be? Are there nanny-cams all over the house?"

He looked up. "What? Couldn't hear you, my mouth was full."

That might have been the stupidest thing I'd ever heard — but at that moment, it was hilarious. I could barely stop laughing.

"He's bad news, Jamie. You gotta know that by now," Tripp said.

Instant sobriety. I wiped my eyes with the sleeve of his sweatshirt. And somehow felt the need to defend Chase. "You can't be talking about Chase O'Brien, because you don't know him. You've never met him."

Tripp grunted. "I don't have to know him, I know his type. He's a classic hanger-on."

"You've gained all this knowledge, what, online? Or whatever it is you spend all day doing in your room."

Tripp ignored my defensive remark. "I've been around

this all my life, Jamie. My mother is a huge movie star in Mexico. When I was little and I lived with her, kids were always trying to suck up to me — just to meet her. After they got their picture taken or whatever, I was of no use to them, so they'd drop me like a ten-ton brick."

I mimicked playing the violin. "So tragic."

Tripp laughed. "It wasn't meant as a sob story. But when you grow up with famous parents, you get so you can sniff that type out. You just know."

Were he and Abby reading from the same script? I sipped some more wine. "So what's your saga, Tripp?"

He shrugged, "I just told you. Poor little rich boy."

"Nuh-uh, you're not getting away that easily. What's with the shadowy act? You appear out of nowhere and do something nice. Then you disappear again. You're nasty, then nice. Are you an actor-wannabe, practicing for the part of a flip-flopping superhero?"

Tripp gazed up at the stars. And then straight at me. "I'm a musician. I play guitar, and I sing lead in a band. And I produce other bands."

"So that was you at House of Blues a couple of Saturday nights ago."

He looked surprised. "You were there?"

"I was — but not really for the music." I explained to Tripp that Abby and I had run in there after she'd bolted from the limo, and Chase.

"Cornucopia," he affirmed. "That's my band. Too bad you didn't really hear the music. Next time."

Tripp told me that, contrary to how it seemed, he actually was in school, "taking classes at Santa Monica Community College for my Associate Degree."

"Then what's with all the secrecy?" I asked. "You're in a band, you're going to school. Why do you stay locked up in your room when you're home?"

He shrugged. "I'm doing a lot of music online. Besides, it's not like Toph is totally down with my choices."

He smiled slowly and I could feel myself melting. It was the wine. That was it.

"Listen, Jamie, about that guy, about Chase. He's a user in a town full of users. What he's doing isn't even considered bad form. It's considered normal."

"So?" All of a sudden, my lip was trembling, "So what if he wouldn't mind meeting Nicole? She is a big star. Is that the worst thing ever?"

Tripp lowered his voice. "The worst thing is letting him get to you, believing he —"

"Really likes me for me? Is that so impossible? I'm just the flabby nanny after all —"

"Stop it!" His harsh tone brought me up short. "You didn't come to LA being so insecure. You were this cool confident chick without pretense, finally someone in the house with her priorities straight — the last person to buy into this bullshit scene. What happened to you?"

I sat up. Why did I have to defend myself?

"Do you have any pot?"

My question tripped him up. "Wha —?"

"I'm ready to take you up on your offer. Remember? The day you swooped into my life and talked me out of quitting? You asked if I wanted a toke. I do now."

He pursed his lips, and looked out over the city below. "No."

"No you don't have any, or no you won't share?"

Tripp looked at me, hard. It was discomfiting, and I squirmed. "This isn't you," he pronounced. "You don't smoke. So, no, I'm not going to give you any weed."

"If you're worried about corrupting the nanny, too late, Tara beat you to it."

"Sorry, I don't buy that you've been corrupted," Tripp insisted. "What I admired is that you weren't like Tara. You're teaching Olivia, you're showing her another way."

I frowned. Was Tripp, ex-Shadow, only helping me because I was helping his sister?

I pointed out, "*You* could exert some influence on Olivia, too."

Tripp sighed. "This lifestyle, the wealth, it's seductive, Jamie. Sometimes you don't even realize how far into it you've fallen until someone from outside shows up — in this case, you — and with her every breath, points it out. The rest of us, me included, we've been breathing this foul air all our lives. But somehow, instead of you influencing us, the reverse happened. *You* bought into the whole scene. Suddenly you've got both lungs full."

I thought of my sister, and swallowed back my tears. I barely heard him when he said, "Listen, it's not just about

Olivia. It's about all of us. The ratings for *Nikki's Way* are down, that's one reason Nicole's so tense. Her producer suggested she needs a stunt to bring the ratings up — to cast Olivia as an orphan Nikki adopts . . ."

"No!" I interrupted, horrified.

Gently, Tripp said, "That's my point. It won't happen — because of you. Because even though it may look like we're not paying attention, we are. My dad sees more than you know. He understands how you've helped Olivia. No way will he ever let her be put in the pressure cooker of cameras again."

"Really?"

"You did that."

My tears tasted salty. The sweatshirt sleeve made a great tissue.

"There's one more thing I have to tell you," Tripp said softly.

"Not sure I want to hear it —"

"It's about Tara."

"Okay, I'm sure now."

"You probably wonder why my family needed a nanny when they've got this huge staff, and . . . well, I'm sure you've wondered why Tara doesn't watch her from time to time."

I laughed. Back in the naïve old days, I'd also wondered what Tara did all day long. Now, I knew. Shopping, backstabbing, partying, and parading around half-clothed were full-time activities. Let alone the daily treat of messing with the nanny —

"She's not allowed around kids. Not by herself."

Tripp had my attention now.

"Seven years ago, when Tara was ten, she lived in Beverly Hills with her dad and Nicole. One Sunday afternoon, they were having a party, a lot of people. The adults stayed indoors, the nannies and kids were out by the pool. Tara and a bunch of her friends were there. One of the nannies skipped out — she told Tara to keep an eye on the kid she was watching.

"This little boy was playing with another kid. He wasn't in the pool. Tara turned away to talk to her friends. It took, like, a second. Maybe he dove in, fell in, or got pushed. No one admitted to seeing what happened. His name was Josh, he drowned a week after his third birthday."

Involuntarily, my hands flew to my face, and the tears started again.

Tripp continued, "Nicole's posse covered it up, of course, made sure the nanny took the rap. But Tara — well, she'd never admit it, I mean we haven't mentioned it in years — she's been traumatized ever since. You might not believe it, but she used to be a cool kid."

Between Chase and this Tara-bulletin, there was a *lot* I would not have believed.

I dumped Chase the next day.

Not only because of Tripp's warnings. Not even because of the boob revelation — though that hadn't helped. Chase O'Brien was what he was — just a dumb, sexy guy who grooves on being part of the Hollywood game, and absolutely believes he'll be a real "insider" one day.

And, dude, there's nothing inherently wrong with that. He's just wrong for me.

Chase didn't take being dumped very well. More to the point, he didn't understand it. "But we're good together," he said over the phone. "I really want to be with you, Jamie. Lemme come over and show you."

I paused. "What if you come over when Nicole's here? I'll introduce you. Isn't that what you've really wanted all along?"

His silence was all the answer I needed.

"Hey, Chase?" I whispered. "I'll have Nicole send you an autograph. Have yourself a bitchin' life, okay?"

There was not a hint of bitterness in my voice. Relief washed over me, and left in its wake a sweet feeling: Abby, and Tripp, whatever their methods or motives, had warned me away from Chase, because they had my best interests at heart.

I knew then what I had to do.

Chapter Nineteen

The Real Garrick

Abby

It was police procedure that the parents of arrested minors had to be notified. By the time I got back to Aunt Molly's in New Jersey, my mother had phoned five times. The first thing Molly said when I walked in the door was, "Call your mother right now! If I get one more phone call from her I'm going to have a nervous breakdown."

I went into the guest room, threw my backpack on the bed, and dialed Insanity. My mother answered with a lilting, "Yell-ow?"

"Mom, it's me," I said.

"ARRESTED?!" she screamed. "Are you trying to kill me? Do you know what you put us through? Haven't I got enough trouble without getting phone calls from the police? Wayne, get on the line quick, it's her," I heard her holler to my dad.

Automatically, an apology was on my mind, in my throat — but it suddenly lodged there. I was sick of feeling responsible for other people's misery — or happiness. And I was tired of not being allowed to have a problem of my own without my mom and/or dad making it a bigger problem for them.

"I'm sorry," stole out before I could stop it, but I did manage to add, "that you feel that way. Mom —" My voice cracked, disguising the outrage I'd meant to inject into the convo. "*I'm* the one who went through this horrendous experience. I'm the one who needs love and support and help. Not you guys. Not this time."

Where had the words come from? Not from the make-it-all-better girl whose job was to calm and cure outbreaks of family crisis. Some other Abby then was scolding her mother, a new Abby who could tell the truth instead of tiptoeing around it.

"Abby, is that you?" my father asked hesitantly. "Your mother is very upset. She wants you to come home."

"Abigail, I want you to come home," my mother said, as if my father hadn't spoken. "There's no reason for you stay there now —"

"There is too!" I cried, frantic at the thought of returning to the Burrows family nuthouse. "I've still got a job to do. I'm not going to leave Dylan." That much was true, even if I didn't mention that I'd been fired.

"You're going to stay in New York? Oh, but you can't, Abby. Your mother is —"

The mother in question quickly cut him off. "Oh, Abby, my baby. Don't you care about us at all?" she croaked, her voice suddenly thick with tears. "Is a stranger more important to you than your own mother?"

Again, the need to apologize, explain, and comfort came involuntarily to me. I beat it back. "Dylan is not a stranger," I said quietly but firmly.

She started to weep. "Put Molly on," she blubbered. My aunt was standing in the doorway of my room, drawn by my surprisingly loud and angry side of the call. I blinked at her as if I'd just woken from a trance.

I hadn't caved. I hadn't put my mother's distress above my own. Excited and exhausted, I handed Aunt Molly the phone and walked out.

While they talked, I tried to catch my breath and figure out what I had to do. I couldn't let Molly know that I'd lost my job; she'd tell my parents. And, even if I could convince her not to, she probably wouldn't let me just hang around her house all day, every day, alone. And I didn't want to, either.

What was I going to do? I could only sightsee for so long. After which I'd need someplace to crash until it was time to head back to New Jersey at night. I didn't want to bother Simon again . . .

Garrick. I phoned his apartment and he was there, happy to hear from me. I gave him the short version of what had happened and listened with relief as he, the only person so far who seemed to feel my pain, helped me figure out what to do.

We agreed that I'd go into the city three days a week, as if I were going to my job. Then I could stay at his place, a one-room studio on West Twenty-second Street, checking out the papers and the internet for a job. Bonus: Garrick could fill me in on how Dylan was doing. He was sure to run into my sweetie pie at the playground or other places where rich kids made the rounds.

It sounded like a plan.

Garrick's one-room apartment was small and dark and faced the brick wall of another building about six feet away. There wasn't much furniture. All that fit into the place was a closet-sized bathroom, an alcove kitchen with a teeny fridge that fit under the counter, a tiny table for two with mismatched chairs, and a single bed decked out with pillows that were supposed to make it look like a couch.

For a gay guy, I couldn't help thinking, he sure didn't have a clue about style.

The third time I was there, Garrick showed up unannounced. I was on the bed, where I'd been leafing through the *Times* want ads. "Just wanted to check up on you," he said. "Are you all right?"

"Sure," I kidded. "Jobless, boyfriend-less, practically homeless. I'm fine."

He laughed and took a beer from the midget fridge.

"Where's DC?" I wondered aloud.

"Morgan's nanny is keeping an eye on him for me. I just wanted to see how you were doing."

As he popped the can open, I peppered him with questions about Dylan. Had he run into him that morning? How was he doing with the stern-and-sour Frau Farber? Did he seem happy?

"He was at the playground — grounded," Garrick said, pausing for a hearty swig of brew. "Farber doesn't let him play in the sandbox 'cause it's too dirty, according to her, or climb the jungle gym 'cause he might fall. He mostly sits on the bench beside her, swinging his chunky little legs and looking miserable —"

I expected the sigh that escaped me but not the tearful moan that followed it. "Oh God, it's all my fault."

Garrick was beside me in an instant, taking me in his freckled arms, smoothing back my hair. "It's okay," he murmured. "He'll be all right. It's you I'm worried about."

I wailed into his chest. "I'm okay, Gar."

"Sure, Abby. I know you are —" He was stroking my back reassuringly, but I couldn't stop crying. "You're all right now. You're all right just the way you are," he insisted.

I didn't know why, but his sweetness only made me cry harder. And made him hold me tighter.

My face was pressed against his neck, my nose nuzzling his skin. I smelled beer — not just the sip I'd seen him take but a boozy smell that seemed to be seeping from his pores. Had Garrick knocked back a few brews before he got to the apartment?

"I can't stand to see you unhappy. I . . . I really care about you, Abby," he whispered into my hair. "I'm not like that arrogant asshole Simon Wagner. I'd never hurt you. You can trust me —"

Suddenly the hand that had been stroking my back slid under my sweater. I knew right where it was heading.

No wonder Margaritte had cracked up when I'd told her

Garrick was gay. She'd probably been through a scene just like this one with him.

The panic whistle blew. "Garrick, stop. Please," I said, trying to squirm out of his arms. "I'm okay. Let go of me."

He didn't. "Don't you like me? Even a little?" he asked, drawing me in closer, his caress suddenly urgent. "Come on, Abby. Give me a chance."

One of his hands, the one under my sweater, had made it to the boob it had targeted. His fingers were cold.

For a split second I actually wanted to say, *I'm sorry. I like you, Garrick; just not that way.* I wanted to *apologize.*

Instead, out of some suddenly awakened dead zone, I shouted at the top of my lungs, right into his ear: "GET OFF ME NOW!"

The deafening command stopped his groping. With a surge of strength fueled by outrage, I shoved him off me.

I still had the newspaper in my hand. It had gotten rolled up in my fist and I was gripping it like a baseball bat. I jumped to my feet and started swatting him with the paper.

Garrick cowered behind his hands, "I'm sorry. Abby, honest. I didn't mean to —"

"Honest?" I snapped. "Honest, you're sorry? How can you even use the word? You lied about who you are and even who Simon was supposed to be. You lied to me about everything! Didn't you?" I demanded. I didn't wait for or need an answer. I hurled the paper at his head, grabbed my backpack, and split.

All the way back to New Jersey I talked to Jamie. I told her everything — what had happened, and how empowered I felt. I said, "You'd be proud of me." I said, "Oh, James, I missed you." I said all this to the Jamie in my mind, though I longed to speak to the real Jamie back in LA.

Chapter Twenty

Making Up

Jamie

It was past midnight in New York, but I needed to get to Abby, even if it meant waking her.

She answered on the first ring. "Jamie?! Oh my God, what time is it? Are you all right?"

"Ab!" I hadn't meant to break into tears, but I was so relieved to hear her voice. "I'm so, so, soooo sorry for all the stuff I said," I sobbed. "I'm the biggest jerk the world."

We talked, alternately crying and laughing, for nearly two hours. And it felt like a bear hug, like the first ray of sunlight after a dark frigid winter, like a lifeboat in a choppy sea.

Chase had used me, Garrick had lied to her. Juliana was still sick, Abby's mom was still making everything about her. Net-net? Everything was still wrong, but one big thing had just righted itself.

Our friendship.

It was enough. For now.

"About Ethan," I said. "I'm so sorry about the way I blurted it out that night. That was messed up."

The old Abby would have said, "Oh, it's okay." Or, "Forget it, no big deal." But the all new "say what you really mean" Abby said what she really meant! "That really did hurt. You were vicious. I didn't think I could breathe."

"I'm so sorry. It's been crazy here. I *am* like a different person. It's all the stress. And Tara, she's evil."

"Which doesn't make her a killer," Abby noted. "It doesn't sound like she was really responsible for that kid's drowning."

"She was supposed to be watching him —"

"She was a child herself," Abby pointed out. "Whoever put her in charge of a baby, there's your murderer."

The nanny. That neglectful nanny had taken the rap, had been arrested — deported back to France, in fact — only this time, justice had been served.

"Which doesn't help Tara," Abby continued. "She's probably had this massive guilt all her life."

"Like I care," I said.

"You don't have to care," Abby advised. "But it might go a ways toward explaining her fear and hatred of nannies."

"C'mon, Abs, it's too psycho-pop convenient." I paused. "Although it does provide motive — in a sick way."

There were more pressing topics to discuss than Tara, anyway. Like Simon.

Abs was bleak about ever seeing him again. "It would take a miracle," she said.

"Okay, then expect a miracle," I advised her.

"Ya think?" she said uncertainly, hopefully.

"I know," I promised, and somehow, I did know. I

was sure about Simon. It was Tripp who continued to confuse me.

"I know this excellent band playing at the Key club on Sunset tonight," Tripp mentioned casually as he ambled through the Great Room, where Olivia and I, our tummies pressed flat against the bamboo floor, were building Legos.

I clocked him warily. Tripp was in his usual outfit, frayed jeans, janky T-shirt, scuffed boots, acoustic guitar slung over his shoulder. "They're called Cornucopia — maybe you heard of them?"

I pressed my forefinger to my cheek in mock concentration. "Hmmm, I think I might have. They're pretty decent, from the little I heard."

That made him smile. "If you wanna go, I could hook you up."

I resisted the urge to show my real feelings, which were "YEAH!" I paused, which he took as a yes. "It's at nine P.M., but we won't go on until after nine thirty. Kip's going, he can drive you." Tripp was already halfway out of the room. "I'll put your name on The List."

I defy anyone to try resisting the surge of power, the feeling of "I'm so cool, and you're not," when you cut the line at a place like the Key club. It feels awesome to inform the bouncer, "We're on The List."

Kip and I were ushered into an already-packed, darkened

room. The clublike setting eschewed seating, the audience stood, crowding around the stage. An emo-punk band called Undertow was on, and kids zoned out on their dirge-rock, swaying and nodding to the trancelike music.

I turned to Kip. "So is this part of your job, chaperoning the nanny to see Tripp's band?" I asked, sipping at the foamy beer Kip had ordered. A perk of being on The List was not having to wear one of those yellow "underage" bracelets.

"Wrong on two counts," he responded affably. "I'm off tonight, and by this time, I think we can agree you're more than the nanny to the Hastings-Taylors."

But am I more than the nanny to Tripp? That's what I wanted to ask.

"After all we've been through over the past few months, you're practically family — or as close as any non-blood relative gets. They don't always use their powers for evil," he joked.

I wanted to agree, but could I really trust anyone in the family, aside from Olivia?

"Besides," Kip nodded toward the stage, where Undertow was wrapping its set and Cornucopia was getting ready. "The kid is a real talent. Stubborn, though. Refuses any help from the old man, won't even talk to him about his music."

The old man, I reminded myself, is the source of family money. The night Tripp had taken me to Mulholland Drive, he'd said that Topher was not "down" with his choices. Translation: The helping hand his family could lend did not come without strings attached. And the only strings Tripp cared about were those on his guitar.

Cornucopia: Tripp and three other guys — bass guitarist, rhythm guitarist, and drummer — were setting up. They were a scruffy bunch, no question, a ragtag pack of random scraggly-tops, one with a soul patch, another donning a do-rag, the drummer with multiple face-piercings. They didn't look like a bunch of rich kids playing at street rock. They neither looked nor sounded like poseurs.

Tripp took the microphone and called out, "Are you ready to rock?" A blast of guitars jolted the audience out of its stupor and got the party started. Tripp's voice, as he sang, was gravelly and deep. Between songs, he joked around, explained what the songs were, who wrote 'em, what the influences were. Tripp Taylor on stage was friendly, accessible.

So this was The Shadow's natural element, I realized. I did an equation: Rodeo Drive is to Tara, as onstage is to Tripp.

Only the music mattered, and Cornucopia's rocked the roof. It was real, achingly raw. Familiar, too. I'd heard random tracks in Tripp's car, both times I'd gone out with him. I was moving, arm pumping, sweating even, and when invited, shouting out. Kip let loose, too. It was very cool to see the family's buttoned-up chauffer get his groove on.

After a slew of rockers, Tripp announced, "We're gonna take it down a notch for this next one, a new one we're playing for the first time tonight."

Tripp strummed his guitar and started to talk. "It was written for a special person . . ." The rhythm guitarist added a layer over Tripp's acoustic strums. "Someone who dropped into my life from . . . well . . . might as well have been another planet." He laughed, and the bass guitarist came in adding a backbeat. "She spun me around, and I didn't know where to stop . . ." Now the drummer came in with the whisks. Tripp finished, "She'll leave soon, and I know I'll never be the same."

And then he sang: *"Jamie, oh, what's your game, girl? You got me wrapped up in knots, dunno how to feel. Your tears rip my heart apart, and then you smile, girl . . . and then you smile, girl.*

"I dunno what to say, the words tumble and stall, scatter and fall, ringing empty in the hall. Oh Jamie, I know you think I don't care . . . but you couldn't be more wrong, girl. Just listen to my song, girl. Let me stop your tears, and let me see your smile, girl. 'Cause all I need is your smile."

I couldn't look at him. My eyes were glued to Tripp's fingers, as they massaged the guitar strings. My jaw dropped to the floor, I could not swallow. My heart knocked around in my chest like a ping-pong ball. And after those first verses, I heard not one single word of the song. Kip hugged me when it was over, but I stood frozen, rooted to the spot, too terrified to look up at the stage.

It was the kind of night you dream about. The lead singer-boy opens his heart, lets the whole world know how he feels. About you. And you feel — I felt — beautiful, and amazing. I was floating on air.

When the set was done, I went backstage, did that obnoxious "I'm with the band" thing and found Tripp. We locked eyes, he took my hand, and led me out back. We sat on the wooden steps behind the club.

And that's when I woke up from the kind of night you dream about.

Because that's when you're flying without a script. When you're face-to-face, the words you want to say are just cheesy, embarrassing, things you've rehearsed in your head, or wrote in your journal — e-mailed to a friend, maybe, but when it comes to actually saying out loud? To the other person?

Not so easy.

If that song had been about me, then Tripp had already said his piece. So was it on me? Did he expect me to go, "Oh my God, Tripp, now I know how you really feel, and yes, I'm all yours"?

Seriously? I could have done it. I was *this* close. And I'd like to believe the words on the tip of his tongue were, "What did you think of my song?"

But neither of us got there. An awkward silence filled the air, which Tripp dove into by talking about the guys in the band, other gigs they had lined up, and a bunch of new songs he was working on.

He never said a word about "Jamie."

Was he trying to tell me, "Don't take that song literally"? Was he trying to say, "Don't flatter yourself, it wasn't really about you: It was just words that rhymed, a melody that worked. I didn't really *mean* it"?

Was I overthinking it? Probably. But the moment when I could have asked the real question went by in a blinding flash of bling. The backdoor slammed behind us, and the distinctive click of Jimmy Choo's advanced toward us.

Tripp swung around and grinned. "Tara-belle, you made it!"

She ignored me. She gripped the railing of the steps, hovering over us. "I'm all about supporting my brother."

"Well, come on down," he said, scooching over — away from me. "What'd you think?"

Tara hesitated. The princess? Putting her sequined tush on a concrete step? Something made Her Highness deign to sit down, however: probably the thought of coming between me and her brother. But then Tara had a news flash to deliver: "As a surprise, I invited some A&R guys — record company scouts — to the gig. The one from Interscope and the one from Sony/BMG want to meet you."

And with those words, I became invisible.

Chapter Twenty-one

Thanksgiving in the Hamptons

Abby

The miracle Jamie had told me to believe in happened — times two!

I reconciled with my parents. I still hadn't told them that I'd lost my job. But I did say I'd try to get home by Christmas. Before I did, I was determined to take in as much of the city as I could.

I bused into Manhattan, armed with maps and guidebooks that I tried to keep out of sight, lest anyone take me for a tourist. First day out, I bumped into Margaritte again, who had the day off. The sight of her cheerful face framed in bobbing, golden dreads made me smile with gratitude for my good luck. She was on her way downtown to do a little shopping. We decided to join forces.

On the loudly rattling subway, I filled her in on what had happened with Garrick. She laughed as I gave her the blow by blow, and confirmed that a more or less similar scenerio happened to her.

We hit Chinatown first — and checked out a gazillion little shops featuring everything from ivory chopsticks and paper dragons, to racks filled with "designer" merch with logos that looked like but weren't Gucci, Vuitton, Prada, and Yves St. Laurent. There were bins of cute cloth shoes and glittering mesh slippers. For less than five dollars, I bought Jamie a pair of sparkly slides, which I'd seen uptown for five times the price. For myself I scored these amazing Manolo knockoffs: black, patent leather, knee-high boots with sexy, spiky heels. Margaritte got the same ones in luscious red.

Clutching our unfashionable recycled plastic shopping bags, we walked uptown to Soho. After wandering through art galleries and over-our-budget boutiques, we popped into Dean & Deluca, the upscale market. Perched at the window bar with our cappuccinos and croissants, we watched a parade of people for whom black clothing was more a religion than an option.

The Meat Packing District was the next stop on our tour. What was once the place where, my guidebook claimed, huge slabs of beef hung from loading platform hooks and the wide cobblestone streets bore the stench of decades of butchering, was now a New York must-see zone. Cool clubs and purposely seedy bars were interspersed with dozens of chic spots — from Stella McCartney to the in-crowd eatery, Pastis.

At the end of the day, Margaritte and I hugged like the good friends we'd become. She promised to look after Dylan for me and to let me know how he was doing.

A warm spell had temporarily banished the November cold. And New Yorkers were primed to sop up every last ray of sunshine before winter set in for real. So on the third day of my walking tour, when my feet ached from midtown sightseeing, I rested along with oodles of others on the steps of the New York Public Library.

Between the famous lions, Patience and Fortitude, New Yorkers of every accent and appetite lounged, chatting, reading, smoking, joking, munching kosher hot dogs, Greek souvlaki, and Middle-Eastern falafel. I loved the place and the people-watching ops it provided. Plus, it was the perfect venue to think about my book again. At last.

I was doing just that, jotting down things my mom had told me about her grandmother, when my cell phone rang. It was Margaritte. She'd phoned to say that she'd just stepped between Ms. Farber and my baby when the rigid nanny was scolding Dyl for getting his hands dirty. Her back to Farber, she'd taken Dylan's supposedly dirty hand and led him over to the jungle gym, which he and Daisy then clambered over like a couple of happy chimps.

Ms. Farber had been flabbergasted, Margaritte reported. (To be "Farber-gasted," we decided, was to be pissed off but too nervous to admit it.)

I was grateful to Margaritte, but the incident was bittersweet. My baby needed me and I was helpless to help him.

The buses to New Jersey were running late, due to some glitch announced over a platform speaker. So my usual forty-five minute trip to Aunt Molly's took an hour and a half. She wasn't home and the phone was ringing off the hook as I walked in the door. I raced into the kitchen and must've sounded as exhausted as I felt when I grabbed the phone. "Hello," I wheezed.

"Are you okay?" a guy asked.

"Who is this?" I was cranky and tired and not up for guessing games.

"It's me, Ohio," a contrite voice said. "You sound whipped."

Simon! I um-ed and uh-ed and suddenly went blank. I couldn't think of a thing to say.

"Are you mad at me?" To my amazement, he sounded uneasy, apprehensive. "I wouldn't blame you if you were. But I'd like to see you, try to straighten things out."

"Okay," was all I could manage, my mouth suddenly parched.

"How about dinner? I know a great Italian restaurant downtown — no atmosphere but awesome food."

A trek back into the city? "Um, I don't know," I answered, to my amazement. My heart was willing but my exhausted body begged to take a pass.

"If you're not hungry, we could get a drink, or grab a cup of coffee, whatever you want. I'd just like to see you, Abby. Curt told me that Lila fired you. I didn't know she was going to do that. Come on, Ohio. Maybe you think I don't deserve it for being such a jerk at the police station —"

"And the gelato place on Broadway," I blurted. I'd told the truth. To someone whose opinion of me really mattered! I kept going. "I want to see you, Simon, but . . . um . . . not tonight. I'm tired and cold and I just got home from the city —"

"I could pick you up —"

"— I'd rather just hang here," I finished my thought.

A pause as silent as my pulsing heart was loud. Was he angry? Would he ever ask me out again? Did I care? Yes! Absolutely. Was I really too tired to see him or was I into petty revenge? No, I was exhausted. Absolutely. But should I make the effort anyway? Should I sell myself out to keep him from getting mad at me again?

"What about Thursday?" he asked.

"But that's Thanksgiving."

"If you've got other plans, I understand —"

"No," I assured him. "I haven't got any plans."

"Well, a friend of Curt's is throwing a Thanksgiving dinner in East Hampton for all us nowhere-to-go, nothing-to-do types."

"Curt Gordevan?" I asked.

"The old lion himself. We could drive out together."

How could I say no?

Couldn't.

Didn't.

"I'll pick you up around noon, okay?"

"Okay," I said.

There's a reason they call the Long Island Expressway the longest parking lot in the world. It was a holiday and the traffic out of the city resembled a panic scene from a disaster movie.

Horns honked, drivers hollered, SUVs and Hummers wheeled wildly from one lane to another.

Simon had found a way to beat the insanity. He'd hired a Town Car and driver (not Mike, sadly) again; warm and plush, the car a cozy cocoon against the madness outside.

By the time we crossed the Nassau County line, we'd gotten most of our issues out of the way. We'd rehashed: I thought Jacqueline was your girlfriend and you were just stringing me along; I thought you were playing games, running out on me; you were so cold; you were so trashed; I thought you were a playboy doing a blonde at a time; you had a boyfriend, remember, that guy in California. Had is the word; we're over; he found someone else. He's clearly nuts. . . .

We'd started out at opposite sides of the backseat, facing each other. But as we continued talking, letting go of the past, without even thinking about it, we'd begun to lean toward each other. We slowly shifted away from our respective corners, mindlessly heading for the center of the soft seat.

Laughing at something I'd said, Simon took one of my hands and began lightly stroking my forearm. I moved closer to him, the length of leg between the tops of my faux Manolo boots and the side-slit Ann Taylor skirt I was wearing warmed against his khakis. Near Bayshore, we met in the middle — Simon's arm cushioned my neck, my head lay against his chest. While I contentedly breathed in his clean, fragrant scent, his free hand toyed with my hair, my neck, my shoulders.

By the time we hit the off-ramp at Exit 70, we were kissing.

Not turbulent sexy kisses, but soft exploratory ones. Just brushing each other's lips, gently licking, first almost ticklishly light, then harder, almost fevered, then back to playful teasing.

"Oh, man, Ohio, you're driving me crazy," Simon whispered.

"My pleasure," I murmured, my mouth still on his lips.

The car pulled into a gravel horseshoe driveway that fronted a sprawling French country-style mansion, set on landscaped dunes against the backdrop of the Atlantic Ocean. A valet parking guy opened the rear door and, reluctantly, Simon and I separated, straightened our clothing.

On the sandy soil at the side of the house, a slate path ran through a garden of beach roses, cranberry bushes, and wild grasses. Following it, we came to a huge poolside deck where about half a dozen guests, drinks and hors d'oeuvres in hand, braved the ocean wind. Expensive hairdos were being wildly tousled; exquisitely tailored Prada, Armani, and Versace paired with casually draped Calvin cashmere was the uniform of the day. Dark was the color. Only one person wore white — Curt Gordevan — in rumpled linen from head to toe, with just a dash of color coming from the Bacardi rum bottle peeking from the pocket of his wrinkled jacket.

I saw him through the wide glass doors that separated the deck from a massive living room. He was swaying next to . . . Lila Matheson! How could I not have known she'd be there? Gordevan was pointing and mouthing off angrily at her. Her lips, pressed together in withheld rage, tilted up at the corners in a forced smile. "Oh man, soused already," Simon said. "Come on." He was heading toward them.

"Um, I'd rather wait here," I said.

He nodded, squeezed my hand, and took off. A moment later, I watched through the glass doors as he gave Lila the East Hampton, two-cheek kiss. Then he clapped Gordevan on the back, and, as if he were his best friend, Simon led the drunken author away from his victim.

Flushed and annoyed, Lila looked around and saw me. Her first response was disbelief; her second was icy disdain. I quickly turned away from her — too quickly — and collided with a waiter carrying a huge tray of hors d'oeuvres.

Black caviar on rounds of toast, smoked salmon dotted with little cream-cheese roses, mini crab cakes, and oysters on the half-shell flew in all directions, starting with the poor waiter's spotless, starched jacket. The tray itself hit the deck like a gong, alerting anyone who hadn't been struck by flying seafood.

I froze. So did everyone nearby. Stunned and blinking, they stared at me. The silence was totally terrifying. And then someone started to laugh. Simon, who'd stepped back out to the deck. And slowly, others joined in. Even Lila, who did this Cruella DeVille cackle. And Gordevan. Especially Curt Gordevan. He lumbered over to me. "Ah, the precocious Ms. Burrows; the jailhouse fugitive —"

Simon, still laughing, took my arm and led me away from Gordevan and the mess I'd made. We did a once around the party, Simon stopping to say hello and introduce me to people he knew. One of the first was a tall guy about Simon's age, with premature gray hair. He grabbed Simon and hugged him, then pounded his back, saying, "I knew I'd catch you here." Simon looked equally happy to see the guy. "Abby, this is Harry, one of my old roommates —"

"And you're Ohio, right?" Harry said, greeting me with the same hundred-watt smile he'd beamed at Simon. "This is a good man, Ohio. He saved my ass — excuse me — my life. This guy saved my *life*."

He knew my name, I thought, almost giggly with pride. Or my state, anyway. Simon actually blushed. After a few minutes of small talk, he said, "Catchya later, Harry."

"Later, dude," his ex-roommate said, and Simon whisked me off to introduce me to some other people.

About halfway through the ritual, I realized that I had this Before and After thing going. Inside my head (that dangerous neighborhood), I was scared and fiercely self-conscious. But outside, I was smiling, nodding, asking questions I actually wanted answers to. And people wanted to know if I was an actress, a model, a dancer? I cheerfully copped to being an unemployed nanny, but with literary ambitions. I wound up talking about the book I was working on and an editor from a small publishing house gave me his card and suggested I call him.

In a dining room so full of orchids that it resembled a greenhouse, a mile-long table groaned under the weight of an opulent Thanksgiving buffet — which, judging by the number of size four women at the party, was doomed to be wasted. The food looked good but I wasn't particularly hungry, so Simon snagged us a plate of cold shrimp, oysters, and clams, and picked up two Diet Cokes. We returned to the deck, which was emptier now, and followed a winding slate path to the beach.

Although it was a cold, clear afternoon, the ocean smelled sweaty, and salty, sensual. Simon took off his jacket and laid it down on the sand for us. We sat facing the water for a while, watching sea birds darting in and out of the waves.

"You having a good time?" he asked.

"The best," I said, squirting lemon juice onto another clam and thinking, *Well, Dorothy, I guess we're not in Shafton anymore.*

I'd read *Lost in Brooklyn* by then; I'd checked it out of the library near Aunt Molly's house. "Is Harry 'Eugene Evers' in your book?" I asked Simon. Evers was one of the three young artists living together in Williamsburg. He was the one who'd overdosed on heroin. "In the book he dies, right?"

"He did die," Simon said, drawing squiggles in the damp sand. "He was practically flatlining when Reef and I got him to the hospital." He dusted off his hands and lay back on his jacket.

"Is that why you got so mad when I asked you about drugs?"

"I guess," he said. "I'm not a fan. Check out those clouds, Ohio."

I looked up and saw mountains of white moving across

the horizon, blindingly outlined by the sun. Rays of yellow and pink light stabbed through the clouds.

Simon patted the space alongside him and I set aside the plate of hors d'oeuvres and lay down, staring up at the sky, until his face suddenly blocked my view, and his body blanketed mine.

"God, you're beautiful," he said. It could have been a line, but it didn't sound like it; it sounded as if Simon meant it and that he was almost as suddenly scared as I was.

"You, too," I said, unable to laugh or even smile. My entire body was flushed with warmth. Every inch of me strained toward him and ached.

We kissed again. Again and again.

"There y'ar," I thought I heard someone say. But the words were slurred.

Startled, Simon and I separated and looked up. Curt Gordevan was weaving above us, grinning stupidly, squinting through bleary eyes. "She's all right, you know? Smart kid."

"Absolutely," Simon said.

"Miriam's here," Gordevan managed, enunciating the words slowly and carefully. "She's looking for you. Go on, I'll show the kid around."

Simon put his arms around me and, holding me tight, whispered in my ear, "Do you think you can handle him? He's better off out here than inside. I'll be back as soon as I can." I pasted a smile on my face and strictly out of habit, did the "Oh, sure. Go on" thing.

Simon squeezed me just enough to set my pulse racing.

Then he headed back to the house. Curt, who'd promised to show me around, fell into the sand beside me. I was angry at myself for being such a wuss. I didn't know who Miriam was or what she meant to Simon; I only knew that Miriam was a girl's name — a girl who'd been looking for Simon.

"Who's Miriam?" I demanded.

He was too far gone to answer. And way too big and heavy for me to attempt to get him back on his feet. He shut his eyes. He looked kind of gray against the gray sand.

"Curt —" It was the first time I'd called him by his first name. "Curt, are you okay?"

Dumb question. If he was okay, he'd be the last to know it.

I poked his shoulder. "Curt. Who's Miriam?" I whispered, hoping to slide the question in under his consciousness. He opened one eye and tried to say something that never got past gibberish. Finally he tried to haul himself to a sitting position, but failed and fell back, frustrated. "I can't get up," he whined.

Fine with me, I thought.

But it was cold and windy and Gordevan was wearing a stupid white summer suit. But I wasn't feeling very *Rescue 911* either. The man had staggered over the dunes to tell Simon, who'd been deliciously nestled on my totally willing bod, that there was a woman who wanted to see him.

He mumbled something. I put my head down, to hear him better. "You gotta help me," he insisted.

"I don't gotta anything," I shot back.

But then I remembered how tipsy I'd been at Columbia

the afternoon Gordevan had lectured there. He'd been concerned, had tried to help me — even though that had consisted
of turning me over to Simon. So I guessed I owed him. My
next thought was the clincher. "I'll make a deal with you —"

"Anything," Gordevan groaned.

He was in no condition for details like, *Ms. Farber, the
woman Lila hired to replace me, is making Dylan miserable;* or
*you owe me because you got Lila pissed at me by telling her that
I did a better job with your manuscript than she'd ever
done. . . .* So I made it very simple for him. "I'll get you inside,
if you get Lila to hire me back."

He nodded, either because he understood what I'd asked
and agreed to the terms, or because his great shaggy head had
gotten too heavy to lift. I preferred to believe the former. "So
that's a yes?" I asked loudly.

"Yes," he rasped. "Christ, I'm freezing."

Kill two birds with one stone. Make that three, I thought.
Find Simon. Check out who Miriam is. Get Gordevan picked
up and stashed somewhere safe and harmless. But I wasn't
physically strong enough to drag the writer in myself. "I'm
going to get Simon," I told him. "Can you wait here?"

"Are you kidding?" he asked gruffly. "Just get back before
the tide comes in."

I hiked back to the house. And from the deck, where I was
brushing sand from my skirt and pouring it out of one of my
spiky heeled boots, I spotted Simon inside.

With a blonde.

With *the* blonde.

The same foxy blonde he'd been with at the gelato place when he'd icily looked right through me.

He was having what looked like a serious conversation with Harry — and while he did, one of his arms was draped casually over the blonde's slender shoulder. She was looking up at him adoringly.

Run, said the old me, crumbling inside, cheeks burning with shame. *Get out now. Take the Town Car back to the city and never look back.*

Grow up, said the nervy new me. *Stand your ground. He brought you here, he'll take you home.* Or else. Or else what, I had no idea. And anyway, his old pal Gordevan needed him — so I had every right to rush inside and reclaim him from this Miriam. But I would *not* make a scene.

Without waiting to put my boot back on, I limped inside. Simon's intense convo had just ended.

I found myself rushing up to him — hobbling, actually — and taking hold of his non-blonde-bearing arm. I looked at the suddenly surprised woman on his other side. "I just need to talk to him for a second," I blurted. "It's all right. I'm his sister."

The blonde looked bewildered. Her big blue eyes widened. She glanced at Simon, then back at me.

"Two different fathers," I frantically improvised. It seemed the new improved me closely resembled the hysterically nervous, blathering old me.

Suddenly Simon was laughing.

"Actually, *I'm* his sister," the blonde said, trying to keep a straight face. "Correct me if I'm wrong, but you've never lived with us, have you?"

Blush much? Neon red. Feel stupid? Totally.

"Kill me," I muttered, leaning against Simon, pulling on my boot.

"Miriam, this is Abby," Simon said, adding, unnecessarily, I thought, "she's here because she's not all there." But he more than made up for it by taking my scarlet face in his hands and planting a major smooch on my lips.

Miriam was laughing by this time. "So this is Ohio," she said. She extended her hand. "It's nice to finally meet you."

"You, too," I managed. Simon had a firm grip on my hand. "Where's Curt?" he asked.

"He's out in the dunes. I can't budge him and it's too cold for him to sleep it off in the sand."

Miriam corralled Harry and two other guys to help us, and we went down to the beach to rescue Curt.

While Miriam and the guys carried him into one of the guest rooms, I ran back to the beach to get Simon's jacket. I was trying to shake the sand off it, when my cell phone rang. Because I'd been thinking about getting my job back, of being reunited with my chunky monkey, I thought it might be Dylan. But I was all out of miracles. It was Ethan.

This is the way I described our conversation in my e-mail to Jamie (who I was *so* relieved to be e-mailing with again):

He said he'd thought it over! Can you believe it? He'd thought it over. Like I still cared. "Thought what

over?" I asked, keeping it light, wanting only to get back
to the party and to Simon.

"I want to see you again, Abs. That thing with Sam?
It was just a fling. It's over. She's going back to Utah
and I'm heading home next week."

"Bon voyage," I said.

"Don't be that way," the loser whined. "I want to see
you. I want to —" Huge swallow, pride going down hard
as my mother's fruitcake. "I want to get back together."

"Whoops, I've got another call coming in." Big lie.
"Hang on, okay?" I put him on hold . . . forever.

Chapter Twenty-two

Revenge & Redemption

Jamie

TO: ABS@OH.com
From: Jamie the lionhearted@OH.com

Great line to Ethan, what satisfaction to dump
him by leaving him holding on! I looooove it. Especially because no one is more deserving than he.
You handled him, Gordevan, and 'specially Simon
magnificently! You the girl!

Anyway, here's the postscript to my night at the
Key club with Tripp.

Picture this: Me, in bed. In hemp pjs, about as
unsexy as you can imagine. The covers are around
me, I'm reading. There's a knock on the door. I
decide to play it dismissive. "Whatever you're selling,
I'm not buying," I called out.

Tripp came in anyway, looking chagrined, looking ... sort of amazing in an "I want to hug him, and
be hugged by him" way. You know? So he perches
on the bed, and apologizes. "*That sucked*, huh?"

You think? was what I wanted to say, but
didn't. He wasn't getting away that easily.

"I'm sorry. It's just that, Tara blew me away — I had no idea she invited record company guys. And that they were impressed, maybe enough to sign the band to a contract, I just got all wrapped up in that."

I shrugged, acted like I didn't care, hadn't been hurt. "No worries. Totally understandable."

He was quiet for a while, just sort of gazed at a spot above me on the headboard. Then he said, "It's like what we talked about, about how the dream of glory sucks you in. I got so excited about the possibility of getting the band signed, I almost forgot you were even there."

"Hey, in a few weeks I won't be here ..." I trailed off, frightened by the lump that had just formed in my throat.

Tripp leaned over, slipped his arm around my shoulders, and pulled me toward him. "I need you to remind me of what's real, of what's important." He moved in to plant a kiss on my cheek.

At that moment, I was thinking, "Maybe that's what you need — but what about what I need?" I pushed back on my elbows to sit up — and acci- dentally — I'm sure — he kissed me on the lips. We should have pulled away quickly.

Only we didn't.

He was smiling when he closed the door and said good night.

Here's what I hate about Tripp Taylor. He hasn't changed one whit from the day he appeared as a shadow on the hallway wall. He acts like he likes me — but only because I'm helping Olivia. He says he needs me, but only to remind him of what's important in life. Any way you add it up, it's all about him.

Abs, tell me that, in his own way, Tripp Taylor's as much of a user as Chase was.

XOXO, James

I tucked Tripp away in a remote corner of my mind. I vowed to spend my last weeks at Casa Verde being super-nanny. I made sure I gave Olivia serious props. In our time together, she'd learned to control her bladder, and was even cool with skipping therapy sessions. This was big stuff, cause for celebration.

Topher gladly signed off on the plan to skip Olivia's usual frenetic, activity-soaked day. "Why don't you take her to the Farmer's Market?" he suggested. "She'd like that — you both would. My treat," he said with a twinkle in his eye and a hundred-dollar bill in his hand.

The Farmer's Market turned out to be several acres of open air stalls offering a deluge of tantalizing goodies, a mix of homegrown, organic food, and campy kitschy souvenirs —

dumb stuff you buy on impulse, then look at later and wonder why. We taste-tested and picked up jars of jams, homemade maple syrup, seven-grain bread, cute hair clips for Olivia, plus a Bobble-Head lawyer-doll for Topher.

As long as Olivia came back with "shoppin" bags, she was one joyful toddler. Adding an ice-cream cone to the booty put her over-the-top ecstatic.

Around four, I decided to get seriously radical. I took Olivia to the neighborhood playground. A place to mix with, dare I say it, real kids. Granted, we're not talking tiny sand-box, an old jungle gym, and a couple of lopsided swing sets. Our nabe was Holmby Hills, hence, the park was state-of-the-art, built to serve its upscale residents.

There were two huge sandboxes, separated by flower-covered trellises and a sculptured-stone water fountain, tire swings, slides, rocking horses, and climbing rocks. Benches with nannies on cell phones surrounded the play areas. Beyond were picnic tables, and areas set aside for lawn bowling, and a putting green. A lazy stream ran through the entire several-acre park.

And inside this park we found children of all ages, engaged in unstructured play. What a concept! Best of all, Olivia was instantly welcomed, and invited to play "Fortress" with Sean, Jennifer, and Harrison. I connected with the other nannies, and did a "same time tomorrow" date for the kids, to which Olivia enthusiastically agreed. It all felt so healthy! And overdue.

After dinner and Livvy's bath, I had just started reading to her when an uninvited visitor appeared in the doorway.

I would have shooed the intruder away, but Livvy's eyes lit up. "Tara! Come see what we're reading! It's a story about a pig named Olivia —"

Tara couldn't hide her knee-jerk revulsion at the words, "pig" and "Olivia" in the same sentence, but gamely accepted Livvy's invitation to come read with us.

Content and tired, Olivia dozed off soon after. I tucked her into her castle bed. "What's with up the big sisterly visit?" I asked Tara coldly.

Shushing me with her finger to her lips, as if she were Livvy's caretaker, Tara whispered, "I was coming to get you."

"For what? Another night on the town?"

Tara closed Livvy's door gently, and sighed. "If you need to be obnoxious, go for it. But right now, come with me. It's important."

"To who?"

"Ultimately, to you."

"Is that an order?"

"Please," she mumbled, "if you wouldn't mind. I really need you to come with me and hear me out."

I shrugged and followed her Tara-ness downstairs — to the gym.

Nicole was there. We caught the star in exercise-flagrante. She and Rick, the family trainer, were decked out in designer workout togs. He was keeping the beat, as she did punishing work on the Nautilus machine. The trainer held his palm up as we approached. "We're in the middle of a hundred reps," he said through gritted teeth, as if it were he, not Nicole, working out.

The star was breathing hard, sweating profusely. She was in top shape, even by Hollywood standards. I wondered how many hours she had to spend at the gym to stay that way. Hours not spent with Olivia, or for that matter, any family member.

As if she could mind-read, the first words out of Nicole's mouth when she'd finished, and taken a long pull on designer bottled water, were, "I am personally so grateful for the wonderful job you've done with Olivia this summer. As you know," Nicole paused so Rick could tend to her, wiping her brow. "She's become quite the little happy chatterbox. Fewer accidents, so I'm told."

Inside, I glowed.

Outside, I shrugged. "She's a great kid."

Tara cut to the chase, "Look, Mom, I know we just barged in on you, but there's something I need to do."

"Sounds serious. Come on, take a load off, the two of you. Rick, grab a few yoga mats for the young ladies and throw me my cigarettes."

She's going to smoke here? Right after she worked out, releasing all those toxins from her body? I couldn't — no wait, I *could* believe it.

What came *next* was the mindblower. Tara just spilled it, matter-of-factly, without remorse, just the facts. "The whole scene with the see-through dress," she began. "It was my doing. I tricked Jamie into wearing it, and I paid the photographers off to take her picture. So she was telling the truth the whole time."

I had no clue why she picked this moment to confess. I chased away the possibility that Tripp had something to do with it. Nicole's reaction was the real kicker. It couldn't have been a more Hollywood moment.

"Rick!" she sang out. "Bring me a pen, or better yet, get Leee. This is genius!" she crowed. "This is an episode of *Nikki's Way* waiting to happen!" She sprang up and hugged Tara. "I get my best ideas from you! We'll do this episode in sweeps week, it'll be a ratings blockbuster!"

Leaving the fitness center, Tara and I passed Leee, who'd come to take down all of Nicole's brilliant and inspiring new ideas for the show. When we were out of earshot, I stopped her. "Just answer me this, Tara. Why now? What made you own it, what made you confess?"

"Tripp."

I gasped, even though I'd suspected it. Tripp *was* looking out for me. What did that mean, though? And why did it make my heart pound so hard?

TO: Jamie_the_lionhearted@OH.com
FROM: ABS@OH.com
Here's the deal, plain and simple. Go knock on Tripp's door, and ask him what he's trying to tell you. Make him tell you straight up — was the song about you? What are his feelings for you, really? Tell him you don't appreciate him messing with your head. Simple as that — and girlfriend, it's exactly what you'd tell me to

do. Tripp is a good guy, so what's the problem? Unless, of course, your sudden bout of shy is because you feel more for him? That would make sense. You're falling for him, but are totally scared to do anything about it.

Discuss amongst yourself.

The next day, I invited Tara to come to the playground with Olivia and me.

"What playground?"

"It's two blocks from here — we'll walk!"

I thought Tara would have a heart attack.

"Livvy loves it, she'll want to introduce her big sister to her new friends. They're sweet kids, her age, and best of all? Not one of them is related to anyone famous. They can't do anything for her, except be her friend."

Tara looked horrified.

"I'll bring the obscenely priced coffee, okay? Just come for a while."

Confession: I had an agenda beyond Tara witnessing the great job I'd done with Olivia. It was time for me to apologize. And help her — maybe if Abby was right — forgive herself.

As predicted, Olivia grabbed Tara's hand, and rushed to introduce her to Harrison, Sean, and Jennifer before dismissing her and vaulting up the ladder to their fortress.

I steered Tara to an empty bench where we could keep an eye on the kids, yet have some privacy. She sipped her latte, and admitted, "This park is pretty. I mean, for the kids and the nannies."

I'd not have guessed it was possible, but we actually made small talk. We compared school stories, and majors. And I found out that Tara was a straight-A student. (Albeit, she could probably buy A's at her school.) Small talk soon morphed into big talk. I needed to understand the why behind Tara's determination to hurt and humiliate me. Tripp had his theory, Abby had hers. But what would Tara say when confronted?

"Raw truth?" she shaded her eyes from the sun, really looking at me.

"Macrobiotic," I replied. "Bring it."

She shrugged. "I just didn't like you."

I shook my head. "Right. Like you're getting off that easily. Just spill."

Now Tara shifted her gaze, searching for something to focus on. She settled on her little sister, whooping it up in her play-fort. "You got here and, like, instantly got into my face, into my business. So I tried to get rid of you."

By now, I was fluent in Tara-ese. And suddenly, I just got it.

The raw truth was that Tara and Tripp saw me exactly the same way. Someone who'd come into their home unexpectedly, and did something good for the family that didn't involve material things.

The difference was that Tripp became truly grateful for my contribution to the Hastings-Taylor household.

Tara became truly threatened. I'd done the one thing she could not: I'd been able to get close enough to Olivia to help the child. Because of her shady "history," Tara had been too afraid to.

Tara sipped her latte. And then asked, in a small voice, how Juliana was doing.

I told her Jules was okay — for now. "How did you know, anyway, about my sister's illness? Did Tripp tell you?"

"He confirmed it," she said, "you dropped a lot of hints."

I had? In her quest to destroy me, Tara had tried to find out everything she could about me. She googled the catchphrases on my Cure It Fast sweatshirt and my Great Strides T-shirt, so she knew exactly what cause was closest to my heart. And then Olivia had shown her the picture Juliana sent when she'd been in the hospital. That's how Tara had put it all together.

"So what's it like," she asked now, "to live like that, with —" She didn't say, "Someone you know will die young." She didn't have to.

I told her the truth: It sucked. My sister, my whole family, has been dealt a raw hand. But having close friends, people you totally trust around you, made it easier.

She nodded.

"So listen," I said, suddenly nervous. "I hope you won't get too pissed, but Tripp told me something . . . about you. What happened with . . . that kid."

She stiffened. "Yeah?"

Quietly, but forcefully, I said, "It wasn't your fault."

She eyed me warily. "What wasn't?"

"The little boy. The accident. You were a kid yourself. No one should have made you responsible for him. You didn't fail him, and you certainly didn't kill him."

Tara's face went icy white, then slowly melted, registering something I'd never seen before. Compassion. And insight. "Thanks for saying that. And, Jamie, you can't save your sister."

I nodded, feeling surprisingly choked up. Tara was a lot more sensitive than I'd ever given her credit for.

Chapter Twenty-three

All's Well

Abby

Cut to the chase . . . and I don't mean the parasite who messed with Jamie's head and heart. Cut to the chase, as in, never mind the details, get to the good part.

I got my job back!

And I slept with Simon. Kind of.

After the Hamptons bash, the Town Car had dropped us off at Simon's TriBeCa loft, which was around the corner from the café where I'd loused up our second date. The loft occupied the entire top floor of a renovated warehouse — and the rickety freight elevator that had carried us up, as tightly entwined as hothouse vines, opened directly into the living space.

Which was humongous and almost blindingly white.

Everything had been painted white, including the old, uneven floorboards. There was a gourmet-looking kitchen to our left as we stepped off the elevator; and in front of floor-to-ceiling bookshelves, a humongous desk surrounded by piles of books and stacks of manuscript pages.

The bed — on which we were now breakfasting — was at the far end of the loft, under a skylight — so the morning sun beamed down like a pale spotlight on the rumpled, 400-thread-count Egyptian linens and us. We were sucking down fresh croissants and coffee that Simon had picked up at the café while I slept in. He'd changed into gray sweats and a black turtleneck sweater. I was still wearing the boxers and ribbed undershirt (and the indelible smile) he'd given me last night.

"So you don't hate me?" I asked for the third time since he'd awakened me with a kiss and a bag of croissants.

Simon shook his head as he'd done twice before. But this time he took the container of coffee from my hands and set it down on the floor, and wrapped his arms around me, which had the effect it usually had, of turning me into a frenzied furnace. He smelled fresher and sweeter than the croissants, and his embrace made my entire body blush.

Last night, I'd said I couldn't.

I couldn't believe it, but I'd said, "No."

In a couple of weeks, I'd be going back to Shafton. What would that be like if I hooked up with Simon? ("Hooked up" — I hated that expression. It reminded me of getting your retainer caught in someone else's braces, which had actually happened to a girl Jamie and I knew in sixth grade.) We'd e-mail each other? I'd tell him about my freshman year at college and he'd tell me about the incredible parties, hot clubs, packed readings, and book signings he'd done?

Last night, he'd held me, he'd kissed the top of my head, he'd whispered, "It's okay. Don't worry."

I don't think I ever wanted anything so much in my life,

but still I said, "No. I can't," while every feel-good bone in my body was going, "More, please. Oh please, more."

"I can wait," Simon said, and tried to clear the love-husky tone from his throat. Pulling back from me, he asked, with a small good-loser's smile on his face, "Did I actually say that?"

"You did, because you're the coolest guy I ever met," I said, close to tears.

"At this moment," he'd replied, holding me at arms' length, "cool doesn't come close to how I feel."

He'd disappeared into the bathroom and I'd heard the shower going. I had to phone Jamie. Right that minute, I decided. But while I was searching for my cell, Simon appeared again, without his shirt, his torso as ripped as an Olympic swimmer. He tossed me some clothes — the pair of boxers and the clean wife-beater undershirt. "Can you stay over?" he'd asked. "I'm too beat to bike to New Jersey, but I'll get you there tomorrow, I promise."

"But where —" I started.

"I'll take the sofa," he said, anticipating my question.

When it was my turn for the bathroom, I turned on the shower to soundproof the enormous tiled room, and phoned Jamie. "I'm in his apartment, his loft, this scrumptious huge place in TriBeCa — and James, I was seconds away from de-virginizing and I said, 'No.' Can you believe it? I said no — and he didn't get ticked off or ask me to leave —"

"Good for you," Jamie said. "You're speaking up for

yourself, Abs. Nothing wrong with that." And we promised to talk again the next day for a detailed report.

True to his word, Simon slept on the sofa. Until about two A.M., when I wandered across the loft, just to look at him. But he was awake. "What's the matter? Are you okay? It gets cold in here. Are you cold?" he asked.

"Yes," I said. "I'm cold. Will you sleep with me?"

"We're talking 'sleep' here, right? Just want to make sure —"

"Well, yes and no," I admitted.

We spent the rest of the night cuddled close, turning and shifting as if we were Siamese twins. About the time the skylight showed the first pink streaks of daybreak, we fell asleep in each other's arms.

It took Curt Gordevan's insistence for Lila to ask Edith to ask me to come back. It was a favor Lila fully intended to remind Curt of the next time he got blotto. Which, since he was going to his AA meetings again, might not even happen.

I was never sure that Lila knew I was still seeing Simon. She never mentioned it. When she did speak about him to someone on the phone, she casually mentioned that Simon's book *Lost in Brooklyn* was coming out in paperback. And that he was going to do a college tour to promote it.

Hearing that made my stomach drop. It only reminded me of how little time I had left to be with him and how different our lives really were. I did wonder whether any schools in

Ohio would be on his schedule. I didn't ask him, though. I didn't want to think about "after" — about what would happen when I went home. So I held back every time I saw him, which was nearly every night after work.

Simon would pick me up on his motorcycle and we'd head off to a movie. We checked out the Christmas windows on Fifth, the trees twinkling with a million tiny lights, the huge electric snowflakes that hung over the avenue, the ice-skaters at Rockerfeller Center. We hit whatever club or pub Reef and the Killer B's were playing at, or wolfed down pasta at a little Italian restaurant strung with colored lights.

It was too wintry to ride the bike to New Jersey, so Simon would take me to Port Authority and wait with me for my bus. And we kissed. We kissed everywhere, and every way: sweet and gentle, hot and frenzied, comfortable as old friends and achingly uncomfortable as frantic new lovers.

I spoke to Margaritte, and she'd told me that while I was gone, Garrick and the murderous midget DC had disappeared. They hadn't shown up at the playground all week. Hiding from me, perhaps.

Margaritte sounded really down. Daisy's dad, an investment banker, had gotten a new job in Denver. The family would be moving after the holidays. They'd asked Margaritte to go with them, but she had a life, a boyfriend, and lots of relatives in Queens. She was truly torn up, though — much more over losing Daisy than losing the job.

In the daytime, I focused all my love and attention on my

chunky monkey. He really needed it. During my first days back, he held my hand all the time, even in the apartment. He made exceptions for martial arts and gymnastics. But even there, he looked my way every few minutes to make sure I wasn't going anywhere.

Forced to sit at the playground while I was gone, Dylan had cried and DC had taunted him about it. Dyl now had no desire to go near the place.

We stayed away from the park, but we'd arrange to meet up with Margaritte and Daisy nearly every day. Daisy was noticeably blue — her parents had told her that Margaritte would not be going with them to Denver. Margaritte tried to hide her own sadness, but often she'd develop "the sniffles" and put on her sunglasses. Dylan noticed. He liked Margaritte and kept asking me why she was sad. We'd started to talk about my leaving. Which was another reason he held my hand so tightly. I'd promised that Ms. Farber would definitely not be his nanny ever again. We were working it out.

But when I finally told him that Daisy was moving and that Margaritte was distressed about it, he frowned. We were walking home, holding hands. He stopped. His forehead wrinkled and his eyes scrunched up. I thought that he was going to cry.

But no, he was just thinking, concentrating.

"I know what," he said. "When you go away, Margaritte can be *my* nanny."

I whisked him up into my arms and covered his brilliant little face with kisses. It was the best idea I'd ever heard.

*　　*　　*

The morning Dylan earned his first green stripe in karate, he refused to change out of his *gi*, so I bundled him into boots and his hooded parka, and slipped his ski pants over his white karate pajamas. He looked proud and adorable and I asked him what he'd like to do to celebrate the great achievement.

His first choice was Party Place, the kids' play palace on Broadway. I could definitely get behind that. Dyl was hyped to the max and I pictured him working off his manic energy in the "ball room."

Snow was floating down in big, soft flakes as we walked over. It was too wonderful outside to take a cab any-where — even if I could have found one. The minute it drizzled in the Apple, every available taxi was hailed, seized, and fought-over like lifeboats on the *Titanic*. When it snowed, the panic went up a notch.

But *this* snow was heavenly. It made the city look like it was inside one of those souvenir glass globes and that some giant hand had shaken it to make the snow swirl. So Dylan and I walked, and threw snowballs at each other, and we arrived at Party Place stamping the snow off our boots. Without waiting for me, Dylan shimmied out of his jacket and snow pants, kicked off his boots, and sprinted for the ball room in his white *gi* — now proudly decorated with a green stripe fastened by a safety pin.

I hurried to catch up with him and, by the time I did, his face was bright red; his little hands were balled into fists; he looked angrier than I'd ever seen him.

308

He was standing outside the room filled with colorful rubber balls. The "room" was actually a gigantic mesh net inside of a room carpeted in rubber safety mats. Inside the net, half a dozen children rolled and jumped and whooped with wild abandon, tumbling into the balls and each other. A familiar, mocking, high-pitched voice taunted above the chaos: "Dylan is a crybaby. Crybaby! Crybaby!"

I caught all this while making my way through a flock of moms and nannies whose attention was focused only on their own kids. Nobody was paying much attention to Dylan. Except DC, who was doing the taunting. And nobody was paying any attention to DC. Garrick was nowhere to be seen.

My first thought was to scold DC. But that, I realized instantly, would only make Dylan look like a sap who needed his nanny to fight his battles. And there was something different about my boy today. He was glaring at DC, but he wasn't crying, or commanding me to make DC stop. In his little karate *gi*, he was standing his ground and giving DC the evil eye. So I backed off.

At that moment, Garrick showed up. He was clearly surprised to see Dylan. He hadn't noticed me yet. "Hey, buddy," he called to Dyl. "Long time no see."

With a tentative smile, Dylan looked up at Garrick, and when he did, DC came racing across the room's rubber safety mat. Hanging onto the red ball he'd probably torn from the grasp of some new victim, DC ran over to Dylan and at point-blank range hurled the ball at Dyl's head.

It connected with a terrible splat. A bright, perfectly ball-shaped mark appeared on my honey's forehead.

The nannies and moms turned toward Dylan with a collective gasp.

For a minute, I didn't know whether to run and comfort my wounded warrior or get in DC's face. Then Dylan made the choice easy for me.

In an instant, he'd assumed his karate stance, his pudgy fingers bent into a two-knuckled curl, his hand pulled back near his shoulder. With a bloodcurdling cry that stopped DC cold, Dyl's arm flew forward, rotating so that his stiff palm faced upward, his cocked knuckles connected with DC's shoulder.

The relentless bully spun backward. The ball he'd retrieved flew from his hands as his feet skidded out from under him. DC fell, his face crumpling, instantly morphing from wily villain to whiny victim.

DC hadn't expected any opposition. Mostly it was the nannies who gave him a hard time; the kids either avoided him or folded. But Dylan hadn't. Whether it was surprise or technique that gave him the edge, the result was the same. DC had gone down.

"I got my green stripe!" Dylan yelled at his fallen foe.

"Way to go, Dyl!" I hollered.

Garrick looked up. He saw me and quickly looked away. As he knelt to pick DC up, he mumbled, "Sorry."

"You ought to be!" I hissed. Garrick knew exactly what I meant. His pasty face grew even paler and two red spots of color bloomed on his cheeks. He looked completely miserable and embarrassed.

My knee-jerk need to apologize surfaced, but I smacked it down as efficiently as Dylan had put DC away. Then, behind us, the crowd of kids, nannies, and parents who'd watched my chunky monkey do his karate thing erupted in cheers.

Chapter Twenty-four

The Inner Sanctum

Jamie

I meant to take Abby's advice. I meant to be up-front, charge into Tripp's room — his hideaway — and confront him. Just ask him what his deal was. Were his feelings for me only about guilt and gratitude, or was there something more lurking in his rock 'n' roll heart? I was leaving soon anyway, what did I have to lose?

Only, the thing was, when I knocked on his door, no one answered.

I went in anyway.

I totally trespassed on Tripp's turf.

It's not like I was gonna do anything sketchy, like dig through his drawers for boxers or briefs. But maybe there'd be some clue here to what was really on his mind. A picture of a girlfriend? That would have hurt, but I'd get it finally. Lyrics scrawled next to the computer about another girl? Or lyrics about me?

I hadn't pictured Tripp's personal crib, but I would not have been surprised to find the walls painted black and covered with posters of Bob Marley, Jerry Garcia, or Snoop Dogg. I figured him for a big-screen TV, a righteous video game collection, and a sound system, maybe a trashed skateboard lying around.

As soon as I opened the door, the sweet blend of incense and weed enveloped me. A tangle of wires, attached to keyboards, attached to sound boards, attached to computer screens greeted me.

A music studio. For serious real.

Guitars, most in their cases, were propped against the wall, notebooks littered the floor beneath what was obviously his workspace. I flipped through one — hey, it wasn't like it was a secret confessional diary! It was filled with handwritten lyrics and musical notes, ideas for tunes and drawings for what I assumed would be videos. Afraid to spend too much time reading his notebooks, I did not find out if there were any other songs with the name "Jamie" in them.

And then there was his bed. Where he slept. It was very Sundance — redwood-framed, double-size, rustic. The magazines he subscribed to were mostly music — *Guitar, Vibe, Blender, Rolling Stone.* Bookcases were stuffed with rock bios of legendary ax-slingers like Carlos Santana, Jimi Hendrix, Eric Clapton. I saw an old Earth Day banner, and a ticket stub from one of Sting's Save the Rainforest concerts. An entire wall — none were black — was covered with a painted peace sign. I touched the one I wore around my neck and remembered Tripp wore one, too, in his ear. There were buttons, bumper stickers, and pamphlets for political candidates he supported. It struck me like a thunderbolt.

This is real. Tripp — Christopher Wylie Taylor III — really cares about this stuff. Almost as much as the girl I used to be.

There was one photo in the room, a framed portrait of a beautiful woman, dark and mysterious, her eyes the same bittersweet chocolate as Tripp's. I picked it up for a closer inspection. I knew it was his mom. The Mexican actress. Was she still there? Did he ever see her? Speak to her?

"What are you doing here, Jamie?"

I whirled, my heart racing. How long had Tripp been watching me snoop through his stuff? "Tripp. I was . . ."

"Looking for me?" he speculated. He leaned on one of the guitar stems.

I fessed up. "Tresspassing. Snooping. Grounds for dismissal — or worse, reason for you to not trust me. To not like me."

He said nothing, and once again, gave away nothing.

Which sent me into babble-mode. "This is so wrong, I know it. I totally invaded your privacy. I know I shouldn't have, but I didn't touch anything. I mean, besides this picture —"

"So what did you find out?" Tripp asked casually. He wasn't pissed off?

I found out that Tripp was exactly who he claimed to be. A musician. Maybe not a starving musician, but a serious one just the same. And a boy who cared about some of the things I did: clean air, honesty, and peace — things money can't buy.

All this I told him, while he nodded, looking thoughtful. Then he pointed to the photo of the dark-haired woman. "My mom," he confirmed. "Alexandra Garcia."

"You look just like her," I noted. "Do you ever see her?"

He shook his head and shrugged. "She's in Mexico, with a booming career on TV, in those *telenovelas,* daytime soaps. She's remarried, has a new family, the whole thing. I don't think she misses me all that much." It was said with only a touch of wistfulness.

"I'll miss you." Okay, there it was — *ka-boom!* I'd said it.

The pause was excruciating. Finally Tripp said, "We'll miss you, too."

Not *I'll* miss you. *We'll* miss you. I fought to swallow my hurt.

Tripp ran his fingers through his hair, and said, "We might not show it, but the whole family knows you've been good for us. You being here resulted in a lot of good things — especially with Olivia."

Nothing about himself, his feelings. *It's okay,* I told myself, *go with it.* I teased, "So due to my influence, you're gonna give all your money to charity, and join the Peace Corps? I can just see Nicole and Tara digging wells and building houses in Third World counties."

Tripp grinned. "Doubtful. After you leave, we'll probably revert to being the selfish, superficial bunch of snobs and slackers you know and love."

I laughed, a little too heartily.

Please say something about the song, Tripp, I begged silently. Those words banged around my head, trying to punch their way out — but I would not let them.

Instead, I went for: "I'm guessing Topher and Nicole have no idea what you're into, do they? Topher wants you to go into the family business. He's not so much about the rock star —"

"Musician," he corrected.

"— the musician thing. So what he doesn't know won't hurt either one of you? Is that it?"

"Look, Topher wants what he wants. And this," Tripp indicated his room, "is not it. I . . . am not it."

"I can't believe he wouldn't listen if you wanted to talk to him, to explain. Maybe he'd want to help you, even?" I ventured.

"The last thing I want is his help."

Of course. Son of a wealthy attorney, stepson of a famous TV star. Wants to make it on his own. And this never occurred to me, why?

"I still think —" I started.

"Let it go, Jamie," Tripp said. "*Devine* intervention is not always needed."

I hung my head, more ashamed of my self-righteous streak than of trespassing. "I'm sorry. I know I have the tendency to think I can fix everyone's problems. You're right. I should just go."

And I would have. I even started toward the door. But I still hadn't found what I'd come looking for.

"That song —"

"That song —"

We said it at the same time. I held my breath. So did he.

"Was it —

"Real. From the heart —"

"Did you mean . . . ?"

"Every word."

I'm not sure why my eyes started to tear at that moment. But I think that maybe there is such a thing as tears of joy, tears of relief. Tears of realization that you've really connected with another person: a person who you didn't know you'd been looking for all your life.

But did I *really* know him?

He read my mind. Tripp reached behind me, and closed the door. As he gently took me by the shoulders and pulled me close, he murmured, "Maybe this'll help you figure it out."

That kiss, *that kiss*. It was everything I'd never dared dream of. It was gentle, and fiercely passionate. It was sweet and fiery. I wanted, and got, more. He wanted, and I gave, more. It was the kind of kiss that could've lasted for days, the kind that expresses all that words cannot. And it told me everything I needed to know about him.

Epilogue

This is Bliss, Ohio

Abby

We're crossing the campus, Simon and I.

He has his arm around my shoulder. My arm circles his waist; my hand, a heat-seeking missile, finding a home in his pocket. It's just after his book-signing at the campus Barnes & Noble and the two of us have been getting sly, sly, admiring glances from just about everyone we pass. Simon, the famous, fine-looking author, draws the most attention; but I'm getting my share, thanks to his unexpected introduction of me as "Curt Gordevan's favorite editor."

I look around, smiling. It's amazingly easy to smile when Simon's heat is radiating through his soft leather coat. There are still patches of snow around us, but all over the sprawling grounds of Ohio State University, spring shoots are pushing through — daffodils, crocuses, and the promising green tips of tulips.

It's April. Still cold and windy. And Simon and I are not so much strolling as being blown toward the local taxi waiting to take Simon to the airport.

Déjà vu, I think, hugging Simon's waist a little tighter.

The last time I saw Simon, he was also on his way to the airport, I remember.

"What would you like for Christmas?" Simon had asked me over the phone. I'd only been home for a few days and I was already missing him like crazy.

"You," I said. Then I laughed to take the pressure off him, to pretend I was only kidding. "Gift wrapped, of course."

"Okay, what would be second best?" he'd wanted to know.

Once I'd pictured Simon gift wrapped, it was hard to think of anything else. "When does your college tour start?"

"End of March, beginning of April," he said. "And Ohio State is definitely one of the stops. Will you be there by then?"

"Definitely," I said. "Jamie and I are starting in two weeks. I can't wait to see you."

"It won't be that long," he promised.

"Only about one hundred twenty days," I wailed to Jamie, a couple of days later. We were in my room, wrapping Christmas gifts. "Just two thousand eight hundred eighty hours; about seventeen thousand two hundred eighty minutes."

"But who's counting?" Jamie laughed. "No, really. I know how you feel, Abs," she segued from kidding to kindness. "I miss Tripp, too."

Passing the scissors and Scotch tape between us, we were taking stock — not of the gifts we were wrapping, but of us.

The summer of our discontent, as Jamie put it, had given way to the fall of our expectations. *Fall*, as in the season we were nannies. And *fall* as in tumble, go down, collapse. Our preconcieved ideas about practically everything had crumbled.

Those months spent on opposite coasts had changed us both, in ways that still surprised us.

The doorbell chimed just then. I looked out the window and saw a UPS truck parked outside.

"Abby, it's for you," my mom hollered. She sounded totally flustered.

"Can't you just sign for it?" I called out.

"Um . . . I can, I guess. But it's too . . . too heavy for me to carry —"

With eye roll and sighs, Jamie and I headed downstairs. The front door was open and my mother was staring bug-eyed at whatever the man in brown had delivered.

Jamie got to the door first. Her eyes went *Boing!* Her hand flew to her mouth.

"What's up?" I began. Then gasped.

There was S. G. Wagner, noted author and studly celeb, grinning his meltingly beautiful grin. I shrieked and leaped at him — my arms clasped his neck, my legs wrapped around his hips — and, right there, in front of my nearest and dearest, he gave me a full-on kiss.

"Hey!" my dad went. "Abigail," my mom huffed. I could hear Jamie laughing.

Simon and I separated. Which was when I noticed the taxi waiting in our driveway. "I'm sorry," Simon whispered. "I can't stay. I'm on my way to Colorado to spend the holidays with my dad. Miriam's at the airport waiting for me right now. I just wanted to stop and see you."

After Simon left, I finally noticed that my mom *was* holding an envelope. It contained a homemade holiday card from Dylan: a collage of pasted cutouts that included Santa Claus, pine wreaths, and Keanu Reeves and Laurence Fishburne doing *Matrix* kicks and karate stances.

On campus, Simon and I move slowly toward the taxi. *It'll be okay,* I tell myself. After all, it's not forever. And Simon knows that. He says, "So I'll see you in June, right?"

"Lila willing." I try to be adorable, the clown with the broken heart, then I give it up. "I mean I know it'll be good for me, being a paid intern at Matheson Press —"

"A very well-paid intern," Simon reminds me.

"I'm going to totally make next fall's tuition. But I'm going to miss being with the little guy —"

"Excuse me?" Simon teases. "Are you talking about me?"

I sock his arm. "Dylan."

We are a foot from the cab now. Simon turns suddenly and hugs me frantically. He lifts me off the ground, kissing my scarfless neck and cold ears, my cheeks and nose and, at last, my mouth.

"I'll call you tonight, Abby," he promises.

And I know he will.

*   *   *

Later, as I walk across the diag, the path that bisects the Ohio State campus, I see two familiar figures making their way toward me. One is Jamie, wearing faux-fur-lined Uggs (a parting gift from Tara) and cradling textbooks against her puffy jacket. The other is a guy — long, lean, shaggy-haired, with the ever present silhouette of a guitar slung over his shoulder.

It's Tripp Taylor. Who transferred to Ohio State. To be with Jamie.

Jamie had worked especially hard with Olivia her last week at Casa Verde, showing her how they would e-mail and call each other, and write letters, too. Jamie even invited her little charge to come visit her at home in Shafton, where she could meet Juliana.

But, over that week, Jamie had also grown closer to Tripp. Which hadn't been any work at all. Before she'd left, he'd written her another song, and played it for her — before they spent the night together. As Jamie later told me, she couldn't help but wonder if *her* first time would be *their* last time together.

Clearly, it wasn't.

I walk over to meet them. Tripp is on his way to his music seminar, so he kisses James good-bye and we all agree to dinner later. Then, it's just Jamie and me, and we can't help but grin at each other. We freakin' did it.

This is the payoff for refusing to "make the best of it," for saying "no" to a mediocre job or settling for a "nothing special" guy. *This*, where even introductory courses are taught by

322

distinguished professors; *this*, a place where every light pole is papered with political posters and announcements of famous speakers coming to campus — this is why we parted ways with Shafton.

This is where we wanted to be.

Don't miss
NEXT SUMMER
A SUMMER BOYS NOVEL
by Hailey Abbott
Available in bookstores everywhere!

It only took one kiss for the hammock to start rocking — a little more violently than Beth Tuttle liked, making the moment feel more *roller coaster* than *romantic.*

"I think the original hammock experience beat this one," her boyfriend George said, slowly ending the kiss as he and Beth swung back and forth underneath the shade of the trees in Beth's backyard. For the millionth time, Beth admired George's eyes — brown and deep, and best of all, always laughing.

"You mean last summer?" Beth asked, planting a soft kiss on his nose. "Yeah, I guess our hammock in Pebble Beach is a little more comfortable for hook ups."

Beth grinned as she untangled herself from George and swung her long legs out of the hammock. She stood up and stretched in the warm June sunshine. Scraping her blonde hair back from her face, she squinted across the yard to the garage where her parents had begun piling up boxes in preparation for another summer in Maine. Beth couldn't believe they were leaving for Pebble Beach in the morning. A whole year had passed since she and George had finally figured out they were meant for each other while cuddling in that *other* hammock.

Beth sighed at the magical memory. If only George would be coming back to Pebble Beach *this* summer.

"Come on," George said, climbing to his feet. "Let's go inside."

He looked down at her with that sly, sexy smile of his and slowly ran his hand down her arm. He took her hand and brought it up to his lips, his mouth gently grazing her skin. Beth felt her breath catch. That was all the encouragement she needed to follow George to Antarctica, the moon, or wherever he wanted to go.

They entered the kitchen, dodging all the summer provisions that were scattered around the room — a huge picnic basket and bags of groceries were strewn about the floor; Beth's father's boat shoes were lying on top of a mountain of sealed cardboard boxes; and a collection of battered tennis rackets cluttered up the countertop. Her mother had obviously been very busy, and Beth knew she needed to start bringing down her clothes and beach gear. But, right then, she had other, more important, things on her mind than packing.

"So you think painting is going to be more fun than the beach?" she asked George sourly, picking up one of the rackets. She ran her hand across the tight web of strings and pressed it against the pads of her fingers. There was a part of her that wanted to beat George over the head with the racket — how could he possibly give up a summer with her to work a job that required him to breath in toxic fumes?

Beth knew that George knew her well enough to recognize

her urge to smack some sense into him, which was probably why he took the makeshift weapon out of her grasp, reached over, and held her face between his hands. He kissed her softly, and then tilted his head away to hold her gaze. George always knew exactly how to distract her.

"This summer is about money, not fun," he said with a sad smile, his curly hair flopping forward. "All the cash I'm going to make will lead to the ultimate Year of George in the fall. I can practically guarantee it." Beth reached over and pushed his hair back so that she could get a better view of him. After tomorrow, she'd be without her boyfriend for almost three solid months.

"I thought it was supposed to be the summer of George and Beth," she said, grinning up at him. "Now it's the *fall* of *George?*"

"C'mon, you know the seasons of George revolve around you, Bethy," George replied with a smirk. "Why do you think I signed up for this gig? I'd like, I don't know, to get you something nice for a change."

"You mean something that doesn't come from the Dollar Tree?" Beth teased.

"Hey, a lot of good stuff comes from the Tree. Like that dashboard hula girl and the lemon-scented Jesus car freshener," George replied defensively.

"Well, they'd be a lot more practical if I had a car." Beth grinned, remembering her birthday presents.

"I've been trying to send your parents some hints. See how crafty I am?"

"If by crafty, you mean stupid," Beth quipped.

"Ouch. I thought you loved the G-man," George said as he clutched at his heart and made a sad face.

"What do you know about painting, anyway?" Beth whined, changing the subject. She hated the way she sounded — needy. She couldn't help it. "You barely got through art class." Not that slapping paint on dorms for the brainiacs at MIT was exactly art, Beth thought. But that was beside the point.

"I know it pays way more money than slaving away at the Mini Mart," George replied. His sly smile was back. He took Beth's hands in his and began backing up, leading her out of the kitchen. "I've worked at that place so long I'm like fifty seconds away from becoming that guy in *Clerks*."

He drew Beth toward the stairs. As Beth followed him, she studied the back of his pale blue Old Navy T-shirt. Beth smiled when she thought about the hundreds of times she had taken that shirt off George over the course of the past twelve months. That blue shirt had landed on the floor of Beth's room after soccer practice, before going to the movies, during their study sessions for history, and every other occasion in between. And, more often than not, George's pants came off, too, Beth reflected, gazing appreciatively at his butt, lost somewhere beneath his baggy dark jeans. Beth loved nothing more than fooling around with George, for hours on end. They had — as her cousin Ella might put it —"done everything but."

Somehow, even after a year of dating, sex hadn't happened yet.

Beth was pretty positive that she was ready. In fact, she and George had come seriously close too many times to count. But there was always either some sort of absurd interruption — like her dad knocking on the door at a totally wrong moment — or some kind of crazy obstacle. Both she and George became obsessed with The Moment, as they liked to call it. That one perfect moment, when the mood would feel just right, and they would both just *know*.

So far, The Moment hadn't happened.

When they reached her bedroom, George immediately shut the door and wrapped Beth in his arms. They fell across her bed together. Beth curled herself around his body as he kissed his way up from her shoulders to her mouth. When their lips met, Beth heard herself moan just a little bit. She loved the taste of him (red licorice — George was obsessed with Twizzlers) and the feel of his body against hers (like a warm flannel blanket in the middle of winter — no matter what the season). Beth rolled over so she was on top of him. George ran his fingers through her hair and then brought his mouth to hers for another succulent, sweet kiss.

In minutes, they were in full make-out mode, and Beth was relishing the feel of George's hands traveling down the length of her body. *Why not now?* Beth wondered suddenly. They'd put off having sex for so long. Too long, maybe. *Why not give us something to remember, since we'll be apart all summer?*

Beth rotated her hips against George's. George loved this

maneuver so much that he had given it a name: The Gyration Sensation. She wiggled a little bit more and heard George groan.

"Shhhhh. My mom is in the basement, not in a sound-proof booth."

"I'm sorry. You know what that move does to me," George sighed, rolling Beth over so she was on her back. She felt dizzy and her body tingled wherever he touched her. But now that she had brought up her mom, she couldn't help feeling all too aware of her parents' presence in the house. Which was so the opposite of sexy.

And did she really want to sleep with George *now*? Who wanted to lose her virginity and *then* be alone all summer? The thought suddenly depressed Beth. One time with George would not be enough. If they had sex now, she'd want to keep doing it with him all summer long.

So Beth slowed down the action by shifting to her side and curling into a fetal position. This was a move that happened more often than The Gyration Sensation, so it should also have had a name, but Beth was glad that George was too sweet to ever tease her about it. His usual response was to cuddle up right behind her. And he did just that. George sighed against her ear as his arms hugged her waist.

"Good call, Bethy," he said, nuzzling her neck. "I have to say, the fact that your mom is doing laundry downstairs isn't much of a turn-on."

Beth let out a hefty exhale. George *was* the world's best boyfriend. He'd never think to pressure her about sex.

"This summer is going to suck," Beth whispered.

Without having to see his face, Beth knew that George was wearing a guilty expression. It was the same one he'd been wearing ever since he'd told her about his summer plans.

"Well, it will," Beth persisted. "I was bummed when I found out Jamie wasn't coming to Maine, because of the Amherst writing program. But your not being there is plenty worse."

"Ella and Kelsi will be there," George said. "And the rest of your entire family . . ."

"It's not the same," Beth cut in. She hated it when he was reasonable. "It's supposed to be *all* the cousins. Jamie, Ella, Kelsi, and me. The four Tuttle girls. It's a tradition, and Jamie's breaking it. And you're like an honorary Tuttle cousin, so you're breaking tradition, too." She pouted.

"Okay, please don't refer to me as your cousin again, because that's just creepy and gross," George chuckled. "As for breaking tradition, I'm just trying to start a new one. You know, where I get to spend money on us without having to ask my parents to dip into my college fund."

"Don't you get it? I don't care about any of that," Beth said. "I just want to be with you."

George repositioned himself so that he was lying down in front of Beth and looking directly into her eyes.

"God, I'm going to miss you," Beth said.

He leaned in and kissed her again. His lips were warm and so right, so *George*. Beth didn't want to be without him, even if it was just for the summer. Because, for her, being without

George was the same as forgetting how to laugh. It was that unimaginable.

But Beth also couldn't believe how clingy she was being. When had this happened? When did she morph from an independent, smart-mouthed jock into this girl who couldn't operate unless she was connected to George at the hip? Was she scared? Did she have, in the back of her mind, the slightest of doubts? George might have seemed cool about their not having sex yet. But maybe if George had a few months away from her, he'd have hours upon hours to think about what their relationship was missing.

Before Beth could get lost in that trail of worries, George calmed her by pulling her across his chest and planting small kisses from her temple and across her cheek to her mouth.

"I'm going to miss you, too," he murmured. "Which is why I promise I'll make it up there, even if it's only for a day."

"When?" Beth said, threading her arms around his neck.

"As soon as humanly possible," he replied. "Really. I know I put on a good act, but I'm a mess without you, Bethy."

Beth grinned, and then ran her hands through George's curly hair, making it frizz out. "You're a mess, period."

"Oh, so that's how you want to be, huh?" George asked mischievously, suddenly kneeling on the bed. He posed as if he were about to attempt a complicated wrestling move.

Beth tensed up but couldn't help giggling. "Take it easy, George. You don't want me to break your painting hand now, do you?"

"The threats only fuel the fire!" George boomed. Then he dove in for a tickle of massive proportions.

Beth squirmed around and shrieked like a little girl as George's fingers worked the backs of her knees and her ribs. "Stop! Stop!" she cried. But she really didn't want him to stop. She wanted to soak up all of George's energy and put it in a bottle so that she could ration it out over the next few months. Even though the room was filled with their laughter, Beth knew that once she set foot on Pebble Beach without George by her side, she would have to remind herself how to smile.

Oh Baby, it's a quiz!
Are you more LA or New York?

Your idea of the perfect day is:
a) Checking out a hot new art exhibit.
b) Hanging out at the beach.
c) Shopping at the mall with friends.

A little black dress is _____.
a) Mega-sophisticated. It goes with everything.
b) Boring. Lighten up! Black is a downer.
c) Fine as long as it's comfortable and I can wear it with flats.

If you could be a celeb for a day, you'd be:
a) Lindsay Lohan. She DEFINITELY knows how to party!
b) Mischa Barton. She's cool, laid back and has an awesome style.
c) Kelly Clarkson. I wish I had her voice.

Your favorite gadget right now is...
a) iPod shuffle
b) T-Mobile sidekick
c) Laptop computer

Which Simpson do you relate to most?
a) Ashlee Simpson
b) Jessica Simpson
c) Lisa Simpson

In which exercise class are you most likely to be found?
a) Kickboxing
b) Yoga
c) Class? I play sports!

When you're off from school, you'd rather:
a) Surf the Web
b) Surf the waves
c) Channel surf

You're craving a slice of pizza. How do you eat it?
a) On the go—folded up like a taco
b) At a restaurant—sometimes with a fork
c) Pop it in the microwave—and serve

 You're more New York. You are a city girl at heart. You like the glamour of Broadway and the fast pace of a city that never sleeps.

 You're more LA. You're laid-back, fun, and never take life too seriously! You like the glitz of Hollywood and you love to be in the spotlight.

 City life is so not your style. High fashion isn't everything to you. You'd rather wear jeans and a baby tee and hang out with friends.

OBQ